U

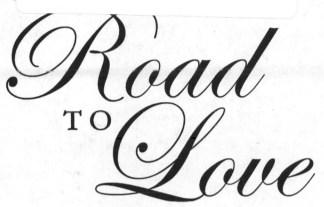

Road

TO Love

UNSEEN
Road
TO
Love

CHELSEA CURRAN

BONNEVILLE BOOKS
An Imprint of Cedar Fort, Inc.
Springville, Utah

ISBN 13: 978-1-4621-2005-5

Published by Bonneville Books, an imprint of Cedar Fort, Inc.
2373 W. 700 S., Springville, UT 84663
Distributed by Cedar Fort, Inc., www.cedarfort.com

Library of Congress Cataloging-in-Publication Data on file

Cover design by Priscilla Chaves
Cover design © 2017 by Cedar Fort, Inc.
Edited and typeset by Casey Nealon and Jessica Romrell

Printed in the United States of America

10 9 8 7 6 5 4 3 2 1

Printed on acid-free paper

To the amazing people who inspire me, for making this story come to life. And in loving memory of my brother, Hunter, who never stops reminding me that even the littlest of faith can make great things happen. I love you all.

Chapter One

⚬⚬

$\mathscr{L}$ogan had to slap the alarm on his radio several times until the loud static finally stopped harassing his eardrums. Blinking in the dim morning light, he flopped back onto the pillow and decided a few more minutes wouldn't hurt. But after what felt like seven seconds of restful bliss, the static went off again and Logan reflexively swung at the radio with enough force to send it to the floor with a *thud*. At least it didn't break this time.

Despite living in the desert region of Southern Utah, the weather was still bitter cold in the mornings during the winter months, especially when his roommate insisted on keeping the heater off to save on utilities. He wasn't opposed to saving money, but the apartment was cold enough to make walking barefoot on the laminate floor a method of torture.

After downing two bowls of cereal, he began to prep himself for one of the biggest opportunities of his life.

Now that he'd be receiving his degree in business at the end of this week, Logan was desperately seeking a job. And thankfully his friend James happened to have a family acquaintance who worked for a financial company in Chicago. He heard through the grapevine of an internship opening that was more than ideal for the both of them. But James still had another year of schooling and was willing to pass it over to Logan like the best friend he was.

Logan had managed to pull a few strings using all the communication skills he'd acquired during his college years to land himself a rare interview. Being fresh out of school, he recognized that this was a rare opportunity, which meant there was little room for error when it came to making a first impression.

Even when attending his business classes, Logan consistently tried his best to look professional and make a statement. But today he chose a dark suit and a red tie that was bold and eye-catching, which was exactly what he needed today—to be remembered.

He blew into his hands in a pathetic attempt to warm them as he walked through the brisk air. Because David Miller, the man conducting the interview, had very little room in his schedule, Logan had agreed to meet him at a coffee shop across town while he was getting his morning order. But because he didn't have a car, he had to settle for taking the bus and sprinting a few blocks to get there on time.

He would have bought his own car ages ago, but over the years he had to think practically while living on a budget. Maybe if he hadn't been so naïve when he first moved to St. George, things would have been different, but there was no use in dwelling on the past now.

After serving a mission, he came home with a newly conditioned mindset to be more focused and committed to his goals. And coming from humble circumstances, he had to put all his focus on mapping out his life accordingly so he wouldn't end up falling into debt.

Putting the two together, the field of finance had sparked his interest, and now he was well on his way to helping major corporations. Or at least he hoped so.

As he entered the warm coffee shop, Logan inhaled the aroma and appreciated the distinct smell that came with the atmosphere.

He ordered a small hot chocolate to warm him up while he waited, but it wasn't too long before Mr. Miller entered through the glass door.

"Good morning," said David as he moved to shake Logan's hand.

"Good morning, sir. I can't tell you how grateful I am for you to see me."

"It's not a problem. I admire your persistence. Plus I get my morning coffee at the same time. Can I get you anything?"

"No thank you, sir. I've been taken care of," he said, raising his paper cup.

"Right then. Well let's get to business."

Once the interview started, time passed by in a blur as he talked about his background and went into detail about his credentials that matched the job he was applying for. When he saw the look of approval in David's eyes, Logan's confidence grew and the interview itself became more comfortable as he answered questions to financial scenarios while expressing his ideas and insights, which David seemed to agree with.

It was when Logan heard the words, "Could you start in two weeks?" that time zeroed in on the moment and a burst of something close to triumph exploded in his chest.

"I know it's a lot to ask considering you'd be moving to a different state, but we're in desperate need of new employees, especially during this time of year when things are more hectic than usual. But I can assure you that the benefits will be substantial enough to make the sacrifices worth it in the end."

Logan couldn't think of a truer statement. Just as he hoped and prayed for, this opportunity was practically being handed to him on a silver platter. But when he opened his mouth to accept, a nagging feeling suddenly crept into his heart that dimmed the excitement he had just felt three seconds ago.

Two weeks? That was a few days before Christmas. It was obviously why they'd want to take him on during a season when most people wanted time off. He could see where his appeal would come from being twenty-five, unmarried, and enthusiastic about joining the workforce. But there was the fact that he wouldn't be with his family during the holidays for the third time in a row.

"Would it be possible to start next month?" Logan asked, already knowing what the answer would be.

He could feel the usual guilt flooding his conscience, dreading the phone call he'd have to make to his mother. But for some reason there was another feeling that lingered uncomfortably in the pit of his stomach, as if he heard someone whisper in the back of his mind, *Don't take it.*

David shrugged. "It is possible, but we have many other applicants who are willing to work sooner than that, and I'm afraid we just can't wait much longer to hire someone new. Two weeks is the most time I can give you before the position will probably be given to someone else. I know that sounds heartless, but it's like I said, you will benefit greatly from this. And I believe our company will benefit greatly from you should you continue with us on your career path."

What he said made sense. Logan could only attribute his doubts to the natural fear of uncertainty and decided he just had to man up and take what the world had to offer. His family would understand, especially when this could mean another stepping stone that would one day give his parents grandchildren.

Sitting up a little straighter in his chair, he forced down all his doubts and said with conviction, "With all that you're offering me, two weeks sounds reasonable. I won't let you down."

After going over further details of what he would need to do to get himself to Chicago, Logan ended the interview feeling like he had conquered Mount Everest.

As he stood to leave, he pulled out his phone to text his friend the good news and how he owed him big time for setting the whole thing up. But being momentarily distracted, he didn't look up in time to see the girl headed in his direction until he slammed right into her.

Because Logan was 6'2" with a medium build, the impact only knocked the phone out of his hands while she lost her footing completely.

"I am so sorry," Logan nearly shouted as he awkwardly offered his hand to help her up. "Are you okay?" When she made no effort to move, he feared the worst until she closed her eyes and started laughing as if her unfortunate end of the accident were the punch line to a hilarious joke.

"I knew this would happen to me someday," she chuckled, finally pulling herself into a sitting position. It was when she picked up a box that he noticed the array of art supplies that had crashed to the floor—no thanks to him.

Without giving it a second thought, he dropped to his knees and began collecting the paintbrushes and pencils that had rolled a significant distance under the tables.

"Really, I'm very sorry. I feel so bad," he said, genuinely meaning it, but it was hard to feel less than thrilled at a time like this.

"It's okay. Really, I'm fine. No blood, no foul."

Taking the hint to shut up, Logan watched her gather the last few pencils in silence and didn't stand until she did. Being around ten inches taller than her, he stifled a chuckle watching her size him up before muttering a quick thanks and readjusting herself.

He was about to ask her why she would be carrying a box of art supplies into a coffee shop when he heard his phone go off from under the table.

"You better get that," she said, appearing amused, but ready to leave the awkward situation now before he made it worse.

With an apologetic smile, he walked past her to pick up his phone, which had surprisingly stayed in one piece.

Seeing James's name on the screen, Logan was brought back to his own moment and right away everything else was forgotten.

He answered to give a full report and the more he talked about what transpired, the more he realized what he'd accomplished in the last hour. He had carried out his first step, and if he stayed focused and played his cards right, everything would go according to plan.

Chapter Two

ive years later.

Logan sped down the highway, admiring the hum of the engine as he accelerated toward the setting sun. The smooth ride somehow eased his nerves and awakened them at the same time. But his brief moment of serenity was short lived once his phone went off and the ID on the screen was one of his assistants. He figured it was likely a problem at work that would force him to turn back around. Hopefully it was something he could pass along to another employee, or perhaps to one of the interns. They were all looking for an opportunity to show how useful they were in hopes of being put on the pay roll once their internships were over.

"Hello," he answered, using the app that connected his smart phone to the car.

"Good evening, Mr. Atwood," came Laura's voice on the speaker. "I'm calling to tell you your 2:30 meeting has been cancelled tomorrow. Mr. Westmont would like to reschedule for next Thursday. The best time for you would be at one in the afternoon. Would that work for you?"

"That works fine. Thank you, Laura."

"Your mother also called earlier this afternoon."

Logan groaned inwardly, realizing he had forgotten to call her back. She left him a message about the upcoming family Christmas party and Logan didn't have the nerve to tell her he couldn't make it. There was too much to get done, and deadlines needed to be met. But mostly, he had no interest in seeing relatives who had practically shunned him from the family. He wasn't interested in reliving the same arguments they had every time he visited, especially with his brother.

"Did she tell you the reason she called?" he asked.

"She didn't say; only that you should call her back at a convenient time."

Now was a good a time as any, but Logan just didn't have the heart to disappoint her . . . again. Instead, he took the coward's route and decided to put it off until tomorrow. By then he'd have an eloquent speech made up and a Christmas gift in the mail. Which reminded him . . .

"Thanks, Laura. Did you send out those packages I ordered?"

"I did this morning."

"Again, thank you."

"No problem. Have a good evening, sir."

"You too."

Logan continued down the busy streets to his home in the city, which wasn't too far away from his work. He parked in the garage, making sure to set the alarm before entering the elevator and pressing the button for the tenth floor.

His place was a spacious two-bedroom condo that he was able to furnish as nicely but as simply as a thirty-year-old bachelor would need. There wasn't much to his décor, save a few framed posters and a calendar he hadn't switched since July. He used his tablet for that anyway, the kind that could connect to his flat screen. It was one of the few things he spent any time doing at home between sleeping and eating.

Logan had barely gotten his keys through the door when he heard the familiar sound of five-inch heels clomping up the stairwell. Instinctively, he quickened his task of getting inside before he was noticed, but he knew he was too late when he saw Sheila round the corner.

"Logan," she crooned, still accompanied by her clomping heels.

"Sheila," he tried to say brightly as he turned to see his neighbor approach him, wearing a tight-fitting dress that barely came to her thighs. Her hair was, as always, bleached blonde with added extensions, but tonight her skin was noticeably tanner and makeup applied a bit darker, which made him wonder who she was dressing up for this time.

"Long time, no see," she said, appraising him from head to toe. "Is that a new suit?"

"Yes, in fact, it is."

"You look like you could be on the cover of *GQ Magazine*. And I see you haven't shaved in a few days. You pull off the scruff look so well."

"Thank you," he said genuinely, since that was the look he was going for. At his age he was finally able to pull it off and he didn't mind the ego boost, even if she did have an agenda. "Is that a new dress?"

"Oh this? Just something from my closet I decided to throw on," she shrugged, and Logan had to keep from rolling his eyes at the cliché line. What woman in their right mind would expose so much skin in the dead of winter?

"The color looks good on you," he said.

She giggled. "You always were the charmer. What are you up to this evening?"

"Just going to finish a few projects, eat some dinner, and head to bed."

"Would you like some company?"

"Not tonight, Sheila," he sighed, knowing exactly what she wanted.

When Logan first moved in, she was the first to knock on his door and invite him over for dinner, which he enthusiastically accepted. He'd already pegged her as high maintenance. He quickly found out she was living off a trust fund and her father had always paid for everything she owned. Right away she wasn't his type, but what man wouldn't want to spend an evening with a beautiful woman who offered him food?

It didn't take long for him to learn she only entertained for men who could offer her something in return. Logan didn't mind this when she asked him to do different things that needed to be done around her place. He fixed a clogged drain in her bathroom and took care of a few issues on her computer, which seemed harmless at the time until one evening she mentioned a loose floorboard in her bedroom.

He knew he should have ran out of there as soon as he figured out her plan, but that small voice of reason was drowned out by thoughts that left him feeling weak and unguarded.

She got what she wanted that night, and the guilt pushed Logan straight to his bishop the following Sunday. But as time went on, his will to progress righteously fumbled as Sheila's advances continued. Not to mention his coworkers enjoyed the big city lifestyle and he never declined an invitation to socialize if it meant him climbing the corporate ladder.

Gradually, as his popularity rose, his church attendance declined until his current lifestyle was all he cared for in his standard of living. He realized being a member had been holding him back, hence the constant disagreements he had with his family every time he came in contact with them.

Right now he could tell Sheila was disappointed that he had declined the invitation. It was about a year ago that he got tired of her antics and started spending time with the women his coworkers were setting him up with. He preferred their company considering they were far less demanding and less, well, annoying.

He was hoping tonight she would leave without putting up a fight, but of course as he walked inside his home, she followed.

"What do you mean, 'not tonight'?" she asked, a hint of venom in her words.

"I have a lot of projects to get done and I don't have time to play games with you."

"You had a lot of free time to spend with me last summer. What happened, Logan? Have I done something to offend you?"

Your entire persona offends me. "Of course not, but what you're looking for, I can't give you anymore," he said, moving to the kitchen to grab a beer. "We've had this talk before. I've moved on."

"Did you meet someone then?"

Logan sighed. "That doesn't matter."

"Why won't you tell me? I thought we were friends."

"*Friends* and *friends with benefits* are two different things. You never told me about your escapades while you had me over at your place."

"That's because there weren't any," she lied.

"Joe, Sam, Derek—" he listed, holding up a finger for each one.

"Okay! So there were other guys and we both knew our relationship was casual."

"Exactly. We had our fun. Now the fun's over and work has taken priority in my life."

"Work has always been your priority. What changed? Did you get promoted or something?"

". . . Yes," he lied. "I have new orders of business and I can't get behind. Maybe some other time."

The words were out before he could take it back. The half-smile on her face clearly told him this wasn't over, but Logan didn't care at the moment. He just wanted her out of his apartment so he could read the news and enjoy the silence for once.

"Call me," was all she said and she sauntered out into the hall.

Logan closed the door behind her and walked back to his fridge to make a salad. But just as he dug in, his phone rang and he answered it without looking at the ID.

"Hello?"

"Logan!" he heard a small crowd shouting in the background. "Where are you?" asked Jack, a guy he recently befriended after helping him out of financial trouble a few months ago. "I just got my new console installed. I thought you were coming over."

"Shoot, I forgot," he groaned.

"Well the party just started. Get over here," was all Jack said before the line cut off.

Logan closed his eyes tightly, rubbing his eyelids in exhaustion. Part of him wanted to stay home and not brave the icy roads all the way to Jack's house just to goof off over video games. But it beat staying home like a loser and not taking the chance to hang out with his friends.

Decision made, he got up to change into jeans, a T-shirt, and a hoodie. Then he made his way to the parking garage. Jack's house wasn't too far away, but traffic was going to slow him down if he took the main roads, especially with the accident on the highway that he'd passed coming home.

He figured the scenic route would get him there just as fast and he didn't mind seeing the Christmas lights on the way. Despite his lack of spirit in celebrating the holiday, there were still a few aspects he enjoyed.

About ten minutes away from home, Logan ended up on a road that had yet to be plowed, so he made sure to stop carefully at the intersection. Thankfully he'd replaced his tires last month, so the traction kept him steady on the ice.

While he waited for the light to turn green, he saw the flash of headlights in his rearview mirror racing toward him.

"Slow down, bro," he breathed.

But he wasn't going to. In the three seconds it took him to realize what was about to happen, the airbag deployed as the impact shoved his car across the ice and straight into the intersection.

In that same time frame, the car's back end drifted into a half circle, until the last thing Logan saw was another set of lights in the passenger window.

And then . . . nothing.

As paramedics made their way to scene, chaos ensued as people in their homes came out to see the damage and help in any way they could.

The three-car collision was just as bad as the paramedics predicted when they got the call. Two of the cars' front ends were crushed in, but the third had received the most damage. When the surrounding crowd flagged them down, the EMTs first attended to the victim inside. A few had already pried the door off so they could get to the man unconscious and hemorrhaging in the driver's seat.

Within minutes they had him on a gurney, inside the ambulance, and on their way to the hospital where staff was on high alert.

ER doctors were ready on arrival and quickly took over as each assessed all the damages he'd received in the accident. One doctor immediately called in a brain surgeon while others noticed the puncture wound in his side. He had a deep laceration in his leg and his vitals were at dangerous levels.

While each doctor gave orders and exchanged information, one finally had the inkling to ask, "What's this guy's name?"

"Uh . . ." one of the nurses drawled as she looked through his chart. "Logan. Logan Atwood."

"Search through his contacts and look for his closest relatives. They need to know he may not make it through the night."

⚬ᗒ

Images of red flashing lights through a haze of cracked glass and falling snow lingered in Logan's mind as he was sure his body was just waking up from a dream. He didn't know where he was or how he got there, but he knew it didn't feel right.

He felt pain one moment, then he was completely numb the next. The feeling of weightlessness and dizziness reminded him of his trips to Lake Powell during his teen years. It was equivalent to riding in the tube on the back of a boat and flying through the air after hitting a large wave.

He was ready to wake up from the dream now until the sound of static from his clock-radio sounded in his ears and he hit the snooze button to silence it.

He let out a sigh of relief as he fell back onto his pillow, happy to be alive and in his warm bed. But as he inhaled the scent of his pillow, he realized something was different.

He lifted his head and saw that the color of his sheets weren't white, but black like the ones he'd had back in college. He looked around and saw the familiar white brick of the apartment he had stayed in as well.

In a panic, Logan's body jerked forward, taking in his surroundings with fear and confusion. The laundry on the floor, the smell of day-old pizza and Axe cologne, the haphazard posters on the wall, books scattered across the desk . . . He was back in college. He was back five years ago!

He jumped out of bed and scrambled to the bathroom. His facial hair was gone and he sported the missionary cut he had when he left for the MTC. Another strange feeling—he was wearing his garments.

He had to be dreaming. Logan tried to think of the last thing he remembered before waking up. He recalled that dizzy feeling, the flashing lights, the cold air . . .

"Good morning."

Logan's head snapped toward the unfamiliar voice and saw a man he had never seen before standing in the doorway.

"Who are you?"

"My name's Thomas, but you can call me Tommy. I know what you're probably thinking, so how about you sit down and take a breather," he said, gesturing toward the living room.

Logan did as he was told and sat on one of the black pleather couches that faced the TV he remembered getting from DI with his roommates. It was pathetic, but it came with a Nintendo and they'd spent endless days playing *Super Mario* and *Smash Brothers* trying to one up each other in the ranks.

He shook his head at the memory and looked up to see the man sitting across from him. He was probably in his mid-thirties, but looked a bit older than that. He was bulky, but not heavyset, and his hair was cropped neatly. He had a kind disposition, but retained a look of authority that left Logan wondering who he was and why he was there.

"I don't understand what's going on."

"That's why I'm here. You were driving to a friend's home and were rear-ended into an intersection. Do you remember anything about what happened that night?"

Logan shook his head. "I think I remember seeing headlights or . . . something. But that's pretty much it." Logan's panic started to rise once he realized the situation. That accident. Him suddenly in a different place in time. "Wait, am I . . . dead?"

"No, son," Tommy said calmly. "In the accident you suffered a serious brain injury that put you in a coma. Right now you're in a hospital while doctors are doing everything they can to make sure you come out of this okay."

"A coma?" Logan repeated, feeling like he was going to throw up.

"I'm sorry that's the case, but I need to get on with the explanation because there isn't much time left."

"You mean time left for me to live?"

"No," Tommy chuckled. "Your interview. You still need to get ready for it."

"My interview?"

"Yes, the interview that got you the job you have now."

"What about it?"

"It's today."

Logan took a minute to process the information he was slowly gathering. "You're saying . . . I'm reliving the day I had my job interview?"

"You're reliving the day you made a serious decision that took you down a certain path. Accepting that job was the path you chose, and this is your chance to choose the other."

Logan got to his feet and shook his head. "This is insane. Why would I want to choose something different than the life I have now? I have a great life. I've been successful and helped many people."

"That may be true, but guess what?" said Tommy, rising to his feet to face him. "You're in a coma. You still have that life you worked hard for. But even the most successful of men have wondered during their darkest moments what they could have done to change things. Even in *your* success, you've wondered what your life would have been like if you had said no. But on this occasion, you've been granted the chance to find out."

"So . . . this is a like a do-over."

He shrugged. "In a sense."

"But if this isn't real, why don't I just skip out on the interview and stay home? In fact, why should I do anything?"

"Well that's why I'm here; to push you in the right direction."

"Who are you anyway?"

"I'm only the messenger, son. A friend, if you will. Even in your subconscious, you don't get off that easy."

Logan squeezed his eyes shut and pinched the bridge of his nose. "Okay," he sighed. "So I have to go to the interview then?"

"That's where it all starts. So if I were you, I'd take a shower because you smell ripe, boy."

Logan didn't argue with that. He moved into the bathroom and took another good look in the mirror. He flexed his bicep and frowned. He had gained a lot more muscle mass over the years and now he was back to his scrawny self with no future.

He tried to keep in mind that he was in a coma and this wasn't real. But the more he dwelled on it, the more depressed he became. Would he continue to live this way until he woke up? Would he ever wake up? What if the decision was made to pull the plug? Who would be making that decision?

The first person that came to mind was his mother. He hated the idea of her in the hospital standing over his body connected to a bunch of tubes. He hated the image of being attached to tubes in general. Why had this happened to him? Was it karma? Was he being punished? Or was it exactly like Tommy said? Was he merely given a chance to discover what life would have been like?

Since he had very few options, he decided to take a shower and clear his head. It was a strange feeling knowing he wasn't quite alive, but everything still felt like he was. It felt every bit like reality and nothing like a simple dream.

Logan got ready just as he remembered doing that day five years ago. It wasn't hard to remember that process, but after he walked outside, it bummed him out to realize he didn't have a car.

"Fantastic," he groaned.

"Don't worry," said Tommy as he brushed past him down the step. "I'll give you a ride."

"You can do that?"

"Of course I can. It's what I'm here for," he called back as he unlocked a very plain looking sedan and climbed into the driver's seat.

"Was this the car you were given?" Logan asked, still wondering how big of a part this guy was going to play during this life evaluation.

"This is the car I chose. I appreciate the simple things, and it gets good mileage."

Logan shook his head as they pulled out of the parking lot. "And that matters while I'm in a coma?"

"Everything that happens here will have the same consequences as you would have had in reality."

Tommy reached over and slugged Logan in the arm with his fist. "Ow! What the heck, man?"

"The same cause and effect. So if I were you, I wouldn't be jumping off buildings or doing anything that'll harm your body. Because the mindset you have here is going to affect your body in the real world."

"Hold on," said Logan, rubbing the sore spot on his arm. "If I *were* to jump off a building and die, would I die in real life?"

"Yes and no," he shrugged. "The mind and the body are very interesting and complex entities that work together to survive. The brain sends a command and the body responds to it. Your heart rate gets quicker when your thought process is immersed in fear. Your hands get sweaty when you're nervous. You blush when you're embarrassed. You get butterflies when you see a good-looking girl. There is always a cause and effect. Having a stressed and negative mindset here will affect the way your body heals itself."

"This is all too confusing."

"Just try not to think about it. It's easier to pretend this is reality and just deal as you go."

"But if I do that, won't I convince myself this *is* reality and I'm not stuck in a coma?"

"You've watched *Inception* too many times. We're here," he said as he pulled up to the coffee shop. "Good luck."

"I really don't want to do this."

"You'll do fine. I'll be around if you need me."

"How do I get ahold of you?"

"You have a phone. My number is in your contacts."

Logan let out a heavy sigh, reaching into his pocket to pull out the phone that flipped open and had no touch screen. "Oh this is going to be fun," he said sarcastically as he got out of the car and slammed it shut.

Chapter Three

❦

It was two in the morning when Peggy Atwood answered the phone and heard the news of her son's accident. She tried to stifle her sobs as she fell to her knees by her bed, but her emotion was too overwhelming as her heart continued to break by the second.

When her husband, Henry, hung up with the doctor, he immediately came to her side providing her comfort while sharing her anguish.

"I prayed so hard for him," she whimpered. "And this is what happens."

"We don't always know the will of Lord. For now let's figure out a way for us to be there for him."

Peggy could only nod in agreement and spent the rest of the night in a fitful sleep. The next morning she cooked breakfast for the family, but decided to start a fast, keeping a constant prayer in her heart for Logan's welfare. When Henry and her youngest son, Mark, came to the table, they agreed to join the fast with her and were glad to put the leftovers in the fridge until dinner.

After Henry came home from work, both sat down at the kitchen table and tried to sort out their finances so at least one of them could travel to Chicago. Henry couldn't afford missing any more shifts with the holidays approaching, but Peggy had the time to go and perhaps stay at Logan's condo so she could be at the hospital for a few days. Although there was very little they could do, she couldn't sit by and do nothing.

While she packed her suitcase, Henry called the rest of their children who were grown and out of the house. Of course they passed along their sympathies and included themselves in the fast, but Peggy had no doubt that they were all thinking the same thing: *Serves him right.*

They were always so candid in their disapproval of Logan's lifestyle. The hurt and dislike they expressed for him in general was heartbreaking, but she always tried to put his good nature in the light despite his decision to walk away from the church.

"Mom?" she heard Mark say in the doorway.

She glanced over at her youngest son, noticing how tall he was for a boy about to graduate high school. He would also be leaving for his mission shortly after and the scene reminded her of when Logan came to her just after he put in his papers.

"Yes, sweetie?" she answered.

"How's Logan really doing? I know you guys aren't telling me everything."

Peggy sighed, wishing she could continue denying the severity of the situation. And if she told him everything wasn't as bad as it really was, maybe she would start to believe it as well. And maybe it would make it all easier for her to bear.

"The doctors say there's a chance he could pull through, but he isn't out of the woods yet. They've had to do several surgeries to repair his leg and brain tissue. But he's on a ventilator that's breathing for him. He still has brain activity, so there's a chance that he'll wake up, but a bigger chance that he won't. Only time will tell."

Mark's eyebrows furrowed as if he were in pain, and the tears that ran down his face pushed Peggy to pull him into a hug. He rested his cheek on her shoulder and silently let go of his anguish. She knew he'd always looked up to Logan, who was the second to youngest and had always acknowledged Mark like a friend instead of a tedious little brother.

"Can I come with you?" he asked.

"I wish you could, but you still have school and we just can't afford it right now."

He lifted his head to look at her. "Christmas break is coming up and I can use what's in my mission fund—"

"No, you won't do that. But I promise we'll figure out another way. Until then just pray that the Lord's will is in our favor."

Mark nodded and wordlessly left, feeling no more comforted than when he walked in. He wandered to his room and remembered the nights Logan had slept on the cot when he came to visit from Dixie. Mark had been eight years old at the time and had always felt privileged to share moments where he'd ask Logan serious questions about life and receive serious answers as if he were his equal. Logan was the one who first inspired him to serve a mission. While Mark had attended primary, he'd watched Logan prepare for the MTC. But it was shortly after he became a deacon that his presence and influence became more and more scarce until eventually it felt like Logan stopped caring altogether.

Mark was sad to find out about Logan's indiscretions and to overhear the heated conversations he had with his other siblings. His parents constantly reminded him that they didn't love Logan any less, but they took extra care in making sure Mark didn't follow in his footsteps. But Mark didn't have much desire to follow a stranger anyway.

Now, picturing Logan's life hanging on line, all he could see was the likelihood of him not being on this earth anymore. With that possibility clenching at his heart, he got down on his knees and prayed out loud, "Lord, please save my brother. Please save my best friend."

☙

Logan sat at the same table of the coffee shop where he was to have his interview. The feeling of déjà vu was almost too overwhelming. David Miller, the man who had been his mentor and confidant during his first year at the company, walked in with the same jovial attitude he always had anytime he came into a room.

It was nice to see a familiar face, especially now, but he had to remind himself this was the first time they ever met.

"Good morning," he said as he approached Logan's table.

"Good morning, David. Words cannot express how grateful I am to see you."

"It's not a problem," he chuckled. "I admire your persistence. Plus I get my morning coffee at the same time. Can I get you anything?"

What Logan wouldn't give for his usual order of a grande mocha with vanilla cream to wake his senses, but the feel of his garments beneath his suit was a constant reminder he was in a time when he honored his covenants. Although his real self would have said yes, he sullenly said, "No. No, I'm fine."

"Well then, let's get to business."

The interview went by in a blur as Logan answered his questions and listed his credentials. He started mentioning certain ideas that left David intrigued and wanting to hear more. Logan could tell he was impressed by his knowledge and knew exactly what to say to appeal to his interests. He was more pleased to be talking to an old friend, especially since he moved from the company two years ago.

And then that pivotal moment came when he asked, "Could you start in two weeks?"

Logan recalled the moment when he had that feeling to refuse, to walk away from the biggest opportunity of his life that had proven to be a successful venture. It had been easy to ignore, but now it was magnified like a loud speaker in his ears blaring, *Walk away, Logan!*

With a wince, followed by a solemn sigh, Logan replied, "I'm sorry, sir. But I don't think that's going to be possible."

"I should remind you that we have many other applicants who are willing to work sooner than that and I'm afraid we won't hesitate to select another applicant. From what I gather, our company will benefit greatly from you and I'd hate to lose a potential employee who I'm certain will be a valuable asset."

"I know, sir. And I greatly appreciate you seeing my potential, but the timing is bad and I'm needed elsewhere."

"I see. Well that is unfortunate to hear. However, I do have your information and if something opens up in the future, I'll make sure to put in a good word."

"Thank you very much," he said, standing to shake his hand.

Logan could sense his slight irritation when he murmured, "Have a good day," and walked out of the coffee shop.

He slumped in his chair feeling more defeated than ever. He thought about lingering for a while, but the smell only tempted him to give in to his indulgence, especially when he was already feeling so depressed.

Standing up, he pulled out his cell phone and looked for Tommy in his contact list. He was about to call for a ride home until he ran into a solid object that stopped him in his tracks. The next thing he knew he was staring at a girl lying on the floor in a sea of scattered art supplies.

"Whoa, are you all right?" Logan asked as he took her hand and helped her to stand. "I'm sorry. I should have been looking where I was going."

She appeared a little dazed as she stood to look up into his eyes and she let out a small laugh that sounded familiar. And that's when it hit him. He had heard it before when he did the very same thing to the same girl after he finished the interview.

"I knew this would happen to me someday," she chuckled, bending down to pick up a box that held all the art supplies that crashed to the floor.

Logan immediately got down on his knees and began collecting the paintbrushes and pencils that rolled across the wood laminate.

"Do you plan on redoing the logo?" he asked, curious as to why someone would bring all this with them into a coffee shop.

"No, I was headed to work and I wanted to stop and get a doughnut on the way."

"Where do you work?"

"The preschool on campus. It's my last day, so I was returning all the supplies I borrowed."

"And you couldn't leave them in the car?"

"I was going to, but I didn't want my brushes to get lonely." Logan had to stop and see if she was being serious and judging by her sarcastic expression, she was only messing with him. He also noticed her heart shaped face and hazel eyes, which he immediately took note of as one of her attractive features.

"My car is in the shop," she chuckled, "and won't be done until this afternoon, so I had to walk here. And because my gift card expires soon, I didn't want to miss my opportunity."

"I see," he said, only partly seeing her justifiable excuse.

When the last pencil was gathered, Logan picked up the box and handed it to her.

"Thanks," she said. "Sorry for not looking where I was going."

"No blood, no foul," he said with a smile as she noticeably blushed and moved to stand in line.

As she walked away, he took a moment to notice her features. Her hair was blonde, but a deeper shade, close to the color of honey. He could tell she owned a modern sense of style wearing red pants with a unique pattern on them, donning a matching hat and scarf over her white sweater. She was very pretty in a natural way, which wasn't very common in his social circle. He was so used to the girls who spent hours on their appearance to attract a certain crowd in loud and sketchy places.

When she offered a gift card to the barista, he watched the kid who looked no more than sixteen say to her, "Sorry, there's only eighteen cents left on this card."

"What? Really?"

"Yeah," he drawled.

"You've got to be kidding me," she sighed.

"I wish I was. Sorry."

"It's okay. Have a nice day."

Logan could see her obvious displeasure in not getting the doughnut her heart was set on. Although it was such a trivial thing to him, he impulsively moved to her side and offered a five-dollar bill saying, "I got this. Would you add a large hot chocolate to that order as well?"

"Sure," said the kid as he moved to grab a paper cup from the stack.

"You didn't have to do that," she said, obviously flustered by his move. "You don't owe me anything."

"I know, but the doughnut looked so lonely and disappointed as you were walking away, I decided to take pity and put it out of its misery."

She raised an eyebrow and then chuckled as she shook her head. "Thank you, you're very generous."

"It was the least I could do," he shrugged.

"No, really. You know when you've been looking forward to something all week and the amazing feeling that comes with finally getting it?"

Logan knew that feeling all too well, and he just experienced the sensation of intentionally letting it slip through his fingers. "I certainly do."

"Then you know you just made me the happiest person on the planet."

Logan laughed out loud. "Well I'm glad."

"What's your name?" she asked.

"Logan," he said as he grabbed the brown paper bag and his change with a "thank you."

"Logan . . . ?" she prodded, accepting the bag while he sipped his hot chocolate.

"Logan Atwood."

"You look so familiar. Where are you from?"

"I'm from Highland. I came here to go to Dixie a few years ago."

"You wouldn't happen to be related to the Atwoods in the Highland Stake, would you?"

Logan nearly choked on the hot liquid. "My parents are in the Highland Stake. Do the names Henry or Peggy ring a bell?"

"No," she chuckled. "But they might to my grandparents. I used to live with them in Highland for a while until I moved down here."

"What a small world. Did you come here to go to Dixie too?"

"Yeah, I actually graduated a few years ago and stayed here to work at the school. But the lease on my apartment ends next week, so I'll be moving back in a few days."

"That's great. Do you have a job lined up?" he asked, taking her box so she could eat her doughnut while they walked outside.

She took a large bite, chewing a few seconds before answering with a half-full mouth, "Sort of." She finished swallowing. "I have an interview with the Salt Lake School District. They're looking for a teacher for one of their preschool programs in the area."

"That's awesome. What made you decide on Salt Lake?"

"It's closer to home," she shrugged. "As much as I love St. George . . ."

"Need a change?"

"More than ever. I'll miss the scenery though. The red rocks are beautiful and the outdoors are certainly more adventurous."

"Very true," he said thoughtfully, recalling the numerous excursions he went on with his friends hiking in Zion National Park. Having lost touch with them since accepting that job, he wondered where they were now and how life had treated them after college.

"I'm sorry to keep talking like this," she said, ending his train of thought. "You're probably on your way somewhere."

"Actually . . . I have nothing else planned today. Are you headed to the school?"

"Yep," she said just before taking another bite of her doughnut.

"Would it be creepy if I walked with you?"

"You seriously have nothing better to do?" she laughed.

"Truth be told, I just turned down an opportunity of a life-time and I could really use a friend about now."

"And during this nine-minute interlude . . . you decided we were friends?"

Logan had been shot down before and he couldn't blame her, having just met under less than ideal circumstances. But he couldn't help feeling a little nervous and downhearted at her reaction. He was used to getting most of the attention from the women he was interested in. Even from women he wanted nothing to do with.

"I'd like to think so. But I guess it's a two-way street, isn't it?"

"Well in that case, good, because I could use a friend right now too."

"Really?"

"Yes. I need someone to hold this box while I eat my dough-nut and walk to work." Logan laughed, not expecting to hear that. "Funny how fate works, huh?"

Oh you have no idea. "Funny indeed. But even though I'm on fate's side, I think I should probably learn your name as well."

"It's Addison, but I go by Addie."

"Addie, what?"

"Garrison."

Logan thought hard, trying to remember any Garrisons in his hometown. The name wasn't familiar, but then again he didn't have much invested interest in his parent's neighbors.

"Addison Garrison," he drawled. "That's a memorable name."

She paid him a courtesy chuckle as they started down the sidewalk. "Yeah, hence why I go by *Addie* Garrison. Roles off the tongue better."

"Hey, a unique name will get you far."

"Hopefully the people reviewing my resume follow that philosophy."

"If it were me, I wouldn't need to look at any of your references. I'd just see your name and say, 'Yes. She's hired.'"

When she laughed again, Logan smiled at the pleasant sound of it. Sheila's laugh was always loud and obnoxious, which he didn't mind until changing circumstances made him realize its equivalence to nails on a chalkboard.

They talked about the trivial things in their lives as they continued to walk toward the campus grounds. They passed the St. George Temple along the way and Logan had a strange feeling in the pit of his stomach as he gazed at the white structure. He remembered going there every other week with a group from his ward and often by himself early in the mornings.

Part of him longed for it, and another part of him hinted at the feeling of guilt; the same that used to pester his senses several years ago. But Logan tried not to let it linger so he could focus on Addie's words.

"Do you have any fun plans for the holiday?" she asked.

"Uh . . ." was all he could say before he remembered this was the year he'd hoped to go home for Christmas. And now that he was jobless, he could easily do that. He just wasn't sure that was the right idea.

"My mom invited me to come home for the holidays. I didn't know if I was able to for a while, but I guess it's possible now. I just have to figure out shuttle schedules," he said, not exactly thrilled to ride in a crowded van for five hours.

"If you like, you can save yourself some trouble and help me out with gas by riding with me up north. I'm leaving Friday morning and have an extra seat."

Logan immediately liked that idea. Saying *yes* would get him back to his family, which is likely the direction he was supposed to be headed. But he'd be lying if he said seeing his parents and siblings again appealed more to him than spending more time in her company.

"Now look who's being generous," he said, glancing over to see her blush again.

"Just trying to save someone from being squished between an old lady who'll snore loudly into your ear and a guy whose cologne is ode to sweat."

"Sounds like you speak from experience."

"If only that was the worst of it. But as useful as public transportation is, I really do need help with gas. My friend was supposed to come with me, but she bailed. So my offer is partially selfish."

"Understandable," he nodded. "Well let me look at my schedule and I'll get back to you later tonight. What's your number?"

"Here, let me put it into your phone."

As luck would have it, Logan pulled it out just as it began to ring. The caller ID said "James" and he suddenly remembered it was his old friend who had gotten him the interview, who he now had to break the bad news to.

Logan pressed the end button. "I'll call him back," he said and she smiled as she put in her number. "Perfect, I'll call you tonight."

"Sounds like a plan," she said, taking the box and entering the building with a spring in her step.

After the door shut behind her, he pulled out his phone and the first call he made was to James. He had to keep telling himself this wasn't reality, that at this time they weren't in the middle of a falling out where James hated his guts for what he did to him just after he moved to Chicago.

Swallowing hard, he found the missed call and pressed send. It rang an agonizing ten seconds before he answered: "Logan! Hey man, how'd it go?"

"Uh . . . hey James, how've you been?" Logan answered awkwardly, and then he rolled his eyes at himself for the stupid reply.

"Seriously, tell me how it went."

"Well it looks like I'm not exactly what they're looking for," he lied, careful not to start any kind of tension with him. "But it's all right. There will be other opportunities."

"Definitely. At least you tried."

"But I still appreciate you setting it up. You're a good friend, James."

"Anytime. I'd like to stay and chat, but I'm in the middle of something. Wanna hang out this weekend?"

"Uh, actually I think I'm going home this weekend," he said, starting to relax a little.

"Nice. For good?"

"I'm . . . not sure yet, but I'll keep you posted."

"Okay. Well then Merry Christmas. I'll talk to you later."

"You too," Logan said before ending the call. He let out a sigh of relief and another pang of guilt hit lower in his gut. He realized this experience was not going to be an easy ride.

He dialed Tommy's number and within two rings he answered with a cheery, "Hello?"

"I'm ready for that ride."

"I'll be there in two minutes," he said before hanging up.

Logan wanted to question how he knew where he was, but didn't overthink it. And exactly two minutes later, Tommy pulled up to the curb and Logan wordlessly buckled himself into the passenger seat.

"So, how'd it go?" he asked with the same cheery voice he had on the phone.

"I turned it down, just like I was supposed to do."

"And how do you feel?"

"Actually . . . not too bad."

"Really?"

"Well it's not like this is real or anything," he said with a hint of sarcasm. After he said it, Tommy slugged him in the arm for the second time this morning.

"Seems to feel pretty real," Tommy retorted.

"Point taken," he grunted. "Just stop doing that."

"I take it you're not too happy with the decision."

"I'm not, but it wasn't a total bummer. Ran into someone . . . literally, from my old stake back in Highland. She offered to drive me back up north for the holidays."

"No kidding. You know *I* can always drive you there."

Logan rubbed the sore spot on his arm. "I think I'll take her company over yours."

"Likely a lot prettier than I am, I'm sure," he laughed. "When are you leaving?"

"Haven't worked out the exact details, but sometime Friday morning."

"How long are you planning on staying?"

Logan thought for a moment and asked with raised eyebrows, "How long am I going to be in this coma?"

"Good point. All I can say is that that depends on you. Just take it one step at a time."

Logan looked out the window and could see the angel Moroni in the distance. "Easier said than done."

Chapter Four

❧

Peggy hugged her coat a little tighter as she entered Logan's hospital room.

Approaching the bed, she looked down at her son lying motionless with the exception of a ventilator making his chest rise and fall with every breath. The rest of his body was hooked to monitors and IVs, his face bruised and bandaged from the trauma.

She pulled a chair as close as she could to his side and tentatively touched his hand. She recalled many people saying—mostly from movies and TV shows—that people in comas could still hear, if not absorb, what their loved ones said to them out loud.

"I remember when you were six years old," she started. "You came in from playing outside and told me you had scraped your knee on the sidewalk from falling off your scooter. You didn't shed a single tear. You just asked for a Band-Aid and went right on playing.

"You called them 'bandans' back then," she chuckled, with a sniff. "And you had a tendency to use them for every little cut and bruise you managed to get. One night I came home to find wrappers all over the floor, and about forty Band-Aids covering your arms and legs. You threw your hands in the air and said, 'Look mommy! I'm all better!'

"I was going to scold you, but I ended up laughing at the whole thing and told you how proud I was that you were able to take good care of yourself. You were such a cute kid, and that didn't change as you got older. In fact . . ." she chuckled again, "when you were sixteen, you were getting ready to go on a date to your first dance. After the day activity, you decided to jump off the roof and ended up spraining your wrist. Despite the pain, you still went to that dance in a brace and made the best you could out of that night. I knew you really wanted to go and didn't want your mistake to spoil your date's evening. Thankfully she was a good sport, but I remember scolding you real good then. I went on about how you needed to be careful for the sake of others, if not for yourself. But this time . . ." Peggy whimpered. "You did nothing to purposely put yourself in harm's way . . . and *this* happens to you. And I can't give you a Band-Aid to make it better."

Gently she brushed a strand of hair away from his forehead. "We've missed you so much. We've been praying for the day we'd get to see you again, and I hate that this is how it turned out."

"Oh, Lord," she cried, "Please save my baby. Please help him pull through this. I can't let him go yet. I just can't."

Logan hung up the phone after his forty-five minute phone call with Addie. Once they confirmed the ride, the topic kept changing to unrelated subjects that further dove into their personalities, allowing them to get to know each other. They were mostly trivial things, but it helped him grow more comfortable with someone he knew less than twenty-four hours, and she was definitely entertaining.

He decided to call Tommy, wondering what it would be like when he went to sleep. Would he dream? Would he even sleep at all being in a coma? But when he asked these questions, all Tommy said was, "Why don't you close your eyes and find out?"

So Logan did just that, all the while hoping this wouldn't be like *Groundhog Day* and he'd wake up to relive the same day over again. But as soon as he closed his eyes, he literally blinked, opening them to daylight streaming through the window, and the calendar on his clock told him that a full day had actually passed.

"That was weird," he said out loud, moving to the kitchen to eat breakfast. Thankfully his roommates were gone for the holidays, so he didn't have to deal with the stress of acting completely normal around them. But the stress of acting completely normal around his family wasn't going to be easy either. A lot was going on at this time, and he had to strain his mind to remember how old everyone would be and where they were at in their lives. Thankfully Facebook gave him some insight and he spent a better part of the afternoon stalking all his relatives and former friends just to catch up on the things he'd forgotten.

Later that evening, Tommy came over with takeout from Durango's. Logan wished it were something a little more organic, but he didn't complain. He currently had very little money to buy the food he was accustomed to and was pleased to have a hot meal.

"Been doing your research, I see," Tommy said between bites.

"Yeah. But unfortunately not a lot of my family members have kept things up to date, so things are still a bit foggy. I have an idea of what everyone will look like, but it's going to be weird. I'd left things on such a bad note and coming home now . . ."

"Won't be awkward then," Tommy finished. "At this time there was hardly any tension between you and your folks, so when you walk through that front door, no one's going to be giving you the stink eye pretending everything's okay for the sake of Christmas."

"But that's just it," he sighed. "In reality, that's exactly what it would be like."

"I'm going to keep telling you this until you get it. You make the right decisions, and you have nothing to worry about. Just keep your head in the game."

Logan ate the last bite of his pork burrito and decided to change the subject. "So Tommy, we've been talking about me this whole time. Who are you exactly? You must have some back story that would bring you to a charity case like me."

"That I do, but I'm not at liberty to say right now."

"Why not?"

"You're very inquisitive," he chuckled. "And bold. I can see how you've become so successful in the business world."

Logan shrugged. "You learn to get over what you have to lose and being bold becomes easy."

"And that, my friend, is part of the answer to why many people end up here. Once you feel like you have nothing to lose, even if those things are good, you become careless in your decisions."

"Being bold doesn't mean to be careless," Logan defended.

"Which is why I only said it was part of the answer."

"Well then what's the rest of it?"

"If I told you, then your trip here would end pretty soon," he chuckled again. "And I don't know about you, but I want to know what happens next in your story. Don't you?"

"Well . . . of course I do, but if I'm here to learn something, I'm pretty sure I already know that answer," he said, remembering the feeling he had as he passed the temple.

"But has your heart accepted it yet?"

"Fair point."

Tommy finished his last bite, wiped his hands on a napkin, and leaned back against the chair. "Anybody can know the answers to a test, Logan. But the reason a person goes to school is to take that information and apply it to their life as they gain experience. Only then will it really matter to them. You have to find that moment when those answers have real meaning for you."

"I'm guessing you're a guardian angel sent here to help me find that moment."

"Good observation, Sherlock. I'm really hoping to get my wings soon."

Logan could hear the sarcasm and he just smiled. "Ah, should have guessed this would be an *It's a Wonderful Life* scenario."

As he downed the Diet Coke Tommy brought, he knew in reality he would have wished it were a cold beer. But oddly enough, in this world, he didn't have that craving. He laughed at how free he felt not having that nagging feeling in the back of his mind when he drank and made a mental note to kick the habit once this was over.

The next day he chose not to overkill on junk food and bought himself fixings to make a salad. Chewing on a piece of chicken, he pulled out his phone and impulsively texted Addie,

> All packed?

> Have been since Halloween. I'm so excited!!

> Haha nice. 7 still good?

> Make it 7:05.

Logan put down his fork and typed,

37

Dare I ask why?

Turns out I'm going to need an extra five minutes of beauty sleep if I'm going to wake up NOT looking like death warmed over.

Or we can still make it 7 and I'll try not be so distracted by such imperfection.

If you can handle it, then by all means we'll make it 6:59.

I always accept a challenge.

Not sure if I should be amused or insulted. lol.

Amused. You could be dressed as a hobo and I'd still be blown away by your lack of need in beauty sleep.

After ten long minutes, she finally said,

Very smooth answer. 7 works fine.

Good. I'll see you then.

The next morning, Logan was awake by six, more anxious than ever. He wasn't sure if he was nervous or excited but would determine that when they arrived in Highland.

It was close to 7:15 when Logan thought about calling Addie to see where she was. But a short minute later he saw her pull up in the parking lot and practically scramble out of her car. He opened the door just before she stumbled inside, out of breath.

"Decided you needed that beauty sleep after all?" he asked.

"I stopped to get gas," she panted, "but then I realized I left my wallet at the pump and had to turn around."

"Well better to figure that out now than halfway to Salt Lake."

"No kidding," she said, taking off her beanie to smooth her hair.

"Well that proves it then. You didn't need the extra five minutes. You look more radiant than ever."

She pointed a finger at him. "Sweet talking is not going to get you out of paying your half of the gas."

He exaggerated a sigh and shrugged. "Worth a shot."

With a laugh, she gestured outside, "Ready to go?"

"Yeah," he said, reaching over to grab his suitcase. But as he glanced toward the hallway, he saw Tommy peak around the corner waving at him, and suddenly he found himself in an awkward situation.

"Uh . . . could you give me a minute? I'm going to use the bathroom before we leave."

"Okay, I'll take your suitcase down."

"You will do no such thing. I'll be down in a minute."

Her face was amused as she shrugged and headed out the door. Logan quickly paced toward the hall to find Tommy standing in his room looking at his pictures.

"You've definitely gotten tidier over the years," he said.

"I'm guessing you're here because you have something important to say, but it has to be quick. I told Addie I was in the bathroom."

"In that case I just wanted to say good luck and Merry Christmas. I'm not going to be around on your trip. Since I have some other things I need to take care of, it's best that I leave you to it."

"So that's it then? Am I not going to see you again after this?" Logan asked, realizing he was going to miss the guy even though he barely knew him.

"I'll be sure to stop by before all this is over. Just follow your heart and you'll do just fine."

Logan accepted the instruction with a nod and headed to the front room to grab his suitcase and computer bag.

Locking the door behind him, he made his way to the teal Subaru parked behind the pool where Addie stood leaning against the passenger door. With the trunk already unlocked, he loaded his bags and climbed in the car that had noticeably survived many years of use. Thankfully it was neat and didn't smell overly used, which said a lot about her.

They made small talk as they merged onto the highway, heading out of St. George toward Cedar City. Eventually shooting the breeze led to her asking, "So what's your family like?"

Logan had to think about it for a second, but finally he was able to say, "My parents met, like many couples do, at BYU. My dad manages the local grocery store and my mom works for the Granite School District. I have two brothers and one sister. Brin is married with two kids. Taylor, also married with two kids and one on the way. My younger brother, Mark, will be fourteen next year."

"Brin? Is it short for Brianna?"

He smiled. "Yeah. Do you know her?"

"It rings a bell. I think I remember her from a youth conference or something," she chuckled. "But that's awesome, and quite the age gap."

"No kidding. Everyone, except for Brin, got the tall genes from my dad, but Mark looks older than he is. I'm pretty sure he started shaving last year."

She laughed at that. "Must be nice. I'm an only child."

"What was it like growing up for you then?"

"Can't say I was too spoiled," she chuckled. "But there isn't much else to say."

There was something in her expression that left Logan wondering what she was avoiding. He'd been around enough people to understand that everyone had some kind of baggage, and he guessed by her vague answers about her family, compared to the detailed ones on everything else, that there was something she had no interest in talking about. He wasn't going to pry, but he made a mental note to steer clear of the sensitive subject.

❦

Peggy stepped out of the cab into the icy wind and gazed at the tall building before her. During the brief phone calls she'd received over the years, she had pictured Logan living in a place like this, so she wasn't surprised to have a doorman open the heavy glass door for her as she entered the spacious lobby.

Despite the complexity of the building, she managed to get to the right floor and find the right apartment number.

As she took out the keys to get inside, she heard a door open behind her and someone say, "Excuse me?"

Peggy turned around to see a woman who looked to be in her mid-twenties with unnatural blonde hair and obvious extensions. She wore a halter top and alarmingly short jean shorts, which didn't make much sense to be wearing in the middle of winter. Peggy wondered if Logan knew her.

"Hi, um . . . who are you?" she said as she approached.

"I'm Peggy Atwood."

"Oh, are you related to Logan?"

"Yes, I'm his mother."

Her face brightened. "Oh wow, I didn't think I would ever get the pleasure of meeting one of Logan's relatives."

"Are you a friend of his?"

"You could say that," she said, using an expression that left Peggy not wanting to inquire further in that meaning.

"Oh, well, it was nice to meet you," she replied, proceeding to open the door.

"Likewise. Tell Logan I said hi."

"Of course."

With that being the last word, she walked inside and shut the door behind her.

She looked around the apartment for the first time and began taking it all in. Everything was neat and tidy with minimal furnishing besides the necessities of daily living. This was strange to her considering how he had lived as a teenager. On average she reminded him three times a week to pick his clothes up off the floor and dealt with numerous pinholes in the wall from the amount of posters he put up. His dresser and desk used to be covered with random trinkets that he insisted he needed but had never given much thought to. Peggy marveled at how things could change so quickly.

Although staying at Logan's place was much more convenient than staying at a hotel, she felt like she was intruding into a stranger's domain. She had no desire to snoop into his belongings, but she came for the secondary purpose of gathering his necessary information so she could deal with the people in Logan's life. Thankfully his assistant knew more than she did and their acquaintanceship had grown enough over the years to make the conversations convenient, but still sincere.

Sitting in his empty apartment, she figured out how to turn on the TV and stared at the news for a while until she changed it to the cooking channel. For a moment she was able to lose herself in a cake decorating show while getting some much needed rest before returning to the hospital in the morning.

As she ended her nightly prayer, she lay down on the couch with a blanket and wondered why she felt such lack of emotion after pouring her heart and soul out to her Heavenly Father. She figured because she had done it so many times already, her heart was accepting the situation for what it was. But pondering her own feelings, she realized in the stillness of the night that someone from the other side was telling her not to worry. The feeling was comforting, but she didn't hear that everything was going to be all right, only that everything was in the Lord's hands now. All she could do was pray that her heart would accept it.

Chapter Five

◈

Logan scrolled through Addie's playlist and couldn't keep from smiling at the variety of music she was into. Her playlists were sorted into interesting categories, such as "Kid's Carpet Time Songs," "My Life Soundtrack," "Cooking," and "Work Out." The last one wasn't uncommon, but the music list surprised him.

"Is there a reason why you enjoy listening to Korean pop music while you exercise?" he asked.

"It's catchy," she shrugged. "I always tell people I knew someone who served in Korea on their mission and they put in on my playlist, but I found in on my own through YouTube."

"Nothing wrong with that. I like country music, but I always told my coworkers it didn't appeal much to me since it wasn't very popular around the office."

"When did you work in an office?"

Oops, that hasn't happened yet. "Just a summer job I had once upon a time," he answered, not really lying, but not saying any more about it.

"There's no shame in it. A few of my friends enjoy going country swing dancing, and I like to go along sometimes, mostly for the music. It all depends on who you listen to."

"True, which is why I had to keep that information to myself."

She chuckled. "How so?"

"I mostly like Taylor Swift."

She laughed harder. "Oh, that would make you the office wimp now, wouldn't it?"

"Hey, she writes some pretty meaningful stuff."

"I can't deny that," she laughed.

"And who's your favorite?"

"Andy Grammer."

"Who?"

She looked at him in shock. "You never heard of Andy Grammer? Did you not go to his concert when he came to Dixie?"

"Oh!" he said, now remembering the year he came to perform. He had gone to that concert, but it was all such a blur. "Yeah, I know who he is. But I only remember the one song that was a huge hit a while back."

Without a word, she took the iPod from his hand and scrolled through until she found the desired song and hit play. Immediately Andy Grammer's recognizable voice came on as he sang "Keep Your Head Up" through the speakers.

He smiled as he watched her nod her head to the beat and tap her fingers on the steering wheel, but he couldn't keep from laughing when she belted out the chorus at the top of her lungs. She looked at him with no shame. "Oh, come on, why aren't you singing?"

"Never been the loud car-singer type."

"Seriously, you never rocked out to Taylor Swift while alone in your car before?"

"I usually do that in my shower."

She laughed harder. "Okay, first of all, TMI. Second, the rule in my car is that anyone riding in the passenger seat has to sing along to the songs of my choice."

"And if I don't know these songs?" Logan challenged.

She shook her head. "Doesn't matter. You have to sing, otherwise you have to dance, and I don't think you'll like that idea more."

"You really don't want to hear my voice," he chuckled.

"If I can tolerate a room full of children singing off key every day, I can handle you."

"Okay, but you asked for it."

The chorus came around again and he sang along as best he could, but not knowing all the words put him at a disadvantage. He hesitated and mumbled through it, but sang as obnoxiously as possible just to prove a point. She smiled and laughed the whole time, but he didn't miss the way she cringed when he went off key.

"I warned you," he said.

"You did that on purpose. But I'm proud of your effort. Most would have downright refused and I would have been sulking the whole way home."

"Well I only aim to please."

Logan looked out the window and noticed they were passing through Provo, which meant they weren't far away from home. When they eventually got off at the exit, Logan started to feel his nervous stomach get the best of him. Addie was a pleasant distraction, but his mind was constantly on his family.

"You're going to have to navigate the neighborhood. It's been a while," she said.

"No problem." Though it had been a while himself, he could navigate his hometown like the back of his hand.

Guiding her around the snow-covered streets, he stared at the breathtaking view of the scenery. After five years of the Chicago city as his view, he forgot how much he enjoyed the look of the mountains and having acres of untouched snow in his backyard. It brought back memories of his dad bringing out the sled when he was kid and pulling it around with the snowmobile.

When Addie pulled up to the front of the house, he took a deep breath and struggled to find the right words to say. He didn't want to leave with just a simple 'thank you' knowing he may not get the chance to see her again. But he figured a heartfelt good-bye would be too much for her.

He sighed. "Well I really appreciate you lugging me all the way here."

"Mind if I come too?" she asked, cutting the engine. "I want to say hi to Brin."

"I don't know if she's even here."

"Well then let's find out." She popped the trunk and quickly went around back, leaving him little time to question her. Logan followed suit to get his stuff, but she already had it out and was carrying it to the door.

"Whoa, what are you doing?" he asked, but she happily ignored him as she rang the doorbell. This was certainly not how he imagined the reunion with his family, but he didn't exactly have a choice when his mom answered the door and all but knocked him over with the hug she gave him.

"You're here!" she shouted and it took Logan a solid five seconds to get out of his stunned phase and return the hug he'd been holding back for a long time.

Although a few lines would appear in the next five years, most likely due to the stress he would put on her, she looked as beautiful and cheery as she always did with her long, red curly hair, which he hadn't inherited. But he did inherit the brown eyes and smile she prided herself on.

"It's so wonderful to see you," she cooed. Letting him go, she stepped back to acknowledge his new friend. "Well, hello, and who's this?"

"I'm Addie. You wouldn't happen to know the Whites, would you? I think they're in your stake. I'm their granddaughter."

"Tawny White?"

"Yeah!"

"Oh my goodness, I do. She and Frank moved into the ward a few months ago."

"That's right. They mentioned moving into a new neighborhood, but not far away. That's great that you know them."

"She'll be so excited I met you. Did you both drive up here together?"

"Yeah, he kept me entertained all morning."

"Well then come in, come in. I was thinking about making pumpkin cookies and now I have the perfect excuse to make them. Will you join us? I don't want to keep you from your family."

"Oh they're not expecting me until later anyway. I most certainly have time for pumpkin cookies," she said.

Logan knew his mom would pull something like this, but he wasn't going to object. Although it was a bit awkward considering he'd never brought any girl home to meet his family besides the dates he took to formal dances, Addie and his mom did most of the talking, which served as a good buffer while he took it all in.

The house was just as he remembered it, though the pictures were a bit more dated than the ones that existed in reality. Daniel and Sarah weren't born yet, and the oldest hadn't started school. Even though he wasn't a part of their lives, his mom had kept him updated through emails and he was glad to have at least some knowledge of his family's whereabouts rather than none at all. He wondered who was coming this year.

"Hey Mom," Logan called as he entered the kitchen. "Am I the only one here? Where's everyone else?"

"Mark and your dad are shoveling out a few driveways, but they should be home soon."

"When will I get to see Brin and Taylor?"

"Brin is spending Christmas Eve with her husband's family, but will be with us Christmas Day. Taylor's spending Christmas Eve with us. Sadly, he has to work Christmas morning, but his wife and kids will be with us too. It'll be different this year, but having you around is a nice change."

Every year Logan's siblings gave him flack for working on the holidays when they understood what it meant to have obligations. There was a lot more to their resentment than that, but it was hard not getting defensive even though none of those issues had happened yet.

"So, Addie, are you in school?"

"Not anymore, but I did go to Dixie and I'm moving back here eventually," she said as she helped roll premade dough into balls for the cookie sheet. "So tell me, what kind of embarrassing stories do you have about Logan's childhood?"

"Wait a minute," Logan stepped in. "No one's telling anyone anything embarrassing as long as I'm in the room."

"Fair enough," Addie shrugged. "Logan, why don't you get out of here while Peggy and I have a chat?"

Logan folded his arms. "I'm not going anywhere."

"Won't stop me," Peggy said. "Back when he was four—"

"This cookie dough looks good, Mom!" Logan shouted as he licked his fingers, threatening to stick them in the dough.

Peggy, who was no fan of anyone double dipping, took the spoon and whacked his hand. "Don't even think about it!"

"I fight fire with fire."

"Well that's a good way to get ice down your shirt," she said, referring to a family argument Logan remembered well. It had to do with him and his brother squabbling over who mowed the lawn last and it ended with Logan getting an Icee poured down his neck. He'd held it against Taylor ever since.

As timing would have it, the front door opened and two sets of stomping boots could be heard in the living room. Within seconds Mark came bounding into the kitchen, chucking his coat over a chair. It took him a solid thirty seconds to notice him standing there, but once he did, he didn't hesitate to give Logan a spine-crushing hug. Mark hadn't hugged him like that in years.

During his brief visits, as Mark got taller and more mature, he decided to graduate to the handshake or a one-armed shoulder hug. It was so strange to have him be a head shorter than him again, and see his shaggy auburn hair grown out instead of the cropped look he had now. But something about Mark's youthfulness made him nostalgic for his own younger life.

"You've gotten taller," said Logan.

"Yeah right. I've given up on that dream." His voice was a bit higher pitched than what Logan was used to. Then again there were some things he didn't miss from his youth.

"Don't worry, the growth spurt will come soon enough. Where did dad go?"

"He's in the garage. Are you staying in my room while you're here?"

"Uh . . . I don't know. Am I, mom?"

"The cot's already set up in there, but you're free to take the couch if you like."

"No, I'll take the cot. It'll be just like old times. Hopefully your snoring hasn't worsened over the years."

"Getting my tonsils out took care of that," said Mark. "But it's likely that the old habit will resurface just for you."

Logan rolled his eyes. "Looking forward to it."

When Logan glanced at Addie, he could see that she was amused by the exchange. "Addie, this is my brother, Mark. Mark, this is Addie."

He reached over to shake her hand. "Nice to meet you. You're the first girlfriend Logan's ever brought home."

"Oh I'm not his girlfriend. We just recently eloped in Vegas. It's nice to finally meet my new brother-in-law."

"She's kidding," Logan said quickly.

"Party pooper," she pouted. "We met a few days ago in St. George and my grandparents are in your ward apparently. We drove up together."

"So does that mean you're single?" asked Mark.

Logan gave him a good shove. "Okay, Casanova. It's time for you to leave."

"But I just got here!"

"Mark, go clean your room," said Peggy.

"Mom!"

"Mark, do as your mother says," they heard Henry say as he entered the room.

Mark sighed and headed for the stairs. "Whoever says the youngest child is the spoiled one, I'm writing them a formal complaint."

"Maybe you'll find some stationary under your dirty clothes," called Peggy.

Logan laughed as more introductions were made between Addie and Henry. When Henry finally looked over at Logan, Logan had to keep himself from getting emotional. The last time he'd seen his father, he was walking with a limp from arthritis. Seeing him whole and energetic made him wish this was the reality he had gotten to know better.

"Hey, son," he said brightly, giving him the tight squeeze Henry was always known for.

"Hey, Dad, it's good to see you."

"Would have been nice to see you sooner. Those walkways took forever," he said, moving around the counter to give Peggy a kiss.

Logan scrunched up his nose. "Gross."

He said it knowing what his father would do next. Henry took his wife into a waltz pose and dramatically dipped her over his knee. She squealed before he kissed her more thoroughly. When he brought her back up, his mom gently swatted him, "You're such a scoundrel."

"She's been saying that for over thirty years, but I know she means charming."

His mom blushed with a smile as he hugged her from behind. He began to reach for the cookie dough when she swatted him for the second time. "Wash your hands first."

Addie giggled, looking at them like she was watching a cheesy romance movie. "I think you guys are adorable."

Logan shook his head. "I still think it's gross. But I should start taking notes cause whatever I'm doing, it's not working."

His dad looked over at Addie. "Seems to be working just fine."

"Not my girlfriend, Dad."

"Yet."

"And we're done here," he said, moving to grab Addie's hand.

"Whoa, where are we going?" she protested. "I haven't had my cookie yet!"

"I'm saving you before she brings out the baby pictures."

"That reminds me," his mother interrupted. "We've baby proofed the house, so don't go into the bathroom without noticing the latch we put on the toilet. We keep it unlocked at night after Mark got up to the use the bathroom, and well . . . you don't want to hear the rest of the story. Just keep that in mind."

"Thanks for the warning," he said, wondering how much more embarrassing it could get.

Just then he realized he hadn't let go of Addie's hand, and quickly dropped his arm, noticing the look his dad was giving him. He decided it was time to give her a tour of the house while the cookies baked. Since she'd made it clear she was going to stay for one, he had to keep her distracted and away from his parents.

"I like your family," she said as they headed downstairs to the family room. It was more like a man cave, but his mom and sister always joined in for every ping-pong tournament and Wii showdown they had.

"Yeah, I've forgotten how crazy they could get."

"Craziness is meant to be embraced, otherwise it'll keep poking you in the ribs until you acknowledge it."

"Did Aristotle say that?"

"I did, actually. I know, I should have majored in philosophy."

"Well there is truth to what you say," he laughed. "I spent a lot of time trying to ignore it. Looks like it got the best of me."

She began browsing through the movie collection. "I would give anything to have someone to tease me."

Logan was mostly referring to his accident, but he pondered what she said. "Well you're welcome to take mine."

"I'll consider that offer," she chuckled, and then she gasped. "No way, you have the first edition of the original *Star Wars* movies?"

"They're my dad's. You a fan?"

"Totally! So was my dad, and naturally he had to pass his nerdiness onto somebody. He'd let me stay up late when I was little and watch them with him. He thought my mom never found out, but she just pretended not to notice."

"Now that's adorable."

"Yeah, I guess so."

"Are you sure your family isn't missing you right now?"

"If you really want me to go, Logan, it's fine. I don't have to stay."

"No!" he shouted a little too loudly. "I mean . . . no, I want you to stay. I just don't want you to feel obligated."

"I was the one who pushed myself in here, remember?" She then turned to the ping-pong table. "Want to play?"

Logan got out the paddles and they spent the next half hour showing each other their competitive edge while simultaneously showing their lack of talent for the game. After the first five minutes they stopped keeping score and just goofed around until his mom said the cookies were done.

Upstairs the family gathered to eat and caught up on old stories while Peggy started dinner. Logan spent most of the time just listening and Addie did the same, but the permanent smile on her face told him she was still enjoying herself. They worked together to make tacos and no one questioned if Addie would be staying or not. Peggy made her feel useful by having her cut the tomatoes and made sure to set an extra place for her.

Once everything was cleaned up after dinner, Addie mentioned the late hour and gratefully excused herself to go home. Hugs were given all around until Logan walked her outside to the car.

"Thank you," she said as he opened the driver door for her. "That was most fun I had in a long time."

"I sincerely doubt that, but I'm happy you enjoyed yourself."

"I wouldn't lie for your benefit, Logan. Your family's great."

"Well thanks for coming. I think having you here added to everyone's amusement."

"I only aim to please," she said, followed by a wink.

After a brief hug, she got into her car and waved before speeding off into the dimly lit sky. He hoped it wouldn't be their last good-bye. But knowing his situation, he had to accept that this would all come to an end eventually. It was best not to get attached, no matter how much he wanted to.

Chapter Six

❧

At the hospital, Peggy had planned to shut her eyes for only a few minutes, but those short minutes turned into a full hour. Waking up, her neck felt stiff and her back ached from the awkward position. She knew the jet lag would catch up to her, but she was powering through it as best she could.

She had only been in Chicago two days and things were already getting taken care of quickly in regards to his insurance, work, and other loose ends that needed to be tied up.

By now everyone was informed and many were calling to give their best wishes and offering their help. Henry called to tell her the Relief Society had been bringing over meals while she was gone. Not that he and Mark would starve without her there, but she was appreciative of their service.

Brin called in regularly to see how she and Logan were holding up. Taylor, however, never called, and while Peggy knew on a deeper level that Taylor cared, she could understand his silence in the situation.

Taylor and Logan had rarely gotten along until they both graduated high school. The dust seemed to settle by the time Logan came back from his mission, but naturally it started up again once he decided to move to Chicago. Taylor was very open about his negative feelings over Logan's actions following those changes and got defensive against anyone who appeared to be on his side.

While the family tried to express their unconditional love, Taylor only felt more isolated until Logan made his formal decision to stay out of everyone's lives. Logan thought he was doing the family a favor, but it only put a rift between Taylor and his other siblings.

They pretended nothing was wrong for their parents' sake, attending holiday and family functions like nothing happened. Brin's heart had softened over time, but privately she had often expressed how much she blamed Taylor for Logan's absence. Peggy kept telling herself that her children were adults and they needed to work things out on their own. But sometimes she just wanted to put them all in timeout like she used to and have them think about what they were doing to each other.

That afternoon she ate lunch in the cafeteria and planned the rest of her week. Though it was painful to consider, Christmas was in three days, which meant she needed to decide whether or not she'd be staying in Chicago or going back to Utah by then. Getting a last-minute flight during the holidays was out of the question, so she had to decide now what her choice would be.

She included that question as she prayed over her meal and then began eating her sandwich. She wasn't a fan of hospital food, but today it served to ease her appetite, though she wasn't really in the mood to eat anything.

By her fifth bite, she heard her phone go off in her purse and dug through its contents to answer it. It was Henry, likely asking for an update or giving one.

"Hi dear, how's the fort holding up?"

"Just fine," he said. "Mark's been a real help since he's on break from school and the house hasn't caught on fire, so we got that going for us."

Peggy smiled weakly. "That's good to hear."

"How are you doing?"

"I'm hanging in there," she sighed, followed by a brief pause. "It's so hard, Henry. I watch him . . . and I wonder what help I'm really doing by staying here. I talk to him, I sit by him. I hold his hand, wanting to believe it's doing some good. But . . . what if it's all for nothing? What if he doesn't wake up? What if it comes down to deciding on discontinuing his life support? No parent should have to think about that for their child."

"You're right," he said. "This isn't fair, Peggy. But it's only been a few days and we can take a better look at those questions in the future. I've been talking to the kids and everyone's pulling together so Mark and I can come be with you for Christmas. Our flight's booked and we're leaving tonight."

"Oh Henry, you don't have to do that."

"I want to be there for my son, and it's not like our other children don't have anywhere else to be for Christmas. They want this to be their gift to us."

Peggy sniffed and wiped away a stray tear. "I can't think of any greater gift."

"I want to be there for you too, sweetheart. I don't want you to deal with this by yourself. I know you're more than capable, but something tells me you need us."

She sniffed louder. "Thanks. I really do."

"Well then, you won't have to wait long. I'll see you soon."

"I love you."

"I love you too. Call me if you need anything."

"I will."

Pressing *End* on her phone, she folded her hands and gave another prayer of gratitude to her Heavenly Father. She wasn't expecting such a quick answer, but it was one more comfort she needed. Hopefully things would only go up from here.

❦

Logan had been staring at the ceiling for nearly an hour. He knew going to sleep would be easy, but wanted to stay awake and think about today's events. He kept smiling at the memories of it and wondered what would come next. It wasn't like he had anything to lose, but he wasn't about to mess up his one chance at seeing how everything could have gone differently.

"Logan," he heard Mark whisper from the bed across the room. "Are you asleep?"

"Yes," he answered, knowing his comment would be ignored.

"Is Addie really not your girlfriend?"

"Why? Are you planning to make a move?"

"Yes, Logan. Because a girl in her twenties would be interested in a fourteen-year-old kid like me. I'm pretty sure that's illegal and messed up on numerous levels."

Logan just chuckled. "Then why do you ask?"

"Because I think she likes you and I was wondering if you plan on doing something about it."

"Since when are you so concerned about my dating life?"

"Because you're an idiot, and it's my job as a concerned sibling to help you look at the big picture."

Logan couldn't keep from laughing at that. "Forgive me for having ignored the advice of someone who isn't even old enough to date."

"Doesn't mean I don't know things. And if you end up marrying her, I can credit myself as the one who nudged you in the first place."

"Ah, so this is for personal glory."

"That's right. I expect you to stand up at your reception and say, 'I owe it all to you, Mark. I wouldn't be here if it weren't for you.'"

"And just because you said it, I'm going to keep that to myself." In the next four seconds, Logan felt a pillow hit his face. "Hey!"

"Sorry, it slipped."

Logan took that same pillow and hurled it back at Mark's face and rolled over to finally get some rest. But only a minute passed when Mark whispered again, "Logan?"

"What?" he groaned.

"What made you decide to serve a mission?"

Now that was a big change in subject. He wanted to drop the conversation altogether, but Logan figured this was part of his test, so he decided to give him the answer he needed.

"I served because I knew it was the right thing to do."

"So you went because it was expected?"

Logan sat up in the cot and turned on the lamp. "No, because I prayed to the Lord about it, and I received a blunt answer that it was what I needed to do."

Mark sat up to face him. "What kind of answer did you get?"

Logan was surprised to remember that reason so quickly, but maybe revelation came more clearly in this coma world.

"I had a dream. It's hard to really explain it, but I was standing in a room with a large group of people in front of me. They were waiting to hear what I had to say, but there were so many people behind me trying to drown me out. They were loud and distracting, and I knew if I wanted these people to hear my message, I had to move somewhere quiet where they could hear me. Within seconds I was on the temple grounds and the same people were present, only there was a silence I can only describe as peaceful. I don't know what I said, but I knew it was essential to their lives.

"When I woke up, I realized there were people out there who needed to hear the truth. The best way to do that was to serve as a missionary in a missionary setting. It wasn't something I could do with worldly distractions. And not only were they relying on me, but so were their ancestors, who were waiting to have their work done."

"Wow," Mark said after he took a few of moments to contemplate that.

"Yeah," Logan agreed, glad he hadn't forgotten it. "But not all answers are going to come so clearly, Mark. And sometimes the clearer ones won't always be enough to keep you on the straight and narrow."

I'm the prime example of that.

"I know. I just . . . I just don't know if I'm all that worthy to serve a mission."

"Well you have a couple more years to work on it. But what makes you say that?"

He hesitated, clearly implying he had done something to make himself feel that way. Of course Logan would likely be able to empathize, but Mark didn't know that.

"I did something," he sighed. "It was only one time, but . . ."

"But?" Logan prodded.

"I was staying the night at my friend's house and his family aren't members. Mom and Dad didn't know that, so they let me go. We just planned to stay up all night playing video games, but a couple of the guys brought some alcohol . . . you know . . . the hard stuff. And I was going to say no, but for some reason I drank it anyway. I don't really know why. It's not like I was being pressured or anything, but I guess curiosity got the best of me."

"Who else have you told about this?"

"You're the only one."

Right then Logan looked at his brother with a different set of eyes. This was the first he heard about it and he wondered if anyone else knew. But considering what his mom mentioned about Mark preparing for a mission soon, Logan trusted that he resolved the situation in reality. But even so, this confession meant more to him than he thought it would. It took a lot of courage and trust to confide such information. Logan wished he had that same courage to talk to someone other than his bishop when he slipped up the first time. It likely would have made a bigger impact.

"I'm glad you told me, but . . . if I wasn't here, would you have told Mom and Dad eventually?"

"Of course," he said and Logan believed him. *That's reassuring.* "But . . . I'm worried."

"You shouldn't be. Mom and Dad are the most understanding people I know. They won't judge or get mad. They'll be disappointed, but they'll be proud that you came to them instead of hiding it until it became a bigger problem. However, something tells me the experience wasn't enough to tempt you again, was it?"

"No!" Mark dropped his head into his palm, appearing disgusted at the mere memory of it. "I got deathly sick that night and the next morning. I told Mom I must've caught the flu or something, but it was the worst feeling in the world."

"That's what a hangover does to you. I know exactly how that feels."

Mark's head snapped up. "You do?'

Logan nodded. "Let's just say I had a few mishaps in my life too. But as soon as you talk to the bishop, and this is the important part, so listen up." Mark leaned forward a little in anticipation. "Once you do that and know that God loves you without reservation, and that Christ already atoned of this for you, you have nothing to worry about."

"I know," said Mark, as if he were ashamed of forgetting the truth in that.

"You have to remember that deathly sick feeling, but it'll help you promise never to do it again. It's one thing to break a promise, but it's another to break a covenant. Not that you won't be forgiven after you've gone through the temple, but the repentance process is a lot harder, and the sin you inflict on yourself is lot more damaging. I'd hate to see you go through that."

Mark nodded. "I'd hate to see the same for you too."

Logan swallowed hard and had to force back another threat of tears. Mark did see him go through that. In reality he still was and a new wave of guilt came over him.

"What would happen if I did, Mark? What if I decided to just walk away from all that I knew to be true?"

Mark hesitated for a minute, but squared his shoulders and said, "You're still my brother, and I'd love you no matter what. But I'd be sad."

"You wouldn't try to knock some sense into me?" he asked, trying to sound like he was joking, but he truly wondered what reality-Mark might be thinking.

"I'd try, but you'd probably beat me up worse," he chuckled.

"I doubt that."

"But honestly, the best thing I could do for you is pray something would knock some sense into you."

Hearing that made Logan laugh, which obviously left Mark confused, but he just looked at him and said, "I really appreciate that, Mark. I have a feeling if I ever do make a mistake, whatever knocks that sense into me, I'll know who to thank."

"Not exactly what I'd want you to thank me for, but I'll accept that as well."

The next morning, Logan woke up to heavy snowfall, so he decided to gear up and shovel the walkway before his dad had a mind to do it.

It had been a while since he'd shoveled anything, but in this life, he wasn't as sore as he thought he would be once he was finished. He was, however, freezing, so he took the liberty of making himself hot chocolate. Coffee still sounded better, but once again, he took what he could get.

"Good morning," his mom said as she entered the kitchen, still in her snowflake pajamas.

"Morning."

"You're up early."

"I woke up before my alarm and couldn't get back to sleep, so I shoveled the drive way."

"Well thank you." She grabbed a frying pan from the cabinet. "That was nice of you."

Logan shrugged like it was no big deal, which it wasn't. But he could see the gratitude in her eyes and it made him happier to have done it.

"Got any plans for the day?" he asked her.

"Tons. I have to do some last-minute Christmas shopping, clean out the storage room, and make the sugar cookie plates to take to the neighbors and ward members."

It didn't sound like a lot, but the amount of time each task took would likely consume the whole day.

"I don't exactly have much to do," he said. "Would you like some help?"

"Sure. What we could do is, while I'm working on the storage room, you deliver the plates and after you come home, I can run to the store."

"Sounds good. You're just going to have to remind me where people live."

"It won't be too hard. I'll write a list for you."

"Perfect." He put his mug in the sink and headed toward the stairs. "I'm going to go shower. Let me know when you're ready."

"I will. And Logan?"

He stopped and turned to face her. "Yes?"

"Thank you for talking to your brother last night," she said in a soft voice.

"You heard?"

"My room is down the hall and you boys are louder than you think," she chuckled, but then turned serious. "I was going to ask you to quiet down, but stopped when I heard the advice you gave him."

Logan sighed, not knowing how to respond, which she must have sensed before she hurried to say, "I knew about Mark's drinking the morning I picked him up from his friend's house. I was going to confront him, but . . . I decided to wait to see if he would come forward himself. I just appreciate you being there for him and saying all the right things."

"Is he in trouble?"

"Mistakes can't go unpunished around here. He's going to have some extra responsibilities and some privileges taken away, but we'll make sure it's after the holidays."

"Fair enough," he said, glad his parents had always been understanding, as he'd told Mark the night before.

"Go get ready. I'll have breakfast on the table soon."

Logan did just that, and by the time he came down, everyone was at the table eating pancakes. He enjoyed the morning spent with his family, and went ahead to take the plates to the neighbors using his mom's car.

Mark insisted on joining him, likely getting out of having to help with winter cleaning. Logan didn't mind since Mark ran the cookies to the door while he waited in the warm car. The awkwardness of encountering old acquaintances was too much to handle.

When they got to the last house, Mark insisted Logan deliver this one personally. He didn't think much of it until he rang the doorbell and Addie answered the door.

"Logan!"

"Addie?"

"That's me last I checked. What are you doing here?"

"Uh . . . my mom is having me and Mark deliver these," he said, nearly shoving the plate into her hands. "I didn't know you lived here."

"My grandparents do."

"Right," he said awkwardly after she pointed out the obvious.

"Would you guys like to come in? Or do you guys have more runs to make?"

"We're still getting stuff done, but . . ."

Logan thought about what Mark said last night and understood now why he wanted to sit this one out. The little punk was
pushing him to make a move, so right there he made an impul-
sive decision.

She waited patiently for him to continue and he finished his
hanging sentence with, ". . . would you like to go out with me
tonight? That is, if you're free."

Her eyebrows rose in surprise, but then she smiled, which
made him hopeful.

"I'd love to," she said.

"Really? I mean, great. Does seven work?"

"Yes," she chuckled.

"Cool. I'll pick you up then."

"I'll be ready. And tell your mom thanks for the cookies."

"I will," he said as she closed the front door and he headed
toward the car.

Sitting in the driver's seat, he looked at Mark and punched
him in the shoulder. It wasn't hard, but it did give cause to shout,
"Hey, what was that for?"

"You setting me up. You knew she lived here, hence your
insistence on having me knock on her door."

"So? You knew I wouldn't let this go. I want to be the best
man, remember?"

"You said nothing about being my best man."

"Wanting to make a speech at your wedding implies that I
want to be the best man."

"You're relentless."

"Which isn't news, bro. So are you going to tell me how it
went?"

"How what went?"

"You said more than 'hello' and 'good-bye.' What happened?"

"No way, I'm not giving you any information."

"You're relentless."

"Not unless you promise to talk to Mom and Dad tonight while I'm gone."

Mark rolled his eyes, but sighed and said, "Okay, deal."

"But if you don't, I'm not going to tell you how the date went."

"A date, you say?"

"I asked her out for tonight and she said yes," he told him, smiling as he said it. He had looked forward to dates before, but didn't realize how much he anticipated seeing Addie again. The only problem was, he didn't exactly have a plan yet.

"Way to go, man. At least while I'm grounded I'll have enough time to write my speech."

Chapter Seven

❦

That afternoon, Logan spent his time making preparations, which turned out to be easier than he thought. He texted Addie to confirm and make sure she dressed extra warm without giving away too much.

He hoped his plan would be a fun experience for the both of them. Being home was nice, but staying on a budget and still using his mother's dated SUV had its drawbacks. In reality he would have treated her to a nice restaurant instead of Plan B, but he tried to work with what he had.

He left the house at five minutes to seven, showing up at her doorstep at 7:03. When she opened the door, she stepped out wearing a long red coat that fit her figure perfectly, with a black knitted hat and matching gloves. She wore a white scarf with sky blue boots that didn't exactly match the ensemble, but they looked good on her.

"You're late," she said.

"I needed the extra four minutes to make myself presentable."

"That's no excuse," she teased.

"Well it's a good thing I plan to make it up tonight." She just smiled as she followed him to the car where he opened the passenger door. "I like your boots."

"Thanks, they're my favorite pair."

He climbed in the driver's side and buckled himself. "I'm flattered you would wear your best pair just for me."

"They happen to be the warmest, and you did say to dress warmly."

"No, I think you're just trying to impress me," he teased back.

"And I think you're being sneaky. You haven't told me where we're going."

"Because it's a surprise."

"Well naturally, and though I do love surprises, I'd like to tell my grandmother where I'm going so she doesn't worry."

"You have a point there. But my mom talked to her over the phone this afternoon. She spilled the beans and happens to know exactly where we're going. My guess is, you asked her and she refused to say anything to you."

"You punk," she chuckled. "You've thought of everything."

He shrugged. "I'm very thorough in my planning."

"Well now I'm impressed. Why go through all the trouble?"

"You'll find out."

The first half of the date went pretty smoothly with dinner at a pizza place where they could build their own and then eat it fresh out the oven.

Addie looked like a kid at a candy store as she added more and more toppings until the dough was completely covered. He appreciated her appetite, having been out with women who were such nitpicky eaters.

"You are my hero," she said, halfway into her third slice.

"Good. I was specifically working toward that."

"Well you succeeded. This was a nice surprise, Logan. Thank you."

"You're very welcome, but this isn't the surprise exactly. I have one more thing planned."

"Seriously?" Her eyes brightened as she said it.

"I'm not giving any hints though."

She exaggerated a sigh, but didn't press him. When they were both finished, they first stopped at a gas station to pick up some hot chocolate they could sip as they drove toward Draper and their next destination.

Heading up the mountain, they passed the Draper Temple and made their way into a neighborhood where the trees were thick and covered in brilliant white powder.

Winding through the roads, they arrived at a large house that belonged to a friend of Henry's. It was large and beautifully decorated, with a yard that merged into the side of the mountain. When Logan parked the car, Addie initially went for the front door, but Logan headed straight for the field of trees around back.

"I'm starting to question your intentions," she said, following just a foot behind him into the unknown.

"Question? Really?"

"Leading me into the woods at night? Either you're taking me to a house made of candy, or you're the big bad wolf."

Logan laughed. "Good theories, but no. If I were the big bad wolf, I'd have kept us at your grandma's house. And if such a house existed, I would have eaten it gone by now."

"Well don't you just have a comeback for everything," she chuckled.

"I just love ruffling your feathers. And it seems you like it just as much."

"You think I like my feathers ruffled?"

"No, you like ruffling *mine*," he corrected. "This is payback. Do you at least trust me?"

She looked thoughtful. "I've trusted you this far, so yes."

"Another goal accomplished," he said, suddenly stopping in his tracks.

He looked around to make sure they were in the right place, then glanced at his watch.

She looked around expectantly. "Are we waiting for something?"

"Just a few more seconds."

What she didn't know was that he had secretly texted the owner of the house to let him know of their presence, so when they were in the right spot at the right time, they would get to see what they came for.

She stared at him anxiously while he gazed down into her eyes. The moon reflected off the snow enough to illuminate her features. Just as he began to memorize them, the lights that covered every tree within two hundred feet flicked on. In a burst of color that made her jaw drop, they were completely surrounded.

She finally responded with a breathy "wow" as she turned in slow circles, taking it all in.

"What do you think?" he asked.

"This is amazing!" she exclaimed with a smile that hadn't faded since the forest came to life.

"Surprise."

"No kidding, this is . . ."

She didn't finish the sentence. Instead she let out a heavy sigh and closed her mouth into a thin line. He noticed her eyes mist over.

"Hey, are you okay?"

Her voice cracked a little. "Did she tell you?"

"Did who tell me what?"

"Nothing, never mind."

Impulsively, Logan took her gloved hand in his. They weren't touching skin to skin, but he felt a distinct flow of energy, which he couldn't ignore despite her emotional state.

"You don't have to tell me, but I'd like to know what you're thinking," he said softly.

Thankfully she didn't pull away from him while she wiped away a tear before it slipped down her cheek.

She sniffed once and said, "When I was eight, I got a really bad sinus infection. It was in early December and I was miserable. Couldn't get any sleep and neither did my mom. But one night . . . she put me in the car, in my pajamas and coat, and just drove me around the neighborhood until I was tired enough to fall asleep. We looked at all the Christmas lights people put up and it was one of the most comforting moments after dealing with . . . difficult things. Since then, every year I would beg her to take me to see the lights, and she always would until I became a teenager."

"And then maturity made you stop?"

"Something like that." She hesitated briefly, but said, "Childhood memories are what I desperately hold onto because it's the happiest I've ever been since . . . well, since things got hard."

Logan didn't know what to say. He remembered how brief and elusive she was when he asked about her family. He figured there was a lot more than she was telling, but now he had a better picture, and his heart went out to her. With how bright and spontaneous her personality projected, it was fascinating to see this deep and serious side of her. But despite it all, her eyes showed strength and determination, and he admired her completely.

"I'm sorry things were rough," he said, and he meant it.

"Me too. But I have a lot to be grateful for. I'm alive and well, and loved by many, so it's gotten easier."

"I'm glad you can look at it that way."

Her smile returned, as did some of the warmth in the atmosphere.

"All right, now that I've put a downer on this evening—" she chuckled.

"Don't say that. Thank you for sharing something so personal."

"Well you did this wonderful thing for me, and I think that deserves a bit of my heart," she said.

"How poetic."

She rolled her eyes. "Ha ha."

"No, I'm serious. You should write that down."

"Oh I have. I plan to be a famous songwriter someday."

He raised an eyebrow. "For real?"

"No . . . but it's one of those things I'd like to try."

"Fair enough. Want to know a secret?" He leaned in close and lowered his voice to a whisper. "I've written songs."

"Let me guess . . . they were all Taylor Swift inspired."

"Ha ha, I meant sheet music on the piano."

"You play the piano?" she exclaimed.

It had been a while since he'd played, but he spoke the truth about spending a lot of time as a teenager trying to perfect the skill. He wasn't amazing at it since he mostly taught himself and watched others. But he had a decent musical ear and sense of rhythm, which his mom delightedly encouraged.

"I did a long time ago," he answered. "I started listening to John Schmidt and he inspired me enough to learn to play just like him."

"And did you succeed?"

"I didn't get quite to that skill level. But I can play some hymns and a few songs from memory."

"That's amazing. I'd love to hear it sometime."

Logan gave it some thought, having no clue how long he'd be in this alternate reality, which made planning ahead a bit difficult. Tommy never gave him a time limit, but he didn't expect it to expire before Christmas. It was, however, two days away, so he wasn't going to plan for any time beyond that.

"How about I make you a deal? I'll play for you, if you come over tomorrow."

"Tomorrow?" She moved to face him, dramatically stroking her chin in contemplation. "All right, but it has to be something more original than *Mary Had a Little Lamb.*"

"I can assure you it'll be much better than that."

Her eyes looked up, making it obvious she was mentally checking her schedule. "I have a dinner to go to at my cousin's, but I'm free after eight."

"I can't guarantee any privacy, but—"

"No worries. We don't have a piano anyway, and I like your family."

"Good, cause they like you too."

They lingered a bit longer after that, taking a dozen pictures per Addie's request so she could savor the memory. When Logan noticed her shivering, he took her hand and headed back to the car. Thankfully it didn't take long for the heater to start working, of which Addie took full advantage by taking off her gloves and holding them against the hot air.

"Sorry, I get cold very easily," she said through her chattering teeth.

"No, I'm sorry for keeping you in the cold for so long."

She rubbed her hands together. "Don't be, it was worth it. At least we have a warm car."

Logan took one of her hands and began rubbing it between his palms. "Wow, your hands are colder than mine."

"I know, I don't exaggerate . . . often," she chuckled.

When he was about to switch the gears into reverse to pull out of the driveway, he realized he had interlaced his fingers with hers. Not that it was a habitual gesture, but the gesture itself felt so comfortable and right that he didn't have to think twice about it.

He wanted to retake her hand and continue keeping her warm. However, his instincts were telling him to keep both hands on the wheel while driving down the snow-covered road. He tried not to think about the fact that he was in coma because of it and that none of this was real, but he deeply wished it were. He wanted his family together, he wanted them happy, and more so, he wanted the woman sitting next him to be there when he woke up.

Logan turned on the radio so Christmas music could fill the silence. It wasn't uncomfortable, but it did add to the atmosphere as he took the long way home so they could see the decorated houses in the area.

When they reached their own neighborhood, Logan pulled into Addie's driveway and walked her to the door. In reality, whenever he took a beautiful or interesting woman on a date, that short walk had him scrambling to think of a smooth way to get him invited inside. And currently, the little devil on his shoulder was telling him that because this wasn't reality, he could do as he pleased without the consequences.

But now, as he looked into her eyes, knowing it was time to say good-bye, he discovered those desires didn't fully disappear, but were overpowered by the desire to see her safe and respected. She already expressed her trust in him and he wasn't going to give her cause to waver in that by making a bold move. Nor was he about to destroy this opportunity to do things right.

"Thank you for the wonderful night, Logan. I had a great time."

She gave him a lingering hug, and he relished the contact between them. He also noticed how nice she smelled.

"Me too. I was hoping you would. So I'll see you tomorrow?"

"Absolutely. I'll call you."

"Looking forward to it," he said as she entered the warm house.

She gave him one last smile before shutting the door, and he went home feeling like a teenager again. And sure enough, when he walked inside, his parents and little brother were all waiting in the family room ready to interrogate him for details.

Peggy stopped with her latest knitting project to ask, "How'd it go? Did you guys have fun?"

"We did," he answered.

"Did she like the lights?"

"She loved them. Remind me, Dad, to send Michael a fruit basket as a thank you."

"I'm sure helping a man to woo his woman was thank you enough," he said as he watched the evening news. There was humor in his voice, but still truth to that statement.

"Were there fireworks?" Mark interjected.

Logan kept his face blank and unreadable. "Maybe. Maybe not."

"Don't worry, Logan," Peggy said. "Mark kept his end of the deal and came clean, so he gets the juicier details."

Logan couldn't hide his smile as he finally took notice in what Mark was doing. As part of a punishment, each family member was forced to write a full five paragraph essay on what he did wrong and how they could do better. It was one of the perks of having a teacher for a mother. With a notebook and pencil in hand, it looked like Mark was still on his introduction.

"Well in that case," he started, taking a seat on the recliner. "I made her cry."

"What did you do?" Mark scolded.

His mom answered that. "Oh honey, when a woman cries on a date, especially when the man does a meaningful gesture, it means she loved it."

Mark exaggerated an eye-roll. "Women."

"Amen," Henry added.

Logan held down the laugh when Peggy glared at him. "She agreed to see me again tomorrow, and it would be really nice if she came over and we had no interruptions."

He didn't miss the way his mom's face lit up as he said it. "As long as you stay in the public areas, we'll try to be discreet. When is she coming over?"

"Sometime after eight."

Mark gave him a knowing look. "You guys plan on . . . watching a movie?"

"She wants to hear me play the piano, dipwad."

Normally he was scolded for calling names, but his mom only squealed, clapping her hands together in excitement. "Oh my goodness! I haven't heard you play in forever! That's so cute! You must really like her," she sighed.

Logan laughed. "I do so far."

"Well we'll give you as much privacy as possible. Won't we, boys?"

"Yes, Mom," Henry and Mark said in unison.

For the rest of the evening, Logan sat back and enjoyed the scene before him. The Christmas tree was lit up with colorful lights and homemade decorations that had accumulated over the years.

It wasn't uniformly decorated like many of the wealthy families he worked with in reality. They always hired people to decorate their homes for Christmas, which meant they always ended up looking beautiful, but each lacked the personal touch Logan didn't realize he missed until now.

He made a note to start decorating his own place from now on. Maybe adding more personal touches would fill up some of the space in his heart.

Chapter Eight

❧

Peggy wanted to go to the airport to meet her son and husband, but the traffic and weather didn't cooperate with that idea. Instead they called to tell her they would take a cab to Logan's place and meet her at the hospital after.

She sat in the hallway so they'd see her when they arrived. But after an hour of waiting, her anxiety and anticipation had grown to the point where she read the same page three times from a book she bought at the hospital gift shop. But knowing her concentration wouldn't focus until her family showed up, she decided to put the book away and just sit while she thought of something else to keep her busy.

Another twenty minutes went by without a single idea, but she didn't have to think much longer when she heard her name called by the nurse's station.

Seeing Henry appear from around the corner, without a care of who was watching, she leapt from her chair and hurried into his arms. Reveling in the warmth and security, she only let go to embrace her son.

"I can't believe you're here," said Peggy.

Henry smiled, but his face fell a little when he asked, "Where is he?"

Peggy led them into Logan's room, which was now decorated in bouquets of flowers, courtesy of his secretary passing them along from his acquaintances.

When Henry sat in the chair next to him, the first thing he said was, "He's certainly not a little boy anymore."

Peggy only half-agreed. Logan had grown into a strong and capable man, but he would always be her little boy.

Mark had found his way to a corner, standing with a concentrated expression and his arms folded. It had become a habit of his, being there so he could see and analyze every part of the room. He hadn't always been so quiet, but this was one of those moments where no one had much to say.

Peggy and Mark left that night, leaving Henry to be alone with Logan. He recalled how Peggy described her helplessness sitting at his bedside. He wanted to tell her how helpless he felt waiting at home, but being at the hospital was more different than he thought it would be. At least they were able to contact his bishop in the area so they could administer a blessing. Unfortunately, the roads were bad enough to delay it until tomorrow, but for now he was able to give a simple father's blessing until the next day.

Now that he was alone with him, there was a lot Henry wanted to say, most of it fueled by past anger. But during the flight, he was prompted to read his scriptures as he usually did during trying times, and he randomly opened the New Testament to the parable of the prodigal son.

Not only was it about a man who left his family and made unwise decisions, but it was about a father who accepted his son back into his home without giving it a second thought.

Seeing Logan now, every negative thought dissipated as he imagined Logan waking up and being able to return the embrace he had desperately wanted to give him since they last saw each other, which he couldn't even remember. Even if he decided to move out of the country, he would never deny him the chance of being there with open arms if he ever changed his mind.

Settling in the chair his wife had spent most of her time in, he opened his scriptures and began reading out loud. If not to comfort his son, then to comfort his own heart for the days he had to take one at a time.

Logan stretched out his fingers after playing the piano for two hours straight. It didn't exactly come back to him like he thought it would when he first sat down. Some of his muscle memory allowed him to play a few simple things, but not without a lot of noticeable mistakes mixed in.

He started off practicing the basics and worked his way up to the harder stuff. His mom had saved his old sheet music in the piano bench, but playing it now, he realized it had sounded much better when he wrote it. He figured Addie would give him praise no matter what, and it would likely boost her confidence level when she saw how little skill he currently possessed.

It was nearly eight when his phone buzzed and Addie texted, saying dinner with her cousins had run longer than she expected but she was on her way.

He spent the next half hour making sure he and the house looked presentable when she arrived. Of course, he didn't have much to wear besides T-shirts and his church clothes, but he decided looking casual would have to do.

She, of course, looked amazing when she walked inside wearing a long-sleeved red blouse and a black, flowing skirt that came to her knees. She wore matching red heels over black stockings that had a floral design on them. Her hair was done in loose curls and the lovely scent she had on the night before surrounded her now.

"You look great," he said, greeting her with a hug.

"Thank you," she replied, kicking off her heels to eliminate the four inches of height it gave her. "Sorry I didn't have time to change."

"No apologies necessary. But you would have looked beautiful either way."

The cold had already colored her cheeks, but her blush deepened the rosy color. He expected some kind of sarcastic remark about his sweet talk, but she just smiled, and he was glad she took him seriously since it was true.

"Well welcome back," he said. "How was dinner?"

"Fantastic. I missed my cousins a lot, so it was nice catching up with them. So many new babies too! I have one cousin who just had a boy a few months ago, and two more who are pregnant. Hormones were flying off the walls, but it was great to see them."

They had moved to the front sitting room, which veered off from the entrance where a slender Christmas tree stood in front of the window to be seen by the neighborhood. It also had a small loveseat, the piano, a few paintings, and some bookshelves.

Logan turned on the piano light and a small lamp, which was the only light fixture they had for the room. It was bright, but it provided a softer ambiance, which was comfortable and warm.

"So, are you ready to be amazed by my mediocre musical skills?" he said as he sat on the bench.

She approached the bench and nudged him to scoot over so she could sit. "Impress me, maestro."

Logan placed his fingers on the keys and began to play a few hymns he put together as more of an intro rather than jumping into his own stuff. She began to sing along perfectly, with an impressive voice. He made a few mistakes along the way, but kept his composure until the end when she applauded.

"Very well done," she said.

"Same to you. You have a great voice."

"Thank you, but I do believe I recognize those songs, Logan."

"I know. This is a song I wrote when I was younger. Keep in mind, I thought I was good then. So . . . here it goes."

Logan didn't have a name for it, but the piece started out soft and then blended into a chorus that repeated a little louder each time. By the end, it became softer once more, leading to a finish that almost faded out. The song only lasted about a minute and a half, but it was the longest minute and a half of his life.

When he looked at her to gauge her reaction, she wore a bright look of approval. "That was amazing. What inspired you to write that?"

"A girl."

"Really?" she asked, obviously wanting the juicy details that came with his answer.

"No," he chuckled. "I just wanted to see if I could write a song."

"Well you succeeded. I really like it."

"I'm glad," he said. "You mentioned before that you'd like to write songs. If you did, what would you write about?"

She gazed in space for a moment, considering his question until she shrugged and answered, "Good question. My dad, probably. He passed away when I was younger."

"I'm sorry to hear that. May I ask how?"

"Uh, well . . . to start off, when my parents turned eighteen, they ran off and eloped, thinking they knew more about the world than they realized. My dad joined the Army and she became a waitress at a restaurant on the base they lived on. He made a really good living as he progressed in rank and died honorably in combat."

"Again, I'm sorry. That must've been hard on you and your mom."

"Definitely. More so on my mom though. After things settled down, she was done living the military lifestyle, so we moved around a lot. By then she was inactive, and went through one boyfriend after another. Eventually she got ahold of her parents and asked them to let me stay for a while until she figured things out.

"Sorry, that's a bit depressing," she said, her face blushing into a rosy red. He took the opportunity to reassure her by lacing his fingers with hers like he wanted to the night before. They were soft and warm, just like her eyes.

"Don't be sorry. It's your life and you've clearly been places. There's no shame in that. What happened next?"

She bit her lip and then continued. "I thought she would be gone a few weeks. But then it turned into several months, which turned into several years. But she visited, and I was always back and forth which is probably why you and I didn't cross paths until now. But at least while I was here, I attended church on Sundays and gained a testimony. My grandparents never forced me, but I always accepted their invitations and they also provided enough security and love I needed so I could make wise decisions in life.

"I really miss my dad, of course. He was more of the nurturing type, as odd as that sounds. He wasn't an official baptized member, but I remember him believing in the church's teachings and making sure I said my prayers at night. With my grandpa's help, we got all of his temple work done, and I can rest easy believing he accepted it and is doing well.

"My mom, however, I'm still trying to figure out. I miss her too, but I rarely see her. Last I heard she was living somewhere in California. But I have hope things will get better with time."

"I think so too. And that whole experience does say a lot of good things about you," he admitted.

She raised an eyebrow. "Does it now?"

"Well despite how things fell apart, you didn't follow in your mom's footsteps. You believed there was something better and didn't settle for anything less."

"Well I may have settled a little bit here and there."

"Is that why you agreed to go out with me?" he teased.

"No," she chuckled. "You asking me out is one of the better things."

Hearing that gave him enough confidence to stand up and play a CD he put into an old stereo his mom kept tucked away in a corner. It had one of his all-time favorite songs to listen to during the holidays.

"I told you how much I loved listening to John Schmidt. Well he put together a Christmas medley that's perfect for a time like this."

"A time like what?" she asked.

"A time to dance."

Both eyebrows went up this time. "Dance?"

"Yes, dance."

"And what makes this the time to dance?"

"Any time is the time to dance," he said. "Mostly I just want to slow dance with you and now seems like the perfect opportunity."

"You could have just said, 'Addie, would you like to dance with me?'"

He brought himself to his feet, looking down on her. "But you would have asked me why anyway, which would have led us to where we are now, and that is me standing here waiting for you to take my hand," he said, extending his hand to her.

With a small laugh, she took it and stood up to join him in a waltz position. Soon the room was filled with the sounds of multiple songs, all with a deeper Christmas meaning, compiled together into a beautiful piano rendition they swayed along to.

Logan kept a respectful distance between them, but it wasn't long before Addie stepped closer so she could rest her head against his chest. Logan tightened his embrace and rested his head on top of hers.

Closing his eyes, he inhaled her scent, and for the first time he felt no feelings of conflict with himself or anything else. He'd been chasing happiness for the last five years, thinking he would find it in a deal, in a bottle, or with a new conquest. But he'd been chasing lies. He was constantly fooling himself, seizing the moment when opportunity struck, but he never took the time to savor it.

It was probably why none of his relationships worked out. He was never looking for love, but for opportunities, which is why he never had the urge to commit. As soon as a deal closed, he moved on. But now, after taking the time to really learn about her, he began to feel something deeper than he planned for, which was both thrilling and disappointing to know that this moment wasn't truly real, no matter how real it felt.

Because it was a holiday mix CD, the next and last song on the track was the classic "White Christmas." He could feel her smile as she starting singing along to the words. That's when she looked up into his eyes, her voice combining with Bing Crosby, which naturally made him smile too.

He just watched her at first as she sang for him. There was something intimate about it that he never experienced before. It was infectious, so halfway through the song, he joined her in the duet.

Their voices were low and husky as he rested his forehead on hers. When the last words became nothing but a whisper between them, he closed the distance completely and lightly kissed her.

The kiss was short, but not at all simple as it left a lasting impression that made him feel warm and lightheaded. He had only pulled away an inch when he heard her sigh. He leaned forward so he could kiss her for a second time, and he felt her willingly wrap her arms around his neck while he pulled her close. It was a good thing they weren't alone in the house, otherwise the temptation would have been a much bigger struggle. But at least he had already reassured her and himself of his intentions, and that didn't involve breaking her trust.

Instead, he took a deep breath and let them both revel in the embrace until he heard her say in a breathy voice, "Wow."

"Wow," he agreed.

The rest of the evening they stayed in the small room, sitting on the sofa as they held hands while she rested her head on his shoulder. He played with her palms and fingers while she continued to go into more depth about her past. Some of it was sad, but mostly she spent time talking about the good memories she had with her dad.

The night ended on a good note when he walked her to her car and promised to call the next day. However, she texted him just as he was about to go to bed and they ended up messaging each other until midnight.

Once again he only had to blink to wake up the next morning feeling well rested like he usually did, but this time he was giddy. He took the liberty of making eggs and bacon for everyone, keeping it warm in the oven for all to help themselves after they got up. He decided to eat a large helping himself before going out to shovel the driveway again so his dad didn't have to do it.

After he was done, he sat on the front porch, suddenly feeling like the weight of the world was resting on his shoulders. Sometime during his shoveling workout, he'd starting thinking about Addie and reality. He'd been successful in suppressing the thought, but the real truth was that he was in a coma. When he woke up, all of this would be gone, including Addie.

While contemplating this, a passerby caught his attention and he gave him a brief glance. But doing a double take, he recognized that man. It was Tommy.

"Tommy?" he said, watching the man wearing a navy blue parka walk up the path.

"Morning, Logan. How are you?"

"Good, thanks. What brings you here?"

"Just checking up on you, and seeing how things are going."

"I didn't think you'd show up so soon," he said as Tommy sat next to him on the porch step. "Maybe on Christmas."

"Well I'm pretty busy on Christmas. It's a big day of recognition for the mortal and spirit worlds."

"I believe it."

"So what's on your mind, kid? You seem lost still."

"I'm not lost," he said in a sure voice. "Just discouraged. Everything about this alternate reality is all I ever wanted, and I didn't know it until now. It's wonderful, but it's all going to end and I'm going to wake up as my old self, surrounded by the huge mess I made."

"I can see why that would be discouraging."

"And Addie . . ."

"What about her?"

"Mark convinced me to ask her out on a date and she agreed. It was just a simple dinner and a trip to see some Christmas lights, but it was the most real fun I have had on a date in a long time. And since then I haven't been able to think about anything else. She came over last night and our conversation got more personal, which was when I learned just how amazing and beautiful she is . . ."

"Sounds like you're in love," Tommy said with a knowing smile on his face.

"No one falls in love in two days."

"Well you've known her longer than that. But if not in love, then you're well on your way."

"But that's not part of the plan."

"Who said there was a plan?"

"I'm here to find out what would have happened if I made a different decision. And now . . . I could have had a much happier life here than the one I have in Chicago." Logan hung his head in his hands. "I feel like this is a punishment. Like everything I could have had is being waved in front of my face reminding me of what I missed out on."

"Well I hate to break it to you, Logan, but this life is something you did, in fact, miss out on." Logan felt him place his hand on his shoulder. "But you also need to know that just because it didn't happen then, doesn't mean it can't happen in the future. Some things are intended to happen, but our choices can make them happen in different ways. Believe it or not, Addie is a real person. She exists in your reality and perhaps this is your wakeup call to get out there and do something that will lead you to her again."

Logan slowly raised his head to look Tommy in the eye. He did have a point, but it was a very small piece of hope that was hard to fully grasp.

"It's five years into the future from now," said Logan. "What if she's married and has kids?"

"You think I'd encourage you without checking to make sure she's available first?" he said, looking more amused than scolding.

"Seriously?"

"Seriously! Get with the program. This isn't fully about you, Logan. There are some people here who have made their own decisions as well, ones that have led them down darker paths just like you. But there is a lot you can do to help change that. The Lord knows it, which is why you needed the extra push to encourage you."

"That . . . is a lot to absorb."

"It's not going to be easy. There will be a lot of bad influences that will try to make you fail. But I'm going to do everything in my power to make sure that doesn't happen. As long as I'm invited, I will be there for you."

"Thanks," he said sincerely. "But why me? Why would you watch over someone who has nothing to do with you?"

"I wish I could say. But like all answers, they will come to you in time when they're supposed to be revealed. You just have to know what you're looking for."

"Can I at least know how much longer I'll be staying?"

Tommy let out a heavy sigh. "Not much longer, I'm afraid."

"Well then I guess I'll have to make the best of every minute."

"That's the spirit. Pun intended."

Logan shook his head, trying to keep down the laugh, but failing as it came out in a snort. He wished he had a friend like Tommy in reality. But then again, he did promise he'd be there in spirit, and Logan was greatly looking forward to it.

Chapter Nine

❧

It was Christmas Eve and Logan did little besides play the piano or watch TV while they waited for Taylor and his family to come over. He was nervous, but having been constantly reminded how things were different here, he decided to not let himself get too worried about interacting with Taylor. He was mostly looking forward to seeing the kids from the good old days when they loved Legos and Barbies instead of smart phones.

Because they were the kind of family who didn't knock, everyone heard the sound of the door open followed by the sound of running children and Taylor's wife, Annie, calling from the entrance, "Hello? Anybody home?"

Carter, who was almost five, and Brooklyn, just a year younger, both came running into the family room to jump in everyone's laps. Annie soon appeared, looking about ready to pop with her baby due in a few weeks.

She rushed as fast as she could to Logan first. "Logan, you're here!"

"Everyone keeps saying that," he said as he gave his sister-in-law a tender hug.

"Well it's been so long and you've gotten so much taller."

"No, you've just gotten shorter," he teased, which he always did considering she was five foot two.

He always liked Annie. She was a loud personality in a small package, always bringing her positive attitude wherever she went.

"You're probably right. Little Daniel here keeps me hunched over so often, I probably have lost a few inches."

Logan just smiled as she continued on to greet his parents. When he saw Taylor enter the room, he couldn't help but stop and stare at the man who had given him so much grief over the years.

"Logan," Taylor exclaimed brightly, which was a first for him in a while. "It's good to see you, man."

"It's good to see you too," Logan said, embracing his big brother like he did when was a little kid. He had always looked up to Taylor, much like Mark looked up to him, and he didn't realize how much he missed their friendship until now. "I've missed you."

"Me too, brother. It's been a while. How are things holding up? How did the interview go?"

"Interview? Oh yeah . . . the interview. I didn't get it."

Taylor gave him a sympathetic look. "Tough break."

Logan shrugged. "Yeah, but it's Christmas and that's all I'm thinking about right now."

"Good idea," he said, giving him a brotherly slap on the shoulder.

This was a lot easier than Logan had thought it would be and he let out a breath of relief. Everything was the way it should be and nothing was going to get him down tonight.

Dinner was already underway before the family showed up, and his mother was now in the kitchen with Taylor getting it prepared. Annie offered to help, but Taylor wouldn't have it. Despite how callous he was toward Logan, he couldn't deny him having always been a good husband and father.

Logan silently prayed he would be allowed to stay until he saw Brin. Out of all his siblings, she had expressed the most reason and understanding during the dark years. But because she and her family had moved to Washington three years ago, she wasn't always in the picture during his rare visits. He missed her children as well, and her husband was a nice guy too. Like Annie, he stayed out of the family squabbles as much as possible, and he didn't encourage Brin to choose sides like Taylor did.

After dinner was served, everyone ate heartily while several conversations went around the dinner table. Extra chairs were brought in so they could all fit while the two little ones ate at a small play table nearby. Shortly after, things wound down while they all gathered to rest after a big meal and eventually put on the Nativity with Brooklyn and Carter as Mary and Joseph. They were more excited to be the center of attention while Henry read the story from the Bible, but they played their parts well.

Mark happily played the role of the donkey before he later joined Logan and Taylor as the three wise men. Brooklyn held onto the small doll wrapped in a sheet tightly to her chest for the entire scene, reluctant to lay it in the manger. But when she did, everyone's heart melted when she kissed the doll's head and said, "Nigh' night, Jesus," before sidling up to her mother who played the angel with her halo made out of sparkly tinsel and tape.

Once it was over, each of the kids got to open the gifts their grandparents got them since they'd be spending Christmas morning with Annie's family. Carter went nuts over the Batman Legos he got while Brooklyn admired the princess dress up set.

Since they weren't going to leave for an hour or so, Taylor and Annie let the kids play with their new toys while they joined the adults for their annual game of Farkle. It was a game played with five dice, and each player rolled to get a certain combination. The player could role as many times as they wanted so long as they kept getting a 1, 5, or any of the combinations that was worth more. But if they took a chance and ended up with a bad number, they Farkled and had to pass it along. The player with the most points won, and Logan distinctly remembered Brin being reigning champ for several years in a row.

It was his turn now, and if he learned anything about taking chances in business, he was going to play the right strategy to get the high score.

"Just going to say this now," announced Taylor. "Y'all are going down."

Henry only laughed. "You say that every year, but it never ends in your favor."

"Well Brin isn't here and I always came in second behind her, so data has proven the odds are in my favor."

"Yeah, good luck with that, honey," said Peggy, patting him on the knee.

The game started, Logan putting as much focus as was needed to play the game, but the rest he kept on his family. He wanted to remember all of them like this. Happy and carefree, no tension with the threat of hurtful words being tossed around. Life was good here, and if he were to carry on in reality, he had to remember this. He just had to.

❦

Mark sighed as he leaned back in his chair next to Logan's hospital bed. His arm rested on the roll out table while he twirled his phone between his fingers. It had become another habit of his since he first got one, but he didn't realize it was a nervous habit until now.

It was Christmas Eve and he was spending it at a hospital in Chicago. Not that he resented it, but it sure didn't sit well with him.

Henry had gone to get Chinese takeout for dinner since it would be the only place open tonight. Mark encouraged his mom to go with him so he could have his moment with Logan. Plus he knew his parents needed some alone time together. Logan's condo wasn't really big enough for the three of them, and they all needed some space.

Mark didn't have much to say, except for, "You big, stupid idiot . . ." He let out a heavy sigh before setting his phone down and leaning forward to rest his elbows on his knees. ". . . is what you would have said to me if I had told you what I did five years ago. You were never alone making mistakes, Logan. If I had told you, maybe you wouldn't have thought I hated you like Taylor and . . . maybe you would have talked to me more."

Mark sniffed, rubbing at the scruff on his chin. "Maybe you would have taken me down with you, I don't know. It's hard to tell how the Lord wants me to see it. All I know is that after that one mistake, I came clean and did everything I could to make it right. I did everything without your help, Logan. But that doesn't mean I didn't want you there, that I wasn't wishing you'd notice me more. Yeah, you were always the good big brother when you visited, but I can count on one hand the times you were really there for me."

He shook his head and wiped away the tear that managed to escape. "I was torn up when I heard what happened. And I don't know why I'm so mad, or why I'm saying all this when you can't even hear me. But I'm afraid it's the only time you'll be around for me to say anything."

His lower lip shook and the tears began to spill more profusely.

"Dang it, Logan," he cried, burying his head on the bed sheet. He stayed like that as he released all his emotion. He didn't necessarily feel better after he did it, but he did feel a bit lighter.

After a few silent minutes, Mark reached into his pocket and pulled out a plastic container full of dice.

"I took these out of the kitchen drawer before we flew here," he said, turning it over in his hands. "We still play, you know. Every year. Brin always used to be the winner, but these days I've managed to climb up the leader board. Last year I was reigning champ.

"I know it's not the same, but I'm not going to let tradition go. As soon as Mom and Dad get back, it's game on."

❧

"Yes!" Mark shouted as he rolled the dice for his final time, receiving the exact amount of points he needed to win the game.

Logan could only laugh and applauded the kid for being the quiet underdog who managed to dupe them all. His strategy was to take the least amount of chances and gain points little by little while everyone else got greedy and Farkled out. Logan had a similar idea, which at least got him second place, but Taylor fell to the bottom of the leader board.

"You're a cheater," Taylor accused, pointing at Mark's chest for emphasis.

"How do you cheat at Farkle?" Mark said, not the least bit intimidated. Taylor obviously wasn't serious, but Mark had tougher skin being the youngest of four siblings.

"I don't know, but I will find out how for next year," he declared.

"All right, boys," Peggy said, intervening as usual. "It's time for bed."

"But mom," they all groaned in unison.

Annie couldn't hold down a laugh. "Yeah boys, Santa's coming and it's way past your bedtime."

At the mention of Santa, the kids jumped up and ran to their daddy's lap. "Yeah, Dad. We need to go home and put out cookies!" Carter insisted.

"And his reindeer needs carrots," Brooklyn added.

Taylor pulled his children close. "Then I guess we better hurry back. Go find your shoes and get your stuff together. There's a package of Oreos Santa is looking forward to."

The two wriggled out of his embrace to run back into the family room.

"This is the only time they get excited to leave," Annie chuckled. "But they sure do love it, Mom. Thanks for having us over."

"Of course! Thanks for coming," she said as everyone stood to say their good-byes.

After coats were on and people were exiting out the door, Logan thought about saying something meaningful. But instead he made one last remark at Taylor and said, "Hey, Santa. Go easy on those Oreos."

He just rolled his eyes with a wide smile. "Merry Christmas, little brother."

"Merry Christmas."

That night, once everyone was in bed, Logan crept down to the family room and turned on the tree lights. With his large comforter, he laid down on the couch and threw it over himself.

He didn't feel like going to sleep just yet, and he wanted some real solitude to think.

He stared at the multicolored lights as they reflected off the shiny ornaments. It reminded him of the evening he spent in the snow with Addie, and the way she was mesmerized by the enchantment of it. He was too distracted by her to really get the full effect, but now that he was absorbing the holiday scenery, he recognized how a small thing, even the beauty of Christmas lights, could bring real joy.

His thoughts soon sailed into the innocent moments throughout his lifetime that brought him true happiness. He once had a mind to forget all of them until now, and by doing so, he had forgotten that at one time something as small and innocent as the birth of a baby brought everlasting happiness and light into the hearts of those who believed in the Savior.

But despite all the happy memories, the burden of the painful reality that was his own doing began to weigh heavier. The emptiness, loneliness, sorrow, and guilt only increased as he remembered what he had done to eliminate that belief of the Savior in himself.

The moisture in his eyes increased and he couldn't stop himself from crying like he was a child again—like he had done something wrong and he feared his punishment.

Logan abruptly sat forward, pressing a hand to his chest as he felt a discomfort seizing him from the inside. It was a sudden and shocking pain that radiated throughout his body. He clutched his chest, breathing hard from the episode, and lay back down.

Eyes closed shut, he felt the ache directly in his heart. Understanding what his body was really going through in reality, he knew something was wrong. Whatever hospital he was at, somehow he was struggling to hold on and the pain was reaching him.

Tommy had specifically told him, *the mindset you have here is going to affect your body in the real world.*

The dark place he put himself in was deteriorating his health. Logan searched quickly through his own reasoning on what he could do to stop this.

He had to calm down. He had to remember why he was here and what he needed to learn. But more importantly, he couldn't do this on his own. He needed help and now was the time to ask for it.

"Heavenly Father . . . please help me," he panted. "I'm sorry. I don't want to live the life I was leading anymore. If I must die . . . then I will accept Thy will. But if I can have another chance . . . I want to use it to make things right."

The prayer was long overdue, but the fear that had enveloped him was slowly fading into a calm that Logan welcomed. Soon his breathing evened out and he began to feel tired, which was a first since the moment he woke up in his old bedroom.

His eyes fluttered closed as he concentrated on taking deep breaths. His body relaxed more and more until the sense of weightlessness carried him to a different place.

He couldn't pinpoint where exactly, or how he got there. But when he awoke, he found himself standing in a bright, clean room empty of furniture. He only had to turn his head to see that he wasn't alone.

"Hello, Logan," said Tommy as he greeted him with a warm smile.

"Hey, Tommy. What's going on? Where are we?" he asked, not alarmed, just unsure of where he ended up.

"We're in Chicago, at the hospital where the staff are working very hard to revive you."

Now Logan was a bit alarmed. "Revive me?"

"You're in good hands, Logan. It isn't your time to go yet, but it is time for you to wake up."

Logan sighed, and nodded in acceptance. "I was hoping for more time."

"I know, son. But you have that second chance. The Savior made sure of that. It's just up to you on how long it's going to take."

"It's going to be hard, isn't it?" It wasn't a question. Logan had a pretty good idea of what it would be like when he woke up.

"Yes it will. But you're not alone. And I don't just mean the spirits who are watching over you. There are many in the mortal world who love and care about you. Some you aren't even aware of."

"You sure about that?"

Tommy laughed. "It's kind of against my nature to lie from where I'm standing."

"Good point," he chuckled. "Well thanks for everything."

"And thank you."

"What did I do?"

"You chose the life that would have brought you real happiness. There are some who make the same choice they made before, and they are particularly hard to get through to. But my guess is, you were able to take something away from this."

Logan nodded. "I guess I did."

"Just promise me you won't forget it."

"I promise."

With a final nod, Tommy walked over and gave him a firm embrace. "Good luck, kid. And promise me you won't forget about Addie."

"I couldn't if I tried."

Tommy took a step back and all Logan had to do was blink before he felt weightless again, turning back into a heaviness that encased him like a vice.

❧

He felt stiff, tired, and very thirsty. He wasn't sure where he was or how he got there, but judging by the smell and the sounds around him, he was in a hospital.

He opened his eyes and tried taking a deep breath, only to realize there was a tube doing that for him.

The light was blinding and the shadows that loomed over him were frantic. Logan knew he had survived something. But what?

He wanted answers, but he decided that question could be worried about later. Right now he just wanted to know how damaged his body was. Instinctively, he wiggled his toes and fingers. The gesture was weak, but possible. His legs were too stiff and heavy to bend, but there was feeling. He wasn't paralyzed.

It was after his assessment that someone finally took out the tube so he could breathe on his own. His throat was dry and uncomfortable, but he was happy to have some independence again.

Amidst the chaos, there was a point where everything became too much for Logan to handle and he fell back to unconsciousness. While he slept, flashes of a different life drifted through his mind. His parents, siblings, plowing snow, rolling dice, and the smile of a woman Logan couldn't recognize. But whoever she was, he figured she was the angel who saved him. A beautiful one at that.

Chapter Ten

❧

Logan woke up facing a window. The blinds were open, allowing the white light of a cloudy afternoon to stream through. His neck ached from the lack of movement, but it felt good to stretch the muscles that were stationary for so long.

"Logan?" he heard a soft voice say.

Logan blinked away some of the fogginess and looked over to see his mother standing next to him with tearful eyes.

"Mom?" he said, his voice sounding low and raspy.

"Hi, sweetie. You're awake."

"Yeah. And you're here. Where are we?"

"You're at the hospital. You were in a really bad accident."

"I was? Oh right . . . I was."

Logan was still a bit dazed, but he'd been in and out of it enough to remember what was going on. He knew he had been in an accident and had gotten hurt. Pretty badly from what he heard the doctors say in his semiconscious state. He also remembered flashes of himself sitting in the car, looking out into the intersection, and then suddenly gazing at the shattered glass of his window. But not much more after that.

"Yes, but you're okay now," she said. Her voice was still soft, but carried the same tone one would use to reassure a child. It was habitual for her, and he was glad that some things never changed. "You were asleep for a long time."

"How long?"

"About a week. You were in a coma. You have some really great doctors though who are taking great care of you. You have a very deep cut in your leg that had to be surgically repaired. Nothing was broken though, so that's good."

"Why does my side hurt?"

"It was punctured, but it just missed your lung, which was really lucky. A few of your ribs were cracked, but those will heal on their own."

"Well that's no fun," he groaned.

"I know. I'm so sorry, dear."

He gave her a small shrug. "It happens. What about my head?"

"You got hit pretty hard. The doctor can explain it better than I can, but basically you received a severe brain injury that took a lot of time to fix. And then of course you were in a coma, but . . . you woke up. The doctors assessed your brain function, and my guess is you don't really remember that part." Logan shook his head and immediately regretted it. "But you were responsive and that gave them high hopes of a full recovery. Now a nurse is on his way to get the doctor to come and see how you're doing now."

Logan turned over his hand and gestured to his mom to take it. He admired her strength during this moment, but he knew her well enough to know that she must have been living in a nightmare this whole time. She was keeping it together, telling him exactly what he wanted him to know. However, he could see it tearing her up inside.

"Your dad and brother are here too," she said.

"Dad and . . . ?"

"Mark," she assured.

"Really?"

She smiled. "Yeah. Merry Christmas. It's today, by the way."

"Well dang, talk about good timing."

They both laughed, though the moment was short lived when Logan grunted from the pain.

"They're downstairs getting something to eat," she said. "I'm going to let them know you're awake."

"Okay," he said as she got up to leave the room, but he stopped her. "This is probably a bad time to ask this, but . . . did I die?"

Her smile turned into a frown as her breath caught. "Your heart stopped, but they revived you. Did someone tell you that?"

"I think I remember some of it. But I just thought I'd ask to make sure."

Logan could see she was doing everything she could to hold back her flood of emotion. He opened his arms so he could hold her and then she let her tears flow freely.

"It was the scariest moment of my life," she sobbed into his shoulder.

"I'm okay, Mom. I'm sorry I scared you."

"It wasn't you're fault."

"I know, I just hate to see you sad."

She stood up straight to grab a tissue and dry her eyes. "Well I'm happy now. And pretty soon there will be a few other happy people to join our party."

"Looking forward to it. We can talk about it later."

"Of course. I'll be right back."

While she was gone, the doctor showed up to do another checkup and order a list of tests. His vitals were normal, and he was given a heavy dose of painkillers that made him drowsy, but kept him alert enough to greet his father and brother for the first time in a while. He wished it were under better circumstances, but at least no one had anything bad to say.

Logan was impressed by how much Mark had grown over the years, but he mostly noticed how quiet he'd become. He figured it was the result of maturity, but he had a nagging feeling Mark was keeping a lot more to himself than he let on.

Logan sipped some broth while his father gave him an update on the family and how everyone was doing. He nodded at all the right moments and enjoyed hearing about his little nieces and nephews. But his siblings had become so foreign to him, he had a hard time feeling any real connection over the events of their lives. Not that he didn't want to, but he figured if he were to somehow jump back into the family boat too quickly, it was going to teeter and sink into the water.

"You want to know the worst part about all this?" Logan said, as everyone leaned in intently. "I can't play video games here."

Mark snorted in laughter, which left their parents looking pleasantly surprised. It made Logan wonder how rare that was these days.

"I thought you were going to say something about the catheter," said Mark.

"Well that too. But not having to get up to use the bathroom would have been a real bonus if I had a gaming console right now."

Peggy rolled her eyes as the discussion went on to the newest games both Mark and Logan enjoyed the most, resulting in their parents' departure at dinnertime.

Phone calls needed to be made and tests needed to be run. But Mark had no reason to leave, so he read a book until Logan was back in his room and visiting hours were coming to an end.

"Sorry I ruined your Christmas," said Logan as Mark handed him a cup of ice.

"You didn't. If anything, you made it better."

"How so?"

"If you were still in coma, or if you . . . died, it would have sucked a whole lot more. Besides, Christmas is supposed to remind us of the day a miracle happened. What better way to remember than to witness one?"

Logan didn't like calling what happened to him a miracle. To him it was more like a wakeup call. But he could see why it would be to others.

"Do you believe in miracles, Mark?" Logan asked.

He looked at him like it was stupid question. "Hard not to when I see them every day."

Logan wasn't expecting that answer, which made him curious. "Elaborate."

"Do you remember the story of Naaman and Elisha?"

"I'm afraid I don't."

"Naaman was a very important man in the scriptures, but he suffered from leprosy. He went to the prophet for help, and the prophet sent a messenger to tell him to go wash in the Jordan River seven times. Obviously Naaman was expecting some great show of his miraculous healing, rather than being told to go bathe in a dirty river.

"But with some encouragement, he took all the faith he had and did it anyway. After submerging seven times, he came out completely healed and whole. Of course it would be awesome to see that, but not all miracles are going to be the parting of the Red Sea. They're little kids who fell off their bikes but didn't get hurt because they were prompted to wear helmets. Or a car hitting you just right so you could make a full recovery."

"Yeah I get it," Logan said dismissively, but Mark wasn't done sharing what he had to say.

"I know you, Logan, so I know sometime in the future you're going to ask why this had to happen to you. You'll wonder when a miracle will save you from it. And I promise you it will come, but you may have to go outside your comfort zone to get it."

Logan was both shocked and impressed that Mark had the guts to acknowledge his stubbornness and scold him for it. He wanted to get defensive, but never in Mark's growing years had he evoked so much passion for something he seemed to truly believe in. Logan knew he had once believed it too, so it was easy to understand where he was coming from. But it was still too much for him to wrap his head around right now.

"I'll keep that in mind," said Logan.

"That's all I'm asking for."

"You're definitely not a kid anymore," he chuckled.

Mark only shrugged, but Logan had dealt with living in the shadow of an older sibling long enough to know it affected him more.

"I've ignored you for a long time, haven't I?"

"Yeah," he said bluntly. "But now that you're bedridden, I have plenty of time to get my payback."

"Hey, remember there's not much glory in beating up a cripple."

Mark scowled. "Who said anything about beating you up? I plan to kill you with kindness."

"No," Logan groaned. "That's the worst revenge there is."

"I would say sorry, but I'm not," he chuckled. "I'm really going to enjoy this."

"Stubborn and devious. You'll make a great missionary," he said, sincerely meaning that.

"You know I put my papers in?"

"You think Mom would keep that from me?" he chuckled. "Did you get your call yet?"

"No, but there's still some time. I have to graduate high school first."

"Dang, you've really grown up. I'm sorry I missed it."

Mark sighed. "You're an adult, Logan. I never expected you to be around all the time. Heck, we're all fine with you living in Chicago. It's just . . . you live differently than we do."

"Biggest mistake I've ever made," Logan said quietly.

"Really?"

"Well in some ways."

"You plan on doing something about it?"

"I don't know. Right now I'm too doped up to think clearly. But I have this feeling that something is pulling me back. It's a good feeling, but at the same time it's scary. I've made mistakes before and tried coming back, but . . ."

"I get it. But you have me this time, so maybe it'll be different."

"Like my spiritual trainer."

Mark snorted and both fell into a fit of laughter. "That was the cheesiest thing I've ever heard you say," laughed Mark. "But I like it. I should make a T-shirt."

"You better not."

"Oh I think I will. I'll even get a whistle while I make you bench press a hundred Book of Mormons."

"I thought it was Books of Mormon?"

Mark just shook his head. "That's a debate I'm not going to get into. But right now, I want to keep the family tradition and play a game of Farkle—with you conscious."

"That's right, you kicked our butts the last time we all played together."

Mark looked confused. "I've never been reigning champion," he said.

"You haven't?"

"Pretty sure I would remember that."

"I could have sworn you beat everyone when you were younger. Weird," he said, pretending to shrug it off.

With that thought came the familiar feeling that he was missing something, something important that he needed to remember. But for now he put that thought away. He had a game to play, and was looking forward to sharing a normal moment with his brother amidst the chaos of his life. It was all he could do, but for now it made him appreciate the simple things he'd forgotten about until now.

⁊ॐ

Logan was feeling better each day, but it came with its chal-
lenges. He spent a lot of time in bed, but was encouraged to walk
around the hospital for a few minutes for the sake of his muscles
and circulation. He needed a walker, and could only move a few
inches at a time before he felt nauseous, not to mention the pain
of his injuries.

Going to the bathroom wasn't a fun task either. He had to
swallow a lot of his pride allowing a nurse's assistant to help him
to the toilet, as well as shower. There was something about feeling
clean that gave him more energy than usual.

"When do I get to go home?" Logan asked his doctor after
another checkup that seemed pretty redundant at this point.

"We've been watching you closely and we'd like to keep you
for another day, but I don't see any problem in having you discharged. Do you live alone?"

"Yeah, but I think I could get by."

"You do seem capable. But emotional support plays a big role
in recovery too. It's not my job to see to that. Just search your
options before you jump into your life. There's physical therapy
and follow ups—"

"I know, Doc. I have a backup plan."

"All right, as long as you get better. Take it easy, Logan."

"You too," he said as the doctor left him to surf the channels on a weekday afternoon. There was nothing but news, which
didn't favor his attention much.

He looked over and saw the Book of Mormon Mark had left
on the table. Instinctively, he picked it up and started flipping
through the pages. He stopped at a random chapter and scanned
the verses, ending up in Alma 12:33, which read, "But God
did call on men, in the name of his Son, (this being the plan of
redemption which was laid) saying: If ye will repent, and harden
not your hearts, then will I have mercy upon you, through mine
Only Begotten Son."

He didn't have to stop and think about it to know it wasn't a coincidence. This motivated him to keep reading until lunch-time. His parents came in just after he finished his sandwich. It was their last day in Chicago, which was a bummer for him, but he knew life would have to restart sometime.

"Where's Mark?" he asked, noticing he wasn't with them.

"He's right behind us," his dad answered. "He stopped to use the bathroom."

"Oh good, because I have something I'd like to ask you. I don't know how Mark would feel about it, but I thought I should run it by you guys to see if it's okay first."

They both stayed silent to tell him they were listening, so he continued, "Even though I'm recovering, jumping back into independence isn't going to be easy the first few days. At least that's what everyone keeps telling me. I could hire someone to help me at home, but I would much rather have someone there who I know and trust instead of a paid stranger.

"So what I'm asking is . . . could Mark stay with me the rest of the holiday break? That is if he wants to and it's all right with you."

When Henry and Peggy looked at each other, he knew they were having some kind of telepathic discussion that Logan tried to determine through their facial expressions. Unfortunately they excused themselves into the hallway, which was frustrating since it would have taken him an agonizing amount of time just to get out of the bed and listen in.

❧

"I don't have a problem with it, if you don't," said Henry, which made Peggy scowl at him.

"Oh right, make me the bad guy if I say no, right?"

"That's not what I'm saying. I'm saying you've seen firsthand how Logan lives. Would it be a bad idea to leave Mark exposed to that for a week?"

Peggy sighed. "I don't know. I trust Mark to make wise decisions, and . . . I trust Logan to be a good influence on him. Logan's made his choices, but he's not corruptive. If anything, Mark may be the good influence, and they never spend time together. Watching them these last few days, seeing at least two of my children getting along has been another miracle for me."

"Mark certainly talks a lot more," said Henry.

"He does! I've never seen him that animated in months. Plus, Mark will only be helping him recuperate. It's not like Logan will be taking him to his favorite party places. At least I hope not."

"We'll set boundaries just in case. But it's like you said, I trust Logan."

❧

Logan was messing with the bed controls when Mark walked in. He had a curious look on his face. "What are Mom and Dad talking about?"

"I don't know. Stuff," Logan shrugged, pretending not to know anything.

"I snuck you a Kit Kat," he said, tossing the package onto the bed.

"Dang, were they out of Butterfingers?"

"I got the last one."

"Dude, really?"

"Be happy I didn't eat yours on the way. I was very conflicted about that."

Logan dug into his Kit Kat, eating only the chocolate sides first, and then going for the middle. Despite him being an adult, some childhood habits never fade.

About half way through his third bite, their parents walked in and Logan scrambled to hide the evidence.

"What are you eating?" Peggy asked.

"Nothing."

She turned to Mark. "Seriously?"

"Whoa, what did I do?"

"I'm a woman, which makes me twice as more sensitive to the scent of chocolate, which I know you have. And as for you." She pointed at Logan. "Are you sure you want this one staying with you until New Year's?"

"Wait, what? Really?" asked Mark, looking at Logan for confirmation.

"Only if you want to. I still need help getting to the bathroom and stuff, just until I'm confident I can get around on my own."

Mark looked at Henry. "Is that okay?"

"It's all right with us, but you have to be back before school starts."

"Sweet!" he shouted, giving Logan a high five. "Does this mean I get to play your video games and eat all your food?"

"All I have is diet food."

Mark took a dramatic pause. "It's worse than I thought. Look at what the big city has done to him. I have to stay, Mom. I must save a man who is clearly crying for help."

Logan laughed and shook his head. This was going to be an interesting week, but he was looking forward to it. Not only would he be spending time with his brother, he wouldn't be spending his time off work alone. Sure, he had friends nearby, but they had their own lives and cared only enough to send best wishes instead of actually visiting him in the hospital.

A few things would have to change during Mark's stay, but they were sacrifices worth making. Logan was determined to get better, in more ways than one.

Chapter Eleven

◈

Logan had never been more grateful to have an elevator in his apartment building. By the time he was settled on his own couch, he was ready to take his pain meds and sleep the rest of the day. His body ached, his head throbbed, and he was nauseous. For Mark, the next week was certainly not going to be one big party, but he seemed to enjoy feeling useful as he set out to help him get comfortable.

Their parents were already on a flight back to Utah and once Logan fell asleep, Mark made himself at home. There wasn't much to do at his place, but he somehow managed to stay busy when Logan didn't need him

Though it was mildly selfish, Logan was glad five years worth of built up pride didn't keep him from asking for help. He wouldn't have been able to do it by himself.

◈

While Logan slept, Mark called his parents and left them a message they would listen to once they landed. He promised to give updates several times a day, which sounded tedious, but he understood their need for reassurance.

He thought about getting on Logan's gaming console, but decided to read a book instead of trying to figure out his system without messing it up.

But about halfway through the first chapter, there was a knock at the door.

Mark got up to look through the peephole and saw a woman standing there with a large plate of cookies. It was something a member of the Relief Society would do, but the way she was dressed didn't give him the impression she was serving on their behalf.

Curious, he opened the door. Obviously the woman was surprised to see him standing there, but her look turned to instant approval.

"You must be Logan's brother, Mark," she said in an overly sweet voice.

"Uh, yes. Can I help you?"

"I'm Sheila, and I've come to deliver these cookies to Logan. Can I come in?"

"He just got back from the hospital today and isn't really up to visitors. But thank you, I can take those and pass along the message."

"I'd rather see how he's doing and deliver them myself."

"Well he's sleeping right now and asked me to let him rest in peace. So if you like, you can come by at a later time."

Sheila pouted, not exactly trying to hide her displeasure. "All right, I guess I can do that. It sure is nice of you to be helping your brother out. He must keep you pretty busy."

"It's actually been kind of boring so far. Not much to do while he's unconscious."

She giggled. "I bet. Well if you're looking for something to do, I live just a few doors down. I can always come over and keep you company."

Mark immediately felt an uneasiness in his gut. It was obvious that she had some of kind of past with Logan, as well as an agenda that Mark didn't want any part in.

"I'll keep that in mind, but I have a lot of homework to do," he lied.

"Good for you. Putting your education first. In that case, I'll be back later. But take a cookie anyway. You deserve it, being the good brother you are," she said with a wink.

Mark graciously took one and gave her a quick "good-bye" before shutting the door. Mark hoped he wouldn't have to deal with her again, but had a bad feeling he hadn't heard the end of it.

❧

Logan woke up in a daze, but felt well rested and hungry. He gingerly sat up in bed and rubbed his eyes, thinking about the strange dream he had during his nap.

Slowly, he limped his way to the kitchen. Mark was already there drinking a glass of juice.

"Morning, sunshine," said Mark.

Logan grunted in response.

"Would you like some soup?"

He nodded.

"Go sit down, I got it," Mark ordered.

Logan did just that, laying on the couch to extend his bandaged leg on a pillow. He picked up his tablet and started browsing through Facebook. He had over fifty notifications, all coming from people he barely knew who sent him words of encouragement, hoping he got well soon.

His nieces and nephews had sent him drawings and cards in the mail, which he assumed had been mostly the result of Annie and Brin. They made him smile just the same.

Mark brought him a bowl of bacon and potato soup and sat with him on the couch with his own helping.

It was quiet for a minute or so until Mark said, "A woman named Sheila came by while you were asleep."

Logan was about to take a bite until he lowered his spoon. "What did she want?"

"She just wanted to see how you were doing. She had a big plate of cookies that she insisted on delivering to you personally."

Logan rubbed his eyes and swore under his breath, which Mark must have chosen to ignore.

"My guess is she's not exactly good company?"

"Mark, promise me you'll never lead a woman on and let her manipulate you into her clutches."

"Hard to avoid altogether, but I'll do my best," he laughed. "Do I get to hear the story behind this?"

"All you need to know is that she craves attention from men who are hard to get. I gave in once and . . . let's just say it's what drew me away from everything I knew was right."

"Why not tell her to leave you alone?"

"I did!"

"Why not change your identity and move to Switzerland?"

"She'd still find me."

Mark chuckled. "Can't say I know how you feel, but I'll keep making excuses for you as long as I'm here."

"No, don't do that. Next time she comes over, I'll deal with her. I'd rather do that than have her asking you for help lifting something heavy and see you tangled in her web."

"I wish you luck," he said, toasting his bowl of soup.

Logan raised his and finished the rest in less than a minute. Satisfied, he pulled a blanket around him and leaned against the cushion.

"I had a weird dream," he said as details from it began drifting through his idol mind.

"What about?"

"I think it might be flashbacks. I keep seeing Christmas lights, but it's not in the right context. I also keep seeing this girl. She may have been one of the paramedics or people standing by, but . . . I don't know her, yet I keep seeing her."

"Does she have a name?"

"Oddly, yes. Addie comes to mind. But I don't remember ever knowing an Addie. I'm not positive its even a name. Whatever painkillers I'm on, it's probably just messing with my head."

Mark looked deep in thought for a minute, then finally responded, "You sure you're not remembering Addie Garrison?"

"Who?"

"She used to live in our stake. I only know because her grandma is Mom's visiting teacher and Mom forces me to sit in on their discussions, even when they're just chatting. I'm pretty sure you guys went to high school together, and even went to Dixie State."

"No kidding, really?"

"Yeah, you should look her up and see if she looks like the girl you imagined."

Logan quickly grabbed his tablet and began searching Facebook for an Addie Garrison from the Utah area. Within a few seconds he was staring at her profile picture, looking almost exactly as he had envisioned.

"How in the world?" he muttered, wondering how this girl ended up in his dreams.

He for sure never met her before. Maybe he passed her once or twice in the hallway, but he would have remembered officially meeting her.

She wasn't the type to post a whole lot to her feed, but he searched a few of her photos just to see if it would jog his memory. "I must have heard Mom mention her too or something."

"Maybe," Mark shrugged. "Is she hot?"

The answer was a definite yes, but he ended up saying, "She's certainly pretty."

"Is she single?"

"Why, you looking for someone to write while you're away?"

"I'm pretty sure she's a little too old for me."

"Not into cougars, eh?"

"Only the BYU ones."

Logan snorted at that as he stumbled upon an album titled "Broncos" and saw that it was the name of a club, one that looked very familiar. The place had a stage and there were numerous photos of bands performing there.

"Wait, I know this place. It's here in Chicago."

"Really?" Mark moved to his side to see for himself. "Was she visiting, or do you think she actually lives here?"

Logan rechecked her information and saw her current location was just outside the city. "She does live here!"

"What are the odds? Are you going to message her?"

"Why would I?"

"To see if maybe she remembers you—jog your memory a bit."

"I couldn't even if I wanted to. Her page isn't open to receive random messages from strangers."

"Lucky for you, there's this new thing called 'sending a friend request' which if she accepts, it'll solve that problem. In fact," he said, snatching the tablet from his hand.

"Dude!" Logan shouted.

Mark stood and walked to the other end of the room, taking advantage of his brother's inability to move quickly.

"Friend request sent. You're welcome."

"What exactly should I be thanking you for?"

"Let's evaluate this. You had a traumatic experience in which you began to dream of a beautiful woman who you used to go to high school with. She even went to the same college as you, and now lives in the area you currently reside in."

"When you put it like that, it sounds creepy."

"My guess is, considering your alternative lifestyles, she didn't do that on purpose. She changed her location from California to Chicago on her timeline only a few months ago, which means she came here on a whim. Not to follow you around. That could only mean one thing."

"That my brother is an obsessive weirdo."

"That fate is intervening! You probably met her forever ago and ignored her. Fate is now getting frustrated and had to literally smack you in the head to get you to remember!"

"You do realize how you sound right now?"

"Yes, but it doesn't matter because . . ." he drawled, staring intently at the tablet. "She accepted."

"Wait, really?"

"Yeah, and now that you have more access to her information, you will come to find that . . ." he took a minute to scan through the page. "Wow."

"Wow, what's wow?"

"Very interesting," Mark said to himself.

"Give me the tablet, Mark."

"Oh, so now you're interested?"

"You're going to make me tear my stitches from trying to strangle you, and I'll be back in the hospital, and it'll be your fault."

"All you had to say was please," he said, handing him the tablet, which Logan dramatically snatched out of his hands.

Logan scanned through pictures he was now allowed to see and saw the band photos she posted were part of a showcase she supported.

She wore a black T-shirt with skinny jeans torn at the knees, with red streaks in her long dark blonde hair as she held a microphone close to her face. Obviously she was one of the lead singers, and she looked like she was having the time of her life.

"Wow," Logan breathed.

"Told you."

"She doesn't look like my type."

"And what is your type? The spider down the hallway?"

"Sadly . . . yes."

"That's depressing. Have you ever thought about branching out?"

"I have, it's just hard to branch out when most of the people I spend time with are work-related acquaintances, and work takes up most of my life."

"Well you have all the time in the world now that you're on leave."

"I'm not exactly fit to socialize, Mark."

"Nothing's stopping you from sending her a message."

"If I'm going to meet someone, I'm not going to do it over the Internet. I may be a part of the modern world, but there are some things I like doing the old-fashioned way."

Mark nodded. "Point taken."

"And who knows? If fate, as you put it, has decided to take action, we'll run into each other on the train or something."

"Oh I was just joking around about that. If everything were predestined, then there would be little reason for us to be living on this earth."

"So you're saying you were kidding about Addie possibly being my soul mate?"

"I never said she could be your soul mate."

"You implied it."

"Okay it may have sounded that way. But maybe she's someone with a problem that you have the expertise to help her with. Or vice versa. Or maybe the Lord is giving you an opportunity to get to know a woman from your past and decide for yourself if you want her to be your eternal companion."

"You do realize where I'm at in my life, right?"

"And we discussed already that I'm going to help you get back on track, remember? I'm your spiritual trainer."

"I knew I'd regret that."

Mark shrugged. "Day one, brother. Your first challenge is to pray about it. You want to know more about this dream, just ask."

Logan knew he was right. The problem was, he hadn't prayed in so long, he'd forgotten how. He also wasn't sure if he'd recognize an answer if he received one. However, when he went to bed that night, he kept a prayer in his heart that he'd remember what he needed to know and would have the wisdom to do what was required to have a better future. It was very general, but he kept an open mind to the idea.

❧

It was New Year's Eve and Logan was feeling pretty good. He still limped and his side hurt if he moved too quickly or laughed too hard. But he could do most things himself and didn't have to take his painkillers so often. The last thing he wanted was to get addicted, and he preferred to take Ibuprofen unless he really needed something stronger.

Mark was busy playing a game from Logan's collection while Logan checked on some projects for work. He was allowed some allotted time to recuperate, but he wasn't going to leave anybody hanging if there were some things he could get done from home. He may be injured, but he wasn't an invalid.

"So what are we doing tonight for New Year's Eve?" Mark asked, his eyes glued to the flat screen.

"Good question. I was already invited to a party a while back, but I doubt it would be any fun. Can't exactly combine alcohol with medication."

"You can't have alcohol, period."

"Right," said Logan, remembering how he woke up the first morning to find all of his beer missing from the fridge.

"Plus you just woke up from a coma like a week ago."

"No, really?" he said with an extra dose of sarcasm.

"Do you have friends you can call? Maybe they'd like to come over so you won't have to leave the house."

"They're all out partying," Logan sighed, then groaned in frustration. "I really hate this. I don't have friends, I don't have a car . . ." Logan groaned again, this time in defeat.

He worked so hard to save up for that car and now it was totaled beyond repair. He had good insurance, but everything was still being processed and there was nothing he could do about it.

"I'm ordering pizza," Logan decided, having the number already programmed into his phone. "Mark, have you ever had Chicago pizza?"

"I've had Chicago-style pizza, but not regular pizza from Chicago."

"No man, Chicago pizza is Chicago-style pizza. Regular pizza from Chicago is just regular pizza."

"I'm confused, what kind of pizza are we getting?"

"Chicago pizza."

"So regular pizza?"

"No. Chicago-style pizza."

"Why didn't you say so in the first place?"

"When the pizza gets here, I'm throwing it at you."

"You don't dislike me enough to waste perfectly good pizza like that."

"You're right." Logan picked up one of his pillows off the floor and threw at Mark's head. It ended up knocking the controller out of his hands, which got him a, "Dude! What the heck? I'm getting ambushed!" He chucked the controller to the side. "Great, now I'm dead."

"I'm dying on the inside, brother."

"Okay, that's it. We're getting you out of the house."

"There's nowhere to go."

"There's always somewhere to go. Where was that party you were invited to?"

"That's irrelevant."

"Well maybe I want to go."

"You're not going anywhere, Mark."

"Why not?"

"Because you're not of legal age, you'd be in a big city by yourself, and I'm not going to subject you to what goes on at those kinds of parties. You'd hate it."

"Then why do you want to go so badly?"

"Who said I wanted to go?"

"It's very obvious, Logan. I know you and you wouldn't have been drawn to that kind of lifestyle in the first place if you didn't enjoy it. Heck, if you hadn't been in the accident, you'd be there right now living it up, getting wasted, and kissing every single girl at that party. And don't say I'm making judgmental assumptions, because we both know I'm right. But guess what, it's okay to miss it, Logan. It's okay to be bummed out over missing all the fun and spending your time with your annoying kid brother. It's called withdrawal."

Logan took a deep breath, pinching the bridge of his nose as he squeezed his eyes shut. "Must you always be the one with common sense? Will there ever be a time when I can give you advice?"

"There will come a time for that. But right now I'm your spiritual trainer, and I have a new task for you. Read the conference talk "Avoid It" by Lynn G. Robbins. In fact, here," he said, picking up the tablet to search for the talk himself. Once he pulled it up, he handed it to him. "Read it right now. It'll give you some perspective."

Reluctantly, Logan took the tablet and began to skim through the words. The talk was on conquering temptation by avoiding it completely. Logan already had an understanding of that, but the analogy of walking into a bakery thinking the smell wouldn't tempt him into submission was accurate.

It started with one cookie, which led to more and more until the cravings were all he could think about.

"I've tethered myself to this life, haven't I?" he said more to himself than to Mark. "I've become so dependent, I don't know how to live without it."

"That's how addictions work. You might think that because it's not completely poisoning your body, drinking is okay. Or because society's definition of the worst that could happen is unplanned pregnancy or STDs, being immoral won't hurt you. When really you're completely unaware that it's taken control and you've become dependent on it bringing you false happiness.

"When I leave, Logan, your next task is learning how to be happy without it. Maybe then you'll have your mind back again, and you'll know exactly what you want."

Logan kept that in mind when he ordered the pizza and decided that being in his own home was safer than being any-where else. Not just for health reasons, but for his spirit. It wasn't going to be easy. He still longed to be of the world, but it wasn't as bad as he thought it would be. He and Mark counted down to midnight, drank Martinelli's Sparkling Cider, and watched YouTube videos until they fell asleep.

In a way, Mark was right. If he hadn't gotten hurt, he'd have been up all night partying—a "what if" that only existed in a fantasy. At least reality wasn't so bad. There was something to be said about having his own mind back. Once that happened, maybe he'd remember how to have fun without the worldly influences. If not for himself, he'd try for his brother. He owed it to him.

Chapter Twelve

❧

Logan insisted on taking Mark to the airport. And by take, he rode in the taxi and walked him all the way to security using his cane.

"You look like Dr. House," Mark said as he watched his brother limp through the terminal.

"You're just jealous because I can pull it off."

"Touché."

"I'm going to miss having you around. Too bad you have school, a family, and a life back home."

"You do too."

Logan opened his mouth to retort, but Mark quickly followed with, "But I know a big extension of it is here. And I know we talked a lot about your mistakes, but you have a nice place to live and a respectable job, and you haven't been involved in any criminal activity. You really do have it good and it's because you worked hard. That's pretty awesome."

In a quiet voice, Logan said, "You're the only sibling who thinks so."

"They were wrong to judge you so harshly, Logan."

"I played a part in it too. But that's an issue that can be worked out later."

"Of course. Thanks for letting me stay."

"And thanks for staying. You're welcome here anytime. Maybe after you graduate, we'll go on a real road trip or something and visit the sites you didn't get to see."

"Sounds good. Take it easy, Logan. I mean it. I'll know if you don't."

"That's right, I forgot you can sense disturbances in the Force."

"You know it," he said, waving his hand from one side to the other. "You will not rejoin the dark side."

"Mark, go home."

"Dang, that usually works on the weak-minded."

"Mark. Go home," he chuckled, pushing him toward the crowd of people who were already boarding.

Logan stayed to watch the plane take off and couldn't keep himself from getting misty-eyed. As he blinked away the oncoming tears and sniffed a few times, he noticed a small child, perhaps three or four, approach him.

"Are you cwying 'cause of your owie?" he asked, pointing at the bandage on his head, likely acknowledging the other bruises on his face.

"Uh . . . yeah, but I'm okay."

"Does it hurt?"

"A little, but I had really good doctors to make me feel better."

"Oh. What happened?"

"My car crashed. That's why it's always important to wear a seatbelt."

At that point, the boy's mother had rushed over, apologizing profusely on his behalf. Logan told her it was fine, brushing it off, but that's when he became very aware of what he probably looked like to others, and decided to go home.

Because he couldn't go to the gym, he made sure to eat a nutritious dinner and do some minor exercises that wouldn't be hard on his leg and knees. At the same time, it got circulation going and kept his muscles loose until he completely healed and rebuilt his strength.

He went to bed that night feeling better, but as soon as he turned off the light, he couldn't stop the feelings of loneliness and despondency as he thought about the painful moments he endured just after his car was hit.

Part of him wished he had died in that accident, that he didn't have to continue on like this. But it was a selfish way to think. He was spared with hardly any long-term injuries and he had no reason to complain. However, it didn't keep him from dwelling on the fact that his heart did stop.

He didn't know how long, only that it happened. He could almost picture it from the way hospital staff had described. But he didn't have that out-of-body experience like some who go through similar ordeals. His mind was just somewhere else.

He kept another prayer in his heart that he would remember something and drifted off to sleep. Once again he stood outside surrounded by falling snow and Christmas lights.

Even though he didn't necessarily feel it, he knew it was cold and common sense told him to go inside the house that suddenly appeared in the night. But once he did, he ended up in a white room where someone was there to talk to him.

He had never seen the man before, but in the dream, they were friends, so he shook his hand like they hadn't seen each other for a while. While doing so, Logan suddenly realized who he was.

"You were there when I died."

The man just smiled and nodded in conformation.

"I'm not dying again, am I?"

He only shook his head to answer him.

"It's good to see you again, Tommy."

He had no idea where the name, Tommy, came from, but it somehow suited him.

Tommy then pointed to another room where there was a bench sitting in front of a piano. Logan walked over to play a few keys when he was stopped by a hand tapping on his shoulder. He turned around to see the same girl smiling at him as if they had known each other for years.

Sadly, Logan woke with a jolt for no particular reason. His body was stiff and his sinuses were congested. He sat up in bed and turned on the lamp, rubbing the fogginess out of his eyes.

Once he was a bit more awake, realization hit him like a battering ram. His heart didn't just stop, but sometime during that coma, he hadn't been alone. The Lord had made sure of that.

A sudden warmth came over him and he knew it was true. It was too painful to recall other details besides the traumatic ones, but at least he now had something comforting to hold on to. He couldn't fully explain it, but there was someone watching over him then, and someone watching over him now. Knowing that, he was able to fall back asleep in peace and go on another day.

The weeks blended together as time dragged on. A month after the accident, he was starting to feel like his old self. Most of his bruises cleared up and his scars were healing nicely without the very conspicuous stitches.

He spent a lot of his free time at the gym, working on the parts of his body that wouldn't put any strain on his leg or ribs. Instead of the treadmill, he used the elliptical to work on his cardio, increasing his time little by little. His doctor told him not to overdo it and that healing a head injury took more rest than rehabilitation. But he'd been seeing a friend who specialized in hyperbaric chamber therapy, a treatment using pure oxygen to better heal tissue damage, especially in the brain.

Although he was off the painkillers, he hadn't touched a drink since before the accident, nor did he agree to go anywhere alcohol was being served. He had to admit that he felt better without it. He appreciated having a more focused mind, and doing so helped him discover most of his "friends" weren't very interesting unless he was under the influence in their presence. It took away some of his entertainment, but it made him that much more determined to find other things to do.

One particular afternoon, while he sat at his computer catching up on a few projects, a knock sounded at the door.

"Please don't be Sheila," he muttered as he looked through the peephole.

Sure enough she stood there waiting, holding a fruit basket of all things. He decided to stay quiet and pretend he wasn't home, but of course she called out, "Logan, I know you're home. You can't hide from me forever."

Logan groaned and opened the door. "Hi, Sheila," he said, not bothering to fake any courtesy toward her.

"Is that any way to greet a friend?"

He rolled his eyes. "Selling your wares from door to door, I see."

"Very funny. These are for you. You never did accept my cookies."

"Thank you. You shouldn't have."

You really shouldn't have.

"I wanted to. You are my friend, after all, and I was so worried about you. I had to find out what happened through Facebook. Facebook! Can you imagine how put off I was that your own mother, who I personally met, didn't tell me?"

"Wait, you met my mom?"

"Yes, she was here, probably snooping through all your things too. She had the nerve to outright lie to my face and not tell me what was going on. You were right about them—"

"Sheila, shut your mouth for once in your life and understand this," he spat, and she stared at him in silent shock. "Despite the disagreements my family and I had, they love me regardless of the choices I make. They were around when I needed them most and I should have never confided in you about them, especially since you have been nothing but selfish and conniving since the day we met. There's a reason why I've been avoiding you and it's because I'm done with your poisonous antics. I don't wish to hurt your feelings, but if you insult my mother, you insult me, and I won't tolerate it."

"How hard did you get hit in the head?" she said, looking up at him with furious eyes.

"Hard enough to knock some sense into me. Go home and put on a sweater. It's the middle of winter for heaven's sake."

He didn't wait for a response. He just shut the door and locked it to prove his point. Although he didn't wish to be so venomous toward her, she wouldn't have let it go without taking drastic measures. And he wasn't about to allow her to speak ill toward his family without defending them.

Sitting back at his computer, he finished the project he was working on and decided to catch up on Facebook for a minute. Looking through the feed, Brin posted pictures of his nieces and nephews playing with their new Christmas toys. She had also posted a picture to his wall of her oldest, Evelyn, with Joshua and baby Sarah, each holding a sign with a word on it so together they read, "We love you." Sarah was ready to put the wad of paper in her mouth, and Joshua had the cheesiest smile a nine-year-old could have.

Though Brin wasn't in the picture, he recognized that he hadn't heard from his sister in in a long time. When he saw the second picture Annie had posted, it was pretty much the same setup, only that each of her children, Carter, Brooklyn and Daniel, all held signs that together read, "Get well soon."

Now his heart couldn't stand it anymore. He wasn't sure if Taylor had any part in this, but it felt like his siblings had raised a white flag for the time being in favor of getting along during the holidays. Sure, it was likely out of pity for him getting hurt, but he didn't care. He was just happy they were thinking about him.

In response to each of them, he found blank sheets of paper, writing one word on each to read, taking a picture of himself with each one. He used a different funny face in every picture and compiled the photos together to send to both Brin and Annie. The words put together read, "I love you too".

He wasn't sure if Taylor would see it, but he hoped he would, just to show him he wasn't always the heartless family black sheep. Maybe someday they could sit down and resolve a few things, but it was something that had to be slowly worked toward.

Going back to the main news feed, he scrolled down and noticed Addie had posted something, which he hadn't seen her do until now. It looked like an advertisement for some kind of showcase going on at a local venue for amateur musicians. He wasn't sure what she had to do with it, but it looked interesting.

It was scheduled for the weekend, which was in two days, and it seemed like a good excuse to get out of the house. He thought about inviting other people, but decided against it since he planned to introduce himself. It still piqued his curiosity that he recognized her. He wanted to solve the mystery once and for all.

Saturday night rolled around and Logan decided to go casual since the venue didn't call for dress up attire. He dressed in jeans and a dark gray shirt, with the new hoodie he got from Mark for Christmas. His other one was ripped and stained beyond repair, which depressed him a bit, but he got over it.

Leaving the house, he saw Sheila walking down the hall with her laundry. She didn't pay him any attention, which was unusual enough for him to do a double take. Not only was she indifferent, but she was wearing loose workout pants and a long-sleeve shirt that covered everything. He didn't know if it was he who had encouraged this, but he smiled at the change.

When he got to his rental car, he sighed, wishing for his old one back, but grateful to have something nice to drive.

It took a while to get to the place and find parking, but it was worth it as soon as he walked through the door. The place was a bit old, yet it had a vintage look to it that set the mood perfectly. A band was setting up on the stage and people were mingling around tall tables near the sides of the dance floor.

There were a few chairs and stools to sit on, but Logan found a spot in the back to lean against. At least he didn't need a cane to be there.

When the music started, he was impressed by the local talent that showed up to perform. It was clear some were there to get noticed by producers, but others were only into it for the experience and love of performing. He was just glad there was a large variety. One guy did a solo act of recording a beat into a machine and then played it back on repeat and sang to it with his guitar.

What surprised him even more was when Addie showed up out of nowhere during his performance with a tambourine and starting singing backup harmony.

As soon as her voice reached his ears, Logan froze as his heart began to quicken. She wasn't just talented, but something about it triggered a memory that brought back the Christmas lights and falling snow.

He tried to concentrate on the moment, but gradually it was getting harder for him to breathe and eventually he had to sit down.

When the song was over, he applauded and watched the rest of the show until a DJ took over and everyone gathered on the dance floor.

He tried looking for Addie in the crowd, but decided it was hopeless after the first twenty minutes. There were too many people and the atmosphere didn't exactly make it possible for an introductory conversation anyway.

Maneuvering toward the back entrance, closer to where his car was parked, he put on his jacket and pushed open the heavy door.

Naturally he had no idea if anyone was behind it, so when he heard a grunt and saw someone land hard on the ground, Logan panicked a little as he jumped to their side.

"I am so sorry. Are you okay?" he asked, and to his immediate surprise and horror, it was Addie.

From what he could tell, she was carrying a box of flyers, which had haphazardly scattered along the pavement. He expected her to respond in some manner of rage or annoyance, but instead she chuckled and said, "If you wanted to get me to fall for you, there are better ways to do so."

Logan tried to laugh, but he was too embarrassed to force one out.

"I didn't see you there. Again, I'm sorry. Let me help you."

"Thanks," she said, taking his outstretched hand.

When he pulled her up, Logan staggered a bit on his weaker leg, which forced her to hold onto his upper arms to steady them both.

He was close enough to look into her eyes, and Logan could hardly believe his luck. He just wished their meeting could have been smoother.

"Would you mind helping me pick these up?" she asked, breaking the daze he was in.

"Oh, of course. I'm Logan by the way."

"Addie," she said.

"I feel really bad."

"Don't worry about it. It's not like anyone is going to take these, but I promised my roommate."

Logan took a good look at the paper and saw it was an advertisement for a blood drive. He was about to ask if her roommate worked for the Red Cross or something, but Addie stopped what she was doing to look at him.

"I'm having déjà vu, do I know you from somewhere?"

Logan stopped as well. He realized he could do this several ways, but didn't know which one made him sound like less of a stalker.

"I don't know, do you get trampled in doorways by strange men often?"

"You'd be surprised how often it happens," she chuckled. "The price I pay for being short. You tall guys see right over us."

"Oh, so it was my lack of peripheral vision that knocked you over? Here I thought you were just falling for me."

She smiled at that, which boosted his confidence. "In all fairness, the door had a lot to do with it."

"Scumbag doors just getting in everybody's way."

"No kidding, right? At least you're not the scumbag. Believe it or not, I was in a similar situation walking into a coffee shop a few years ago and this guy knocked me right over. He helped me pick up my stuff and apologized, but it wasn't my ideal way of starting the day."

When she said it, her description brought back a memory that was uncannily similar to hers. He knew it was a long shot, but he had to ask. "Where did it happen?"

"I was living in Utah at the time."

Logan's eyes widened. "Hang on, did happen in St. George?"

"Excuse me?"

"Were you carrying a large box of art supplies, wearing a red hat and scarf?"

Now it was her turn for her eyes to widen. "No way. It couldn't have been you."

"I was at Dixie five years ago . . . just before Christmastime."

"Oh my heck," she laughed. "I don't know how it's possible, but this is novelty right here."

Logan laughed right along with her, happy she was being a good sport about it. He was also happy to finally pinpoint when and where it was he knew her from. He just wished it wasn't such a brief and awkward circumstance.

"I suppose I deserve the title of scumbag, especially now," he said.

"Heavens, no. I'm glad we could share this moment. Fate must be having a lot of fun with this."

"Well then I definitely have to get your number now, even if it's just to see what fate has in mind."

Logan knew it was forward of him to say, and almost regretted it when her eyes flickered a little in apprehension.

"I'm sorry, was that the wrong thing to say?" he asked.

"Oh, no, no. It's just . . . was that you asking for it?"

"In a roundabout way, yes."

She briefly looked conflicted, but eventually put down the box to take a single flyer out and a Sharpie from her back pocket. Normally when he asked for a woman's number, they programmed it into his phone. Her way was old fashioned, but somehow it seemed more personal.

"I forgot to say I really enjoyed your performance. You're very talented."

She blushed and subconsciously twirled a piece of her hair between he fingers. "Thanks, I'm glad you liked it."

"Well I don't want to keep you from your evening, but enjoy the rest of your night."

"I will, and you too."

Logan opened the door for her to walk through and watched her disappear inside. He was reluctant to let her go, but his leg was starting to ache from the cold air and he didn't want to linger any longer than he should.

While his car warmed up, the conversation he had with his brother came to mind. They had briefly joked around about fate, and after tonight, fate seemed like a good label to give it. But

Mark spoke the truth about what is predestined, and the Lord only giving people certain opportunities to grow.

Given the circumstance, obviously *something* was meant to happen the first time he'd knocked Addie to the ground, and he had chose to ignore it. Now that the Lord was making another point, he definitely planned to stick around this time to find out what it was.

Chapter Thirteen

❦

When Addie got home, she went straight to her bed and flopped face first on the mattress. She was so tired and ready to be done for the day. But sadly, she remembered the stack of projects she had to finish for her class on Monday and debated with herself whether or not it was important enough to stay awake to do it.

Indecisive, she moved to the bathroom sink to wash her face when she heard her roommate call from the next room, "Hey there, sunshine."

"Hey, Savvy," she called back. "I didn't think you'd be home."

"I just got off work. I've only been home ten minutes. How did it go tonight?"

"It went great," she said, truly happy with how the event turned out. She originally did it as a favor to a friend whose backup singer bailed last minute. Okay, she wouldn't call him a friend. More like a guy she briefly dated and decided to take a step back from once he got pushy. But she enjoyed performing on stage, and the experience itself was fun and thrilling.

"Any hot guys?"

It was Savannah's favorite question, and one she asked even if she went to the mailbox. It was always responded by a curt "nope" or "I didn't notice". But for the first time in a long while, she had a story to tell.

"Just one in particular," Addie said nonchalantly before she started brushing her teeth.

Within a few seconds, Savannah slowly peered around the bathroom door so she could exaggerate a shocked stare from behind her. When Addie saw her in the mirror, she snorted at her dramatics.

"Details, woman!" Savannah exclaimed, all but shaking her.

Jokingly, Addie starting speaking garbled words against her toothbrush, which got an exasperated eye roll.

"Come on, Addie. You can't expect me to hear you say something about a hot guy and not pester you for details! Was it someone you saw from afar? Did he talk to you? Did you talk to him? What's the deal?"

Addie spat and rinsed her mouth. "He opened a door in my face."

Savannah looked confused, but Addie proceeded to explain the whole story in full detail, which got a few laughs until she ended with, "and then . . . he asked me for my number."

"Shut up. Really?" she gasped, but then her expression quickly sobered. "Wait, did you actually give it to him?"

Addie bit her lip. "I did."

This time Savannah actually took her by the shoulders and shook her back and forth. "Good for you! You're finally moving on!"

"But that's just it, I have no idea what this guy is all about, Sav. He could be exactly like every other jerk from my past."

"I know experience would immediately bring that to mind, but . . . what does he look like?"

"Tall, dark, handsome . . . cute dimples next to a gorgeous smile that just screams, 'I'm a heartbreaker.' "

"Yum. Sounds like our type."

"No kidding, except our type includes being a worthy priesthood holder, and I didn't exactly get around to asking him that."

Savannah looked thoughtful, knowing very well it was a sensitive subject for Addie. "Well you won't know unless you learn about the man, so at the very least learn about the man, and then go from there. If he turns out to be sleazy, at least you know how to detect that early and you can hightail it out of there."

"He hasn't even asked me out yet, let alone called. Odds are he'll lose my number or forget all about me."

"You're just a constant downer, huh?"

"Savvy, you are a twenty-three-year-old woman who is set in her career and adored by the limited number of men in the singles ward." It was true. Savannah Davis was tall, blonde, and the happiest person Addie knew. Not that she begrudged her for it, but Addie attracted a different kind of crowd and it was hard to understand each other's worlds sometimes.

"Here I am, a few years away from thirty, a school teacher with very few dating prospects because . . . well, you know."

Savannah just shook her head. "I would very much like to kick every guy in the shin who made you see yourself as less than the amazing person you are. But guess what? You're moving on and I say we forget about them tonight, because you know what time it is?"

Oh please, not the happy dance.

"It's time for the happy dance!" Savannah yelled. "Come on, a really cute guy asked for your number. You know you want to."

Addie had to admit it did feel pretty good. So like a high school girl who had just gotten asked to prom, they jumped up and down, giggling and squealing at the top of their lungs until the neighbors below them started pounding on their ceiling.

"Sorry!" they shouted together, but resumed their giggle fest at a lower volume.

Although it was a bit nerve-racking, it had been a long time since a guy she hadn't met over the Internet had shown actual interest in her. She wasn't sure if the guy had an agenda or not, but Savannah had a point. She wouldn't know unless she gave him a chance. Hopefully that chance would come sooner than later.

Logan used to have a system when it came to asking out women. But they were easy women looking for a good time, which he wasn't about anymore. He could tell just by the way she spoke and her body language that she was classier than that, which was attractive in an unexpected way.

But as he stared at the number held by a magnet to his fridge, he felt like he was in high school again. He wondered how long he should wait before asking her out. Or if he should ask her out at all.

The night before, he glanced at her page again and saw the pictures of her standing outside the temple with friends and attending YSA activities. Clearly she was LDS, which meant there was a chance she wouldn't like the idea of going out with someone with a bad reputation. Even though he was working on that image, he hadn't officially come back to the church yet. Even though Mark was helping him, he still had a ways to go.

He'd talked with Mark on the phone that morning, and Logan recapped everything to him. His response was, "Are you nuts? Of course it's a second chance! Every doubt you have is Satan trying to get you to think otherwise. You're going to see that girl again, Logan. Don't make me come back there."

After that pep talk, Logan made his decision, but timing was still important. He didn't exactly have a plan in mind, either. Where does one take a wholesome girl on a date in Chicago in this weather?

Thankfully the answer came just as quickly as the dilemma started. Pizza. Nothing could go wrong with pizza, unless she had a serious problem with it. Her trim figure looked like she would be the health-conscious type, but something about her personality gave the impression she'd be into it. And he knew just the place.

❦

Addie was sitting on the couch writing in her lesson plan calendar when her phone started ringing. The sound made her jump, which made Savannah giggle at her reaction.

"Who the heck is this?" she asked out loud when she saw the number she couldn't recognize.

She thought about letting it go to voicemail, but answered it anyway. "Hello?"

"Hey Addie, it's Logan."

Addie was almost stunned silent. But in three seconds, she managed to put her hand over the receiver and exclaim to Savannah in a whisper, "Oh my heck, it's Logan!"

Savannah immediately jumped to her side as she returned to the call. "Hey Logan, how're you doing?"

"I'm doing pretty good. What are you up to?"

"Work stuff, actually."

"Really, what kind of work stuff?"

"Lesson planning. I teach fourth grade."

"Wait, so you're saying you're a teacher by day and a talented singer by night?"

"I guess so," Addie chuckled. "I don't know about being talented . . ."

"I'd like to hear more about it."

"Well what do you want to know?"

"How about you tell me in person this Wednesday night?"

It took every ounce of will power to force down the delight that bubbled up inside her. Usually if a guy she met through dating sites had asked her out, regardless of how attractive he was in his picture, she'd be indifferent until she met the guy. But even when they did meet and went out a second or third time, she still couldn't remember when she last felt excited for a date.

"This Wednesday night?" she asked.

"Yeah, I'd suggest this weekend, but that's too far away for me."

Again, she giggled, twirling her hair like a teenager. "I'd love to. What time were you thinking?"

"I was thinking six, if that works for you."

"It works perfect," she said, grateful she didn't have any meetings that night.

"Great. Be sure to text me your address and I'll pick you up then. Oh and bring your appetite, because we're going to one of my favorite places."

"And where might that be?"

". . . It's a surprise."

After he said it, her stomach twisted a little. The last time she heard that, the "surprise" was everything less than pleasant. Even though he didn't appear the sketchy type, she learned quickly that anything could have a decent wrapper but still be toxic.

"Yeah, considering we just met," she said, "I think you should let me know what to expect. In fact, if you tell me where it is, I can meet you there."

There was an awkward silence, and Savannah gave her a look that made Addie almost regret suggesting the idea, but she wasn't going to risk having the past repeat itself.

"If you're more comfortable with that, that's totally fine," he assured, and Addie sighed in relief. "Have you ever been to Ronaldo's?"

"I haven't, but I think I've heard of it."

"Well prepare yourself, because you're going to be amazed."

Addie laughed. "I'd better; I have a feeling I won't be disappointed."

"Good, I'm looking forward to it."

"Me too."

"All right, well I won't keep you from your lesson planning, so have a good rest of your weekend, and I'll talk to you later."

"Okay, have a good night."

Hanging up the phone, Addie smacked her palm to her forehead. There were a thousand ways she could have been a lot smoother, but it could have been worse. She had a date on Wednesday!

"I have a date on Wednesday!" she yelled.

Savannah cheered along with her as they proceeded to rummage through their wardrobes to find the perfect outfit to wear. It was moments like these Addie was grateful to have a friend to help her with things like this.

Even though she'd been raised by her grandparents in the Church, when Addie decided to live with her mother in California, she gradually became inactive and starting making some mistakes that left her in a bad place.

But it was a Sunday afternoon, when Savannah knocked on her door as her visiting teacher, when her life started getting better.

She figured it would be a one-time deal, but that wasn't the case. Savannah was not only persistent, but she was also genuine in caring about her welfare. She showed up every week, never with a Relief Society lesson or treat of some sort, but a simple plan to just hang out like normal friends, which was exactly what Addie needed.

Most of her time was taken up by her part-time job as a substitute teacher or spending time with men who encouraged her inactivity in the first place. This resulted in long nights spent alone while her mom was off doing who knows what. She never did say, but Addie had a pretty good idea. She moved in because her mom begged her to, and she hoped it would give her a chance to share the gospel with her like her grandparents had done with her. But that never happened. Anytime she brought it up, she would either pretend to listen or make an excuse to leave.

Addie sought support in the all the wrong places after discovering dating apps she didn't see the harm in using. At first it was fun and exciting to meet guys who found her attractive and fun to be with. But most of them didn't share gospel standards, and the ones who claimed to weren't very sincere about it.

Those relationships never lasted considering they always left her feeling guilty and shameful for compromising her standards. She didn't feel worthy to attend church, especially when her friends began to pull away after she confided in them.

Addie continued to date, but mostly out of habit instead of trying to find someone to have a real connection with. In the process, she met guys who didn't take no for an answer, which pushed her to stop dating altogether. It took some time, but eventually she learned to live without relying on the attention of others to make her happy.

The bitterness still lingered, but it got better as soon as Savannah showed up. When Savannah graduated from the nursing program, she wanted to move back to her hometown in Illinois, and practically begged Addie to come with her. They had grown to become true friends and she recognized it as a blessing to get her away from the past and start over again. She still loved her mom, but she needed to figure life out for herself and let her deal with her own problems.

Her skills in teaching in low-income areas helped her find a job quickly. But the best part was being able to start fresh in a place where her past didn't matter. She hadn't dated much since then, save for a few guys who introduced her to the music scene, but at least it gave her a new outlet and escape. She liked to think it would lead her to something new and exciting, and judging by

Logan's looks and charm, she believed she was in for the ride of her life.

Chapter Fourteen

❧

On Wednesday, Logan confirmed his date with Addie and texted her the address, getting to Ronaldo's fifteen minutes early.

He found a table near a quieter area of the establishment and sat in the chair that faced the doors. Time dragged by, and gradually kept slowing down once it reached 6:15 and she still hadn't shown.

He was about to call her when he heard the doorbell chime and saw Addie rush in looking winded and frazzled.

"I'm so sorry," she breathed. "I couldn't catch a cab to save my life for some reason."

"It's no problem. I'm glad you made it," he said, moving to pull her chair out for her.

She sat down with a bright "thank you" and hurried to smooth her hair down. The day happened to be windy, and the cold added a rosy blush to her face that complimented her well.

"So what kind of place is this?" she asked, seeming to admire the cozy atmosphere of the restaurant. It had the artistic style of Old Italian architecture, but with a few modern accents that made it more casual and welcome to families.

"It's my favorite pizza place in the city," he said, watching her eyes light up.

"I. Love. Pizza," she pronounced and Logan's liking for her increased. "Seriously, I could eat it every day."

"Well that's good, because this place is a novelty."

Once they ordered, she was quick to ask him about his life starting from the beginning, and Logan happily went into detail answering the classic questions he'd expect on a first date.

He talked about his job, interests, and hobbies. But when he got to his family, she stopped him and asked, "Wait a minute, did you say your last name is Atwood?"

"Yeah," he said, knowing where this was going.

"I think I've heard that name before. Did we live in the same neighborhood?"

Logan wasn't going to feign ignorance. "If we're both from Highland, it's a huge possibility. We probably have more connections in common than we even know about."

"Wow," she laughed. "That's insanely awesome.

"What about you? What's your life story?"

Just then the waiter came to their table with the pizza, and her eyes lit up at the sight. Giving him another gracious "'thank you," she stared longingly at the platter, which was a thick crust topped with barbeque sauce, cheese, chicken, bacon, red peppers, and spices, all baked to perfection.

"This looks incredible," she said.

"Tastes even better."

She took a piece to put on her plate, and right away she caught him staring. "Aren't you going to have any?"

"Of course, but for any newcomer, I love watching them take their first bite."

"I don't know how I feel about you watching me eat."

"Well I'd be watching you anyway."

"There's a difference between social eating and being observed."

He stared her down. "Humor me."

She shrugged before she took a huge mouthful, chewing slowly and then fluttered her eyelids closed for emphasis of obvious approval. "This is the best thing I've ever eaten."

Logan exhaled in dramatic relief. "Good, we can be friends now."

"Really?" She shook her head. "Man, first date and I'm already in the friend zone."

"No, that's not what I meant—"

"I'm kidding," she chuckled.

"Good, because I look at you and don't put you anywhere near the friend zone category."

"Oh? And what category do I fit in?"

"I haven't figured it out yet, but you're definitely moving up the list."

"Smooth answer," she said. "Safe, but smooth."

"It'll probably be the only smooth thing I say all night. I'm actually a nervous wreck and humor is really carrying me right now."

She laughed at that. "Well it's working for you. I appreciate a man with a good sense of humor. Quick wit is just icing on the cake. But I don't see why you would be a nervous wreck."

"Why not? You're smart, beautiful, talented, and have this amazing life where you worked from the bottom to successful independence. I'm a little intimidated."

"Compared to a man with a corporate job, his own condo, and natural good looks?"

"First of all, thank you for thinking I'm good looking," he said easily. "Second, working with kids takes a special kind of person no one should take for granted. And third, dating someone with the exact same lifestyle doesn't make much for interesting conversation, which by the way, was left off at your life story."

"Darn it, I was so close to keeping all the good stuff from you."

He leaned forward. "You have my attention now. No going back."

She exaggerated disappointment. "Well . . . life after living with my grandparents wasn't always the best. I'm LDS by the way, and I was sort of raised in that lifestyle, but didn't fully live by it until my mom left. But when she tracked me down, and I went to live with her . . . I left the Church for a while, but eventually came back and I'm happy where I'm at now."

Logan was surprised and almost relieved to hear it. It meant that she faced difficulties and overcame them, and more likely that she would understand him more deeply.

"I also grew up LDS," Logan started. "I served a mission and pursued my career after that. But during that time I made a few mistakes that I'm not proud of and it really did a number on me and my family. I'm still working on coming back, but it's something I really want," he told her, not realizing how much he wanted it until now.

"That's wonderful," she said, and he could tell she looked genuinely pleased.

Topics changed rapidly for the rest of their meal, which transitioned into lighter subjects of most embarrassing moments, first kiss stories, worst date experiences, and acknowledging all their favorite things. Deeply engrossed in conversation, neither realized the restaurant was closing until a waiter had to point it out.

Logan made sure to leave an extra good tip, insisting he pay even though she offered to help with the bill. It impressed him that she would while knowing he could afford it. Many women often chose the more upscale places because of that and never took a second glance at the check.

"Well as long as we're having a good time, would you like to splurge with me and get a cupcake?" she asked. "I remember there's a really good bakery down the street."

"Would they still be open at this time?"

"Right now they're getting rid of their day-old goods, which means they're half price. Honestly I don't taste the difference between fresh and day-old, but it does make a difference on my wallet."

"Sounds good to me," he said, opening the door for her on the way out.

Thankfully the wind had died down, but it was still cold enough for each of them to pull their coats tighter and keep their arms folded.

It wasn't that much of a walk, but Logan didn't like the distance between them and decided to pull the oldest trick in the book. He hadn't done it since college, but given the nature of the evening and the chemistry between them, he figured she wouldn't object.

When they got to the crosswalk, they both waited for the sign to change, and once it did, Logan took her hand and started to run, pulling her in tow.

"Whoa, what's the rush?" she called, trying to keep up.

"We want to make it to the other side before it changes back to red."

"I'm sure we had a few more seconds to spare," she panted after their half sprint.

Now that they were on the sidewalk, Logan didn't let go, but instead laced his fingers with hers. He could feel her gaze on him and he chanced a glance to see a knowing look on her face.

"Keep on denying it, but that was pretty smooth," she said, squeezing his hand a little tighter.

"Thank you, I call it flirt running."

She only chuckled in response, but when he felt her lean into him, he relaxed and let the comfortable silence allow him to take in the moment.

He already figured out how much he liked her personality, her lifestyle, and her looks. They shared certain interests and goals, with differences that weren't deal breakers, at least for him. But he began to wonder how much she liked his qualities in return.

The women he dated had always been forward with their feelings, mostly because it fit their no-nonsense personalities.

Addie seemed more easygoing, but carried a lot more opinions and thoughts than she had yet to express this evening. He could also tell she was a guarded person, with every reason to be. But he wondered if there would be a time when she would come to really trust him and open herself up a bit more.

When they got to the bakery, the first thing he noticed was how opposite the place was compared to Ronaldo's. The walls were covered in modern, pastel wallpaper with circles of various sizes as decoration. The walls were adorned with glass cabinets stocked with old-fashioned sodas and bagged treats. The front counter was filled with of a wide variety of cupcakes and other pastries. The one that caught his eye was the "Elvis," which was a banana bread cupcake with peanut butter frosting and chocolate ganache on top.

"I want that one," he said, already making up his mind.

"Sounds good. I want this one," she said, pointing at a chocolate cheesecake brownie that looked equally delicious.

"Now you're talking. Normally I don't indulge like this, but you bring out the funner side of me. Wait, is *funner* a word?"

"It's not, but adults get a free grammar pass when it comes to that word."

He laughed. "Good, I was worried for a second."

Both sat down at the table and quickly agreed to share half of what they got so they each could sample. He'd have to work off the calories tomorrow, but it was worth it.

When he moved down to readjust his shoelace, apparently one of his scars from the accident peaked out on his ankle just enough for her to notice and say, "Wow, how did that happen?"

"Oh, I got this just before Christmas," he started. "I was in a car accident. Driver behind me slid on the ice and pushed me into oncoming traffic."

Her expression changed from curious to shock like the flip of a light switch. "Dang! It happened just over a month ago?"

"Yeah, it put me in the hospital for a little while, but my family came to visit and I got better very quickly."

"That's insane, but amazing that you walked away from that. Well not literally, but you know what I mean."

"I do," he chuckled. "It was quite the experience. I miss my car, but because things have been pretty rocky with my family, it was worth seeing my parents and younger brother again. He stayed around for a while to make sure I was okay on my own before he went back home."

"You mean Mark?"

"Yeah, he's a good kid."

"Sounds like it," she said almost sadly. "I'm an only child, but I do have a lot of cousins who are pretty much my siblings."

"That's always the best. I don't have any kids, but I do have nieces and nephews I get to spoil."

This information made her smile. "Do you have pictures?"

"Of course," he said, pulling out his phone to show her. After sharing stories of their antics and comparing them to her students, closing time was upon them once again and it was time to leave.

"Would it be okay if I drove you back to your apartment? I'd hate to have you catch a cab, and I'd also like to walk you to your door, if that's okay."

She pursed her lips for a second, looking conflicted, but much to his relief, she nodded and said, "Sure."

So many thoughts ran through his mind as to why she looked so reluctant, but because she agreed, he put it aside and only focused on finishing the night properly.

They walked to his rental car parked in the garage just a few blocks away. By the time they got there, her lower lip was shaking from her shivering. Logan could tell she was doing her best to hide it, but he immediately turned on the heater and draped his coat over her lap so she'd warm up quicker.

"Oh, you don't have to do that," she said, clearly trying to be courteous, but Logan could play that game well.

"I'm too warm, actually. I produce a lot of body of heat, so it's actually a relief. My coat might as well be put to good use while I'm not using it."

"You know, that's three on your smooth list. I'm starting to think you're more skilled than you say you are." He only chuckled in response. "Thank you, I appreciate it," she said, pulling his coat higher on her lap.

She directed him to her apartment building, which was a lot farther than he anticipated, but it wasn't a problem at all taking her home. Their discussion had turned to their musical interests. Addie seemed to thaw out as the heater warmed up and her voice grew more animated over the songs and bands she loved.

"Andy Grammer is my favorite," she said.

"I've only heard a few of his songs, but 'Keep Your Head Up' has become one of my favorite songs to listen to this last month."

"It's a good mood-changer song if you're ever feeling low. But if you ever get the chance, listen to his newer stuff. They're quite clever and creative. Not to mention catchy."

"I like that you're the musically creative type. I used to be once upon a time."

"You had my curiosity, but now you've captured my attention," she said.

"I use to play the piano and write my own songs."

"What?" she exclaimed. "Why didn't you say so before?"

He shrugged. "You didn't ask."

"Well now I have to hear you play."

"Oh no, it's been too long. I probably lost every ounce of talent I had during my teenage years."

"No way, music is instinctive. Plus, I work with fourth graders. I know I've heard worse, so you don't have to worry very much."

Logan briefly gave it some thought and came up with the perfect excuse to see her again. He wasn't going to wait a few days like last time to ask her out, so he went ahead and said, "Okay, I'll make you a deal. First of all, are you sports fan?"

"Can't say I follow it very often. Why?"

"A friend of mine gave me two tickets to the Chicago hockey game next weekend. I don't know how much you like hockey, but if you're interested, I'll let you hear me play if you go with me."

"Hmmm, it's quite the tempting offer. I've never been to a hockey game before."

"And everyone needs to go at least once, especially in Chicago."

"Then it's a deal," she said, and Logan was pleased to see the lack of hesitance this time.

When they got to her building, Logan parked in the hidden lot behind an alley, which didn't sit well with him considering her safety. But he put that thought aside for the moment and fell in step with her as they headed up the stairs.

He was grateful his leg didn't choose now to give out, but he moved slowly behind her up the seven-floor walk up to the fifth level.

"Sorry about the stairs," she breathed.

"It's no problem," he lied, feeling the usual twinge in his knee. He'd have to ice it tonight, but it wasn't an issue he needed to address. "I can see why you're in such great shape."

She had already dug the keys from her shoulder bag, but he noticed the way she lingered, fiddling with them as women usually do while stalling.

"I don't know about that," she said, then boldly followed up with, "would you like to come inside?"

And there it was, the vulnerability Logan usually looked for when the date drew to a close.

In the past he never had to pressure. Typically she would offer, he'd accept, and things would escalate from there. He figured with her, given her standards, she was likely only being friendly. But he knew himself, and it was a tempting situation he didn't want to put himself in, especially where she was concerned.

"I'd love to, but it's late and I'm going to be bluntly honest . . . I like you. A lot, actually, and I'm going to make sure I end a perfect night being a gentleman."

Her eyes widened a bit and the blush in her cheeks turned three shades deeper in seconds.

"Oh," she giggled nervously. "Well then I appreciate your chivalry. In fact . . ." Her expression changed from amusement to true sincerity. "It means more to me than you imagine."

"Then I'm going to say goodnight, and I'll call you tomorrow," he said, giving her a long enough hug to take in the subtle but sweet fragrance she had in her hair.

"Goodnight, Logan. And just so you know, I wasn't inviting you in for . . . well, with the intention to—"

"I understand. I trust you completely. I just don't trust myself at the moment."

"You should. You're a good guy, Logan," she said, unlocking her door. "And for the record . . . I like you a lot too."

With a final smile, she closed the door, and Logan stood there for a couple seconds to absorb her words. He regretted saying no, but he didn't regret ending the night on a good note. After all, they were going to see each other again, and for the first time in a long while, he was looking forward to making plans.

Chapter Fifteen

❧

As Addie leaned against the front door, she let out a heavy sigh of excitement, satisfaction, and wonder. She jumped when Savannah walked in and said, "Girl, you are redder than the Free Parking space on a Monopoly board."

Addie smirked, making a mental note to add that to her list of things she compared her blushing face to. It ranged from an apple, to well . . . the Free Parking space on a Monopoly board.

"I like him," she giggled, and Savannah let out a loud whoop. "Details, woman!"

After bringing out the moose tracks ice cream, each plopped on the couch with the carton and two spoons as she dished on everything that happened that night.

"He's LDS too," Addie said, "but he's coming back after being inactive, which isn't a bad thing. But considering my past, which I didn't fully share, it makes me wonder about his—if there's any deal breakers or bad habits I should worry about."

"I get you on that, but don't worry about it until it comes up. For now, enjoy his company and see where it goes. It sounds like you two have a great connection."

Addie nodded in agreement as she thought about what he'd said before he left. She, herself, had gone further than what's morally acceptable, which helped her understand how hard it is to withdraw from those desires. But she admired him choosing to do so anyway, not because he wasn't interested, but out of pure respect.

She still had a lot to learn about him, but at least she had something to smile about in the process.

❧

Addie woke up on Saturday earlier than usual to get chores done and caught up on shows. She checked her phone regularly, but decided not to fret about it, remembering that Logan had promised he would call her eventually.

It wasn't until she was in the bathroom that her phone went off, and she had to scramble to the living room just in time to see the *missed call* notification. However, when she saw who it was from, she didn't recognize the number. But the area code rang a bell and Addie's heart sank a little.

She hesitated to call back, but in case it was something important—and there was a good chance it wasn't—she redialed and put the phone to her ear.

The line only rang a few times before someone answered.

"Addie?"

"Hi, Mom," she said in a weak voice.

"Hey, dumpling, how are you?"

Addie blinked, grateful that she sounded sober, but still wondered what she wanted. "I'm doing well. How are you?"

"I'm good. Just . . . living life. How's work?"

"Fine. Is there a particular reason why you called?" she asked, cutting to the chase.

"I just wanted to see how you were doing. And I was wondering if . . ."

Oh, here it comes. What is it this time? Another loan? To be picked up at a random bus station? To be bailed out of jail . . . again?

". . . if I could come visit," she said, which surprised Addie in more ways than one.

"Visit?"

"Yeah, it's been a long time and I miss you. I know you can't get off work this time in the school year, so I thought it would be nice if I came to you instead."

Her voice was sweet and motherly, which came out from time to time, but on very rare occasions. Usually those occasions preceded bad news, and considering she was suggesting making the trip out to Chicago, it had to be serious.

"Is there something wrong? What's going on?" Addie asked bluntly.

"Nothing's wrong, honey. I mean it. I missed you over the holidays and I want to give you a late Christmas present."

"You do realize how strange this sounds to me."

"I know. And you're allowed to say no. I won't pressure or guilt trip you. But I'm hoping you let me do this at least once in your life."

"So you can make up for all the times you weren't there before? You really think one visit will do that?"

Linda Garrison had always been a defensive ball of energy, which came out when the alcohol got to her head. Sometimes it came out when anyone challenged her, including her own daughter. But for some odd reason, she wasn't taking the bait.

"I don't. Nothing will make up for everything I did. But it isn't going to stop me from showing you how much I love you, okay? Take it however you like, but that's the bottom line."

There was a long, tension-filled silence after her declaration, and although Addie wanted to refuse her, something, perhaps insanity, softened her heart and said, "Okay, if you visit . . . you're welcome to stay here. But I only have a couch to offer."

"I'd take the floor if that's all you had."

Not that you aren't used to passing out on floors anyway.

"Then let me know when you're coming and I'll plan for it."

"When's the best time for you?"

"The end of February, actually." She wanted to plan for any disasters after her next date with Logan, as well as Valentine's Day. Not that she was planning on doing anything special for it, but in case her mom stuck around long enough to be around, she didn't want to deal with the depression of reliving the previous Valentine's Days, which had included a drunk mother.

She sighed. "All right, I'll wait until then."

"And Mom? Only a few days, okay?"

"Sure thing. It'll just be long enough to see you, maybe do something fun together, and I'll go home."

She had never been this accommodating before. Whatever she wanted, or whatever news she had, it must be big.

"And it's just you, right? Because Lars isn't invited," she said, referencing her most recent boyfriend.

"Lars isn't in the picture anymore. No need to worry."

"Sorry to hear that," she said, though she didn't mean it.

"No you're not. And I'm not either, trust me. But anyway, I'll let you go and we'll talk again when we know our schedules better. That way we can coordinate."

"Whatever you say."

"I love you."

". . . I love you too," she said, meaning it wholeheartedly, though it didn't come out that way.

Addie hung up the phone, confused and emotionally drained. Not as much as she had been during previous conversations, but this one really took the cake.

Ironically, it was only a minute later when her phone rang again and she saw that it was Logan.

This time she answered in a more sincere and cheerful voice. "Hey!"

"Hey, yourself. How's it going?"

"Pretty good," she lied. "How are you?"

"I am bored as ever, but can't complain. You'd think I wouldn't get tired of Netflix, but now that I've finished all my favorite shows . . . I'm out of ideas."

The conversation stayed casual as they moved on to random topics that kept them entertained until late in the evening. It eventually drifted on to personal childhood stories when Logan mentioned his trip to Disneyland when he was sixteen.

Apparently his favorite experience had been the *Winnie the Pooh* themed ride, mostly because it submerged him in the nostalgia of his childhood.

"It was my favorite show when I was little," he said. "I watched it in the mornings while eating Cheerios before I went off to kindergarten. It's one of my earliest memories."

"Now that's adorable."

"If any of my friends during high school found out about that, my life would have been tarnished forever."

"I doubt that. In fact, I'm pretty sure all the girls would have swooned at your sensitivity, making all those guys jealous as heck. And then they'd start admitting their own personal childhood quandaries, creating this giant sympathy pool that would change the bad boy image forever. You could have changed the world and been a legend."

He laughed loudly into the receiver, enough for Addie to pull the phone from her ear.

"Darn it, I could have! Guess I'll have to settle for the successful, good-looking man I am today."

"Arrogant much?" she giggled.

"Just confident and happy where I'm at. Naturally I have regrets, but it's like that monkey said in *The Lion King*, 'The past can hurt. But the way I see it you can either run from it, or learn from it.'"

"Every child's first teacher in wisdom."

"Indeed. Walt Disney is right up there with Dr. Seuss."

"Funny enough, I've lived in California for quite some time, but I've never been to Disneyland."

There was a brief silence before Logan responded, "You know what this means, right?"

"That I didn't go to Disneyland?"

"It means we're going to Disneyland."

Addie huffed a laugh. "Sure, Logan, let's go to Disneyland."

"I know you're being sarcastic, but I'm totally serious. Everyone deserves at least one trip to Disneyland, and if you thought I enjoyed watching you eat Ronaldo's pizza for the first time, wait until you see how much I enjoy watching you on the Dumbo ride wearing a pair of Minnie Mouse ears."

Addie began to recall the moments when the men in her life got carried away in fantasies. They were romantic and exciting things that nobody did in real life, and she had every reason to believe this was another fantastical moment, but something made her want to believe him and that he would actually take her to Disneyland on some whimsical adventure.

"You're just one big softy at heart, aren't you?" she said.

"I'll probably lose my street cred for admitting to that."

"Don't worry, your secret is safe with me."

"Can I ask you a serious question?" he said.

"Of course."

❧

Logan sat back in his work chair, staring at the artwork that came with the décor of the office. Even though it was Saturday, he was tired of working at home and needed a change of scenery after he found an old photo in his files.

It brought up a question that was related to a topic he wasn't too thrilled to acknowledge, but felt inspired to ask Addie her opinion.

"Have you ever done something that you really regretted; that you would do anything to go back and change?"

"I think everybody has, but yes," she answered easily.

"I won't ask you to elaborate, but . . . what if you had a friend that you wronged? Even if it was years ago—another lifetime ago—and you still carried that guilt in your heart . . . what would you do?"

"Depends. How did you exactly wrong him?"

Logan sighed, pinching the bridge of his nose.

"You don't have to get hypothetical with me, Logan. But no pressure."

"I just think it might be a little early sharing the gritty details of our lives, but . . ."

". . . but, it could be a deal breaker."

"Exactly," he said, hoping it wouldn't. "But that's only half the reason. I legitimately want to know what I should do to fix this and I'm looking for some good advice if you have it."

"I'm glad you feel that way. And for what it's worth, you're talking to someone with a lot of regrets, which makes me less judgmental than some."

"I appreciate that."

"So what happened?" she asked, and Logan thought a few seconds to where he should start his story.

"Back at Dixie, I had a really good friend named James. He was my first roommate and we were like brothers since the day I moved into the complex. It was after we came back from our missions, and we both served in Spanish-speaking countries, so we had that in common. He loved to hike and go canyoneering, so he taught me how to rock climb and we explored a lot of what Utah's nature had to offer. I taught him how to snowboard and he came along on a lot of our family ski trips."

"Sounds like a true bromance."

He gave a pained laughed. "I guess so. Eventually time and educational goals separated us, even though we had the same major. But we still managed to keep the friendship alive. Because I graduated before him, he used a connection he had through a friend of his dad's to land me the career I have today. He was the one who basically set up the interview just before he left to attend BYU."

Logan always hated dwelling on the part that came after, which is why he repressed it for so long.

"After he left for Provo, I made the decision to leave for Chicago. We kept in touch for a little while, but I needed to continue my education and train for what I was interning for, so naturally it became my focus, and I actually stopped communication with a lot of people, including my own family. But as I excelled, I ended up making mistakes. I'm not proud of it, but I had a problem with morality and also drinking. I was never an alcoholic, just a social drinker, but it still provoked me to enjoy the partying lifestyle that came with it."

"It's called temptation for a reason, Logan. No one gives in unless it's enjoyable to some degree."

"I know, but I knew better. And there was one occasion where I came home to visit. I was planning on seeing my family, but we ended up having a huge falling out and so James was nice enough to let me stay with him in Provo for the rest of the trip. And in gratitude . . . my idiot self took him to a bar.

"He didn't want to go, so I went by myself without telling him. When he called to see if I was okay, he could tell how drunk I was, so he drove over to pick me up before I got behind the wheel.

"He came inside to find me and I was with a group of people who I just met—a completely shady crowd all keen on getting after the good ol' Mormon boy doing his service. A few of the guys started to harass him, saying nasty words, shoving him around, and even dumped a full glass of beer on his head. It was all kind of blurry, but I remember not doing anything about it.

He wouldn't leave without me though, and eventually he got me out of there just in time for me to throw up all over his shoes.

"He took me to his place that night so I could sleep it off. During my massive hangover, I remember the very loud argument that ensued between him and the guys in the apartment. I have never heard him get so defensive of me before. But apparently after I left, rumors spread like wildfire and someone had gone to the school's administration and . . . he was kicked out."

"Oh no," Addie sighed.

"James was expelled and it was all because of me. Last I heard he moved back home and . . . I don't know what became of him since then. He never responded to any of my texts or messages. He blocked me on every social networking site and . . . that was it."

"I'm so sorry, Logan."

"Why do you feel sorry for me? I was the scumbag who did it."

"Well yes, but you've had to carry that for a long time. Regardless of wanting to turn your life around, your past doesn't just disappear. That's the funny thing about repentance."

"And trust me, I never got wasted like that since then. I haven't touched a drink since before my accident either. But I haven't made things right, Addie. I just don't know what to do."

"First of all, thank you for learning that lesson the first time. But answer this, do you feel like you need to apologize to James, or do something to make up for it?"

"Both."

"Okay, then since it's a delicate situation, I would do as much research as you can before deciding your next move. I'm sure you know what I mean."

"I do. I've been looking into ways of tracking him down and it shouldn't be too hard to see where he's at in life."

"Then make that your first step and let me know what happens."

"I will," he said, grateful she hadn't been so appalled with his actions. At least, she didn't sound like it. "Has your opinion changed about me?"

"Of course not. Everybody screws up one way or another, but I'm always going to encourage people to do the right thing. I've spent a lot of time in counseling because of the events in my past and the negative reaction I had to them. I learned a lot about healing and the difficult process that comes with it. So I feel for you, Logan."

"That's . . . not what I expected to hear. But I'm relieved to hear it."

"Good. So I'll see you at the hockey game next weekend?"

"Definitely. But I'm picking you up this time."

"Deal."

Chapter Sixteen

✑

$\mathscr{L}$ogan was walking the isles at the grocery store when his mom called him. He leaned forward on the cart, still browsing the canned foods section when he answered. He didn't have time to say hello as she all but shouted, "Your brother got his mission call!"

"Whoa, really? Where's he going?"

"We don't know. He hasn't opened it yet. We're still waiting until the family can all be at the house and find out together."

"When do you think everyone will make time to be there?"

"We're thinking next Monday for family home evening. I know it's short notice, but we would love for you to be here. Mark especially."

Logan more than anything wanted to be there for the big event, but with the account he was working on, he wasn't sure if his superiors would allow it.

"I would love to be there, Mom, but . . ." He paused, figuring his mom was expecting the usual "I can't" to follow up. However, impulsively he responded, "Never mind, I'll see if I can change my schedule."

"Oh Logan, that would be fantastic. And if you're too busy, or can't book a flight, you can still watch him open it via webcam and everything will work out."

"Well then at least we have a good backup plan. And Taylor can't exactly punch me through a computer screen, so still a win-win."

"Logan," his mom sighed, but he cut her off.

"We don't need to talk about it. Family squabbles won't keep me away this time. Mark must be itching to break that seal."

"No kidding. I saw him sitting at the kitchen table, staring at that envelope for twenty minutes straight last night."

"He didn't look worried, did he?"

"No. In fact, he suggested right after to skip the party and let everyone know through social media so he wouldn't have to wait. Everyone, especially your sisters, threw a fit of course, so expect a call from them too."

"Naturally," Logan laughed. "But I think it's great. This will be the last time we'll do this until Carter gets his call."

"I know. All my babies are grown up."

"We're still a bunch of babies though."

"Won't deny that," she chuckled. "But I do get grandbabies out of the deal, so it balances out. Speaking of which—"

"Don't even go there, Mom."

"I wasn't gonna, but . . . I did hear through the grapevine about a certain young lady you met recently."

"Okay, first of all, Mark has a big mouth. And second, we've only gone on the one date."

"Considering this is the first girl I've heard about since your Dixie days, you can't blame your mother for being curious and excited for more grandchildren. I'm just sayin'."

She had a point. "I know, but let's not start planning a wedding. I mean, she's wonderful, but it's very brand new and out of the norm of my social life."

"So I hear. I'm also aware she's the Whites' granddaughter. They're in our ward and I've heard nothing but good stories about her. Funny how things work out, isn't it?"

"No kidding," Logan breathed.

"Do you plan on seeing her again?"

"Yeah, tomorrow actually."

"And if things go well, a third time?"

"That's certainly an option. You're already planning the wedding, aren't you?"

"Actually . . . as your mother, I'm just here to say I hope you know what you're doing." He could hear the warning in her voice, which was just as she intended it to be.

"What do you mean by that?"

"I'm not trying to pick a fight. I'm just making sure that you're making changes for the right reasons. I know Addie has just come back to the Church and I know you've expressed having that same goal recently—"

"Mom," he cut off, "I know what you're thinking and thank you for being concerned, but I didn't decide to come back to church to get a girl. Nor am I pretending to get on her good side, only to bring her down again. It's nothing like that. I've been working on this since Mark left and it hasn't been easy, but it's a start. And I've actually been looking into contacting my bishop, but the old one has been released, so it's still a work in progress. Things are changing because I feel like it's the right thing to do, regardless if Addie slaps me in the face tomorrow and says she never wants to see me again."

"Oh honey," she chuckled, sniffing loudly through the receiver. "I'm sure you wouldn't be surprised to hear how much that means to me. And I know this is your life, so I'm not going to press you about it or give you advice. But you do have our support and we're here if you need us."

"Thanks, mom. I know you are, but it's always nice to hear."

"I'm glad. Well I won't keep you on the line any longer. You'll hear from one of us soon."

"Good, I'll be sure to call Mark tomorrow."

"He'll appreciate that. Love you, sweetie."

"Love you too, Mom. Goodnight."

As he said it, an elderly lady pushing a shopping cart smiled at him and patted his arm as she passed. Logan just laughed to himself and proceeded down the produce aisle, happy he made at least someone's day.

Addie had never considered herself a hockey fan until she sat next to the ice and felt the adrenaline and excitement of the game in person. Logan did well to explain all the fundamentals of the game as it progressed, and she found herself getting into it more than she expected.

Logan had a good laugh when Chicago scored the winning goal and Addie leapt to her feet, sending the nachos in her lap exploding all over her boots. She tried to laugh it off as he came to her aid with a bottle of water and napkins. Although she was humiliated, which he clearly noticed, it gave him cause to put a reassuring arm around her, and instantly all her chagrin was gone.

"That was so fun," said Addie as they exited the ice arena.

"I didn't think you'd become such a die hard fan so quickly. I was more entertained watching you than the game."

"I bet. Me and all my clumsy glory. But it was the most fun I've had in forever. The halftime show had to be the cutest thing I've ever seen."

A few of the junior hockey players had gone on the ice to score goals against the pros. Afterward, they gave the kids their hockey sticks and by the looks on their faces, it was like they were given the Holy Grail.

Impulsively, she took her hand out of her coat pocket and laced her fingers with his. He gave her an encouraging squeeze, and she leaned into his shoulder. They walked in comfortable silence until they reached the car where he opened the door for her.

The lot was packed, so it took a while to get onto the main road, but once they were on their way home, Addie asked what his plans were for the weekend. Logan looked nostalgic as he told her about his brother's mission call. But his eyes quickly changed to disappointment when he mentioned the talk he had with his boss. Apparently he took some time off after his accident, which set him back a little, and he needed to make up for that lost time.

It was flattering to him and impressive to see that he was good at what he does. But her heart went out to him. Not being able to see one's family during the big moments was always hard.

"So it's going to be a busy week for you, then," she said.

"It will, but I'll survive. Any fun plans for you?"

"It's Savannah's birthday, so we plan on celebrating all week of course. A friend of mine wrote a new song and he wants me to help him work out the harmony."

"Is it the guy you sang with that night at the club?"

"Yeah, I don't think I'll be performing it this time, but it's fun just to jam out. Which reminds me, you owe me a song."

Logan exaggerated a groan. "That's right. I guess I have to pay up now."

"After me spilling nachos on my shoes, I'm expecting a full concert."

"I can't guarantee good quality, but I know a nice place with a piano where you'll at least get all the bells and whistles."

"Can't wait. Are you free next Saturday?"

Addie chided herself when he hesitated, both knowing very well that next Saturday was Valentine's Day. But finally to her relief he answered, "I am, if you are."

"Good. But don't feel obligated considering we both know what that day is."

"Do we, now?" he teased.

"You know, the day people raise awareness on those who have, or haven't, a significant other. Or you could see it as recognizing Saint Valentine who was executed for marrying people against the king's orders."

She was rambling off all the wrong things, but she couldn't stop herself when she was nervous.

"Well I can't think of anyone else I'd rather celebrate the death of a saint with."

"Awe shucks," she chuckled. At least she didn't freak him out.

Addie bit her lip and wished he didn't have to keep his hand on the gearshift, liking the way her hand felt in his. But they were only a few minutes from her apartment anyway, and knowing that made the butterflies in her stomach soar.

It was their second date and occasionally when things have gone well at this point, it would end with a kiss. Naturally she had kissed other guys before, but after a long break from dating, the excitement and anticipation of it seemed more daunting than she remembered.

"Addie?"

"Yes?" she said, noticing they were in her parking lot and the car was off.

"Are you okay?"

"Oh, yeah. I'm fine," she said, hoping to convince herself that was true.

They started walking up the stairs when Addie had a feeling something wasn't right. She could hear music in her apartment and it was an oldies classic that her mom loved to obnoxiously sing along to on every road trip they took during her childhood.

"Oh no," she breathed, knowing exactly what was going on, and sort of wishing she was dead. She whirled around to look up at Logan. "I had a great time. I'll call you tomorrow, okay?"

"Is something wrong?"

"Of course not. I'm just . . . tired."

It was the lamest excuse in the book, and she desperately hoped he wouldn't take it the wrong way.

"Okay," he said. "Can I call you tomorrow?"

"Of course." She sighed a little in relief. "Let me know how the project goes."

"I will," he said, giving her a chaste kiss on the cheek, which left her both thrilled and deflated at the same time.

He was about to leave and Addie thought she was home free, until the door opened and the unthinkable happened.

❧

Logan could tell something was going on as soon as Addie froze at the door. It was as if she sensed an army of assassins ready to attack on the other side. He was worried about her reasoning, but he trusted her and it wasn't his place to know everything about her personal life anyway.

But just as he was about to leave, the door opened and a woman, looking in her mid-forties, stepped out and said, "Dumpling?"

Addie winced before turning around. "Mom. What are you doing here?"

Ah, so this is why she wanted me to leave.

"I wanted to surprise you," she exclaimed, pulling Addie into a hug against her will. "Savannah let me in before she left for work. Oh, it's so good to see you, dear."

Logan couldn't keep from smiling a little at the scene. It was a classic mom thing to do, but seeing Addie's obvious discomfort, she wasn't too happy about the surprise visit.

He didn't want to make things more uncomfortable for her. However, he didn't know exactly what to do considering none of his adult relationships had involved meeting the woman's parents.

"And who is this?" the woman asked as she stood back to take a good look at him.

"I'm Logan," he said, extending his hand to shake hers.

There was no doubt that the two were related. They shared the same hair color, face shape, and smile, though her features were more sullen and lean with age. She wore khakis with a designer black top, and large silver hoop earrings. But there was something about her eyes that didn't look right. They were tired and very aged.

"It's nice to meet you. What's your last name?"

"Atwood."

"Atwood, that sounds so familiar. You wouldn't happen to be related to any Atwoods in Arizona, would you?"

"Um, no. I don't believe so."

"Huh, oh well," she shrugged. "Boy, you sure are tall. Are you Addie's boyfriend?"

"Mom," Addie scolded.

"Not yet," Logan answered, trying to force down a laugh as he watched Addie's face go from a soft blush to bright red in seconds.

"Sweetie, why didn't you tell me about this handsome young man?"

"Mom, I thought you weren't coming for another couple of weeks."

"About that . . . we can talk about it later. Let's get inside. I made cheese biscuits."

"Logan actually has to get home."

"What a shame. Some other time then?"

"Of course," he said. "But it was lovely meeting you. Good night, Addie."

Logan headed down the stairwell, wishing the night would have ended more smoothly like he had planned, but he would have to settle for another time. He'd definitely call her tomorrow to make sure she was okay. Until next time, he had some things to take care of. He could only hope it wouldn't take long. For his sake and for Addie's.

Chapter Seventeen

❧

Addie pushed passed her mom inside her apartment and slammed the door shut.

"What are you doing here?" she demanded. "We spoke on the phone and I specifically told you the end of February and that we'd discuss the details. What happened?"

Linda sighed, lowering her head. "I . . . I'm sorry, Addie—"

"No, don't do that. Don't give me the 'I'm sorry' routine and play the wounded bird. You always do this. I just want an explanation."

Linda held her hands together, fidgeting with her fingers a moment before taking a step forward. "I know over the phone I tried to pass things off as casual, that everything was fine and that I just wanted to see you. And that still is the case, but circumstances have changed and . . . I needed to be here as soon as possible."

"What could be so crucial that you would feel the need to travel a thousand miles and surprise me at my apartment? Were you that afraid I would say no over the phone? Is this a new way for you to manipulate me into doing what you want? How did you even figure out where I lived?"

"I called the hospital and asked for Savannah. She told me," Linda said calmly, despite Addie's rampage.

"Wow, you really went behind my back. I just don't understand why."

"It's . . . Lars."

"What about him? I thought you both were done."

"We are. I ended things with him as soon as shady events started happening. He was acting strange . . . some of my things were going missing. One of our mutual friends tipped me off that he was selling my stuff for drug money. Once I figured out who was supplying him, I went to the police. But while they were busting the dealer, Lars was with him. He was arrested for possession, but now he's out on probation. I heard through mutual contacts that he isn't happy and is looking for me."

Addie moved to the couch and sat down, taking a minute to process the information. She was so used to being angry or disappointed, she didn't know how to respond. All she could think about were the final months she spent in California before moving away. Lars had just come into her mother's life, and all she could do was gush about him, going on about how he loved her and wanted to give her the world. But all Addie saw was a freeloader mooching off of everything they had.

She had made sure to watch her mother carefully, looking for any signs of abuse, but there wasn't anything she'd noticed besides her growing affection for a man with big aspirations and no prospects. She wanted to be the one who motivated him to be a better man, but it was only a matter of time before it all crashed and burned once she figured out his agenda. And it looked like the agenda was far worse than they both thought.

"Mom, why didn't you tell me about this sooner?"

"I was afraid to mention it over the phone in case someone was listening. Lars may be a criminal, but there's a reason why he's not in prison. He can be smart when he has a clear head. It's why he fooled me for so long. I also didn't want to worry you.

This isn't your problem; it's mine. I'm moving somewhere where he can't find me. I'm making a fresh start. I just wanted to see you and give you a few things before I do that."

"Don't talk like that," she pleaded. "I'm sure it's not as bad as it seems. We can go to the police and figure this out."

"I've already gone to the police, Addie, but there's only so much they can do. They can't exactly put a protection detail on me for a man who had all charges dropped against him."

"How long ago was this?"

"About two months ago."

"If he's been out of jail for that amount of time, why wouldn't he go after you sooner?" she asked, trying to make sense of this, trying to see if there was a different option.

"Lars has a . . . past. He's been involved in criminal activity before and knows how to deal with people who rat him out. He waits it out for a while, until the betrayer feels like they're in the clear . . . and then he pulls the rug out from underneath him."

"You make it sound like he's part of the mafia or something."

Linda forced a chuckle. "Not that dramatic, but it's not far off. He really wanted me to be a part of it all. He wanted me to help him, but I left before I knew too much. If I did, he wouldn't have let me go. I just knew enough that I had to do something."

Addie wrapped her arms around her torso in a pitiful attempt to keep herself from falling apart. "I can't . . . I don't even . . ."

Linda scooted closer, resting her hands on her shoulders briefly until she pulled her into a hug. It had been a long time since she shared any kind of affection with her mother. But in her vulnerability, she returned the embrace and let her mom cradle her as if she were a little kid again.

She smelled exactly like she used to before she started drinking, and it surprised her to remember it so fondly. It reminded her of the times they spent together while her dad was still alive.

"Don't be scared," Linda whispered as she stroked her daughter's hair.

Addie tried to force back her emotion, but her attempts were pointless. Her eyes kept burning with fresh tears as her body shook in quiet sobs.

"I haven't been threatened in any way. At least not yet. And I've been thinking about starting over in a new place anyway. I'm not here because I need your help or want anything from you. I know it's what I've done in the past, and I'm grateful for your maturity and everything you've done. But that wasn't okay," she said as her voice broke slightly. "As your mother, it's my job to take care of you. To comfort you and help you when you're in trouble or when things get hard. Instead . . . you did all those things for me."

Pulling back to look at her, Addie saw genuine fear and sorrow in her eyes, combined with a sincerity that she had never heard in her voice before. At least not soberly. Her mom may have been a little eccentric and dramatic at times, but this was a new low she hated seeing. She wanted nothing more than to help her find a way out of this and discover the good life she found. It was the whole reason she went back to California.

"You're really leaving."

"I am. But not without giving you some things that I feel you should have. They're not valuable, but I think you'll find them quite endearing," she said as she moved to the duffle bag sitting by the door. She pulled out a shoebox sealed with a few pieces of duct tape and ripped a few off to remove the lid.

Inside were stacks of photos and letters saved over the years. She saw that they were from her dad to her mom, and a new set of tears spilled over Addie's cheeks.

"These were when your dad was in Saudi Arabia. And these were taken when you were just two years old," she said, holding out a picture of her dad wearing fatigues, holding a toddler version of herself in his arms.

"I remember that mustache," Addie chuckled.

Linda laughed along with her. "I hated it, but I never said anything because he always mentioned how manly it made him feel. As if the semi-automatic rifle didn't make him feel manly enough already. But for the last anniversary we spent together, he shaved it off for me."

"Wow," she breathed. "Am I allowed to read these?"

"Of course. It's why I'm giving them to you. I put them away all these years because I was too stubborn to think lingering on the past would help us any, and it was too hard to be around anything that reminded me of him." Her voice lowered to a whisper, old memories likely resurfacing. "I was angry. Angry at myself, at the world . . . and at God for taking him from us. I just wanted to run away."

"God didn't take him away, Mom. It was his time to go home. He died honorably and I'm proud to say that about him."

Linda was getting choked up again and Addie thought about giving her another hug, but she was already rummaging through the box again to pull out another letter from the bottom. The sealed envelope looked like it hadn't been broken, which meant it was either never sent, or never read. And when she saw that it had her name on it, her heart tightened in her chest.

"Your father knew what he was risking when he joined the military. He knew there was a chance he wouldn't come back, even though I refused to believe it. But he wrote this for you just in case he wasn't around for the most important time of your life. It was something that I couldn't just send you in the mail. I would like you to read it as soon as possible, but not tonight. Do it on your own time, when you feel it's right."

Addie held the envelope carefully as if it would disintegrate in her hands. Part of her wanted to be upset at her mom for having kept such a thing from her all these years. But she was unbelievably happy to have something so special, especially sitting next to her mother in the right state of mind. She just wished the circumstances weren't so critical.

"Would you have told me if your situation didn't push you to come here sooner? About Lars, I mean."

She shook her head. "Probably not. I wanted you to think my trip was about you. Not another pit stop to another town."

"I appreciate that, but I'll take what I can get. I'm sorry this is happening, Mom. I'm sorry for being angry with you earlier."

"You have every right to be. I deserve it. I'm sorry for embarrassing you too. But my goodness, what a hottie you found! How in the world did you meet him?"

"Oh my heck, Mom," Addie chuckled, rolling her eyes. "Only you would go from serious mom to boy-crazy in two seconds. But while we're on that topic . . . cheese biscuits? Really?"

"I was just being polite," she defended. "And they're getting cold. Do you want some?"

"It's okay, I'm not hungry."

"More for me then. But while I eat, I want to hear all about him," she said, jumping up toward the kitchen. "He looks so much more put together than the guys you had in California. How did you two meet?"

Addie couldn't believe how drastically her night had changed, but she wasn't complaining. If she only had a few days to spend with her mom before she left for who knows how long this time, she would make the most of it.

After Addie got home from work the next day, they went out to dinner and saw some of Chicago. But later that night Linda took the bus out of town to Texas where her sister and most of Addie's cousins lived. It bummed her out that she didn't have a real chance to get to know her mom better and share with her the happiness she'd found through the Church and the gospel. But she hoped when this all blew over, she'd get that opportunity again. Somehow she felt the Lord wanted it too.

❧

Logan chucked his pen on the desk and rubbed his eyes as the evening dragged on slowly. It was Monday night, the night Mark was supposed to open his mission call and he wasn't there. He managed to get his project finished an hour ago, which only depressed him more knowing that if he hadn't been faced with those setbacks, he could have caught a flight to Utah.

He apologized profusely to his family, and they all seemed to understand, especially Mark, but he owed him more than just an apology.

It was almost eight o'clock his time, which meant any minute now he'd be getting a video call to watch the whole thing. At least he wasn't missing out completely.

Interrupting his thoughts, a knock sounded at the door and he yelled for whoever it was to come in.

"Mr. Atwood?" said Laura, only opening the door wide enough to peek her head in.

"Yes?"

"There's someone here to see you. Addie Garrison?"

Addie? She's here? "Oh, um, let her in."

"Right away."

Of all things to surprise him, this was the last on his list. When he described the fundamentals of his job and where he worked, she seemed enthusiastic when he told her she was welcome to stop by anytime and check it out. He just didn't believe she'd be interested enough to do so, especially at this late hour.

Thinking quickly, though, he scrambled to straighten up his desk and fix his tie. He only had a few minutes, but he wasn't going to turn Addie away.

Another knock sounded at the door and Logan stood up as Laura ushered her inside.

"Thank you, Laura. You can leave the door open."

"Of course. I finished that scheduling conflict, so I'll also be heading home now," she said.

"I appreciate that. Have a good night," he told her before she disappeared down the hallway.

Logan turned to Addie, who momentarily took his breath away. She was wearing a burgundy dress that fit her at the waist and flowed down to her knees. Her hair was styled in loose waves, and the four-inch black heels brought her eyes closer to his eye level.

This was the first he'd seen her all dressed up, and she pulled it off beautifully.

"Hi," Addie said, once the two of them were left alone.

"Hey, what are you doing here?"

"Sorry, I hope this isn't weird or intrusive of me."

"Of course not," said Logan, moving to give her a hug. He didn't miss the delicate perfume she wore, which he liked very much. "You look great. What's the occasion?"

"Actually, I just came back from a Valentine's Day themed FHE, which I helped make the brownies for. We had some leftovers, and I thought you could use a pick-me-up," she said, holding out a container he hadn't noticed until now.

"Thank you. That's very thoughtful of you. I'll admit, it's a surprise, but I'm happy you're here. Come on, sit down. Tell me how your weekend was."

Logan grabbed the chair on the opposite of his desk and placed it next to his so they could sit closer. She sat down to tell him the story about her mom and the reason for her surprise visit. He was sorry to hear about the sketchy circumstances and hoped everything would turn out okay. But he was touched when she explained the reason she had wanted to see Addie in person, and he could tell it was something that meant a lot to her as well.

"How's everything going for you?" she asked.

"Pretty good, but I do have an important video call to make here in a minute."

"Oh, was this a bad time? I can leave."

"No way. I was actually hoping you would stay. It's with my family. Mark is opening his mission call."

"That's great. Are you sure you want me to stay for that?"

"I'm sure. Mark would be thrilled."

"Wow, two dates and I'm already meeting your family."

"Well you sort of already know my family through association anyway, so there's not much you have to worry about. My mom loves your grandparents, and therefore she already loves you."

"Your reasoning is very stretched, but I'll take it," she said just as the video chat started to ring.

Logan turned on the camera, and immediately the screen displayed a living room full of people all waving and shouting their greetings. Mark was sitting on a stool in front of the fireplace, looking eager as ever.

"Bro, so happy you can make it," Mark called out.

"Wouldn't miss it for the world."

"Who's that with you?"

"Everyone, this is Addie Garrison," he said, adjusting the camera so she was in their view.

Addie leaned closer to wave, and Logan noticed the look on Mark's face that was both surprised and knowing at the same time. He really hoped no comments would be made about their relationship, but thankfully the little kids were too hyped up to keep the conversation going much longer.

He heard his father settle everyone down in the background, and all who had phones were pointing their cameras at Mark, who was now ripping the seal of the envelope with both care and enthusiasm.

He pulled out the letter and in a clear voice, he said, "Dear Elder Atwood, you are hereby called to serve as a missionary of The Church of Jesus Christ of Latter-day Saints. You are assigned to labor in the . . . Japan Nagoya Mission."

As soon as it was announced, everyone cheered and applauded while Mark continued to stare at the letter as if it were the winning lottery ticket. There were many congratulations, hugs, and pats on the back, and Logan leaned back in his chair, both nostalgic and ecstatic on his behalf.

Eventually everyone moved to the kitchen for chips and dip, but Mark purposely stayed behind to talk to Logan personally.

"Congratulations, little brother. Japan . . . how do you feel?"

"Honestly, it hasn't quite processed yet."

"And it probably won't until you're halfway through. But you're going to be great. I'm proud of you."

"Thanks, Logan. We can talk later, though. I can see you've got a date with fate right now."

"Bye, Mark," he said quickly, snapping his laptop closed.

"What did he mean by that?" Addie chuckled.

"Nothing, just my little brother being obnoxious."

"Well I'm happy for him. I know a few people who served in Japan and they loved it. I have no doubt he's going to have a wonderful experience."

"I believe so too. But now that that's done, didn't you say something about brownies?"

"Oh yeah!" she said, taking the lid off the container she brought. Inside were thick, cakey brownies with chocolate frosting on top. It looked like a lot of effort was put into them and they smelled delicious.

"It's a special recipe I got from a roommate back in St. George," she said. "They're made with zucchini, so they're the healthiest brownies you could eat. That is if you minus the frosting and the chocolate chips that I added to the mix."

"Nice touch." He rolled up his sleeves to take a corner piece. "Are you going to join me?"

"I had two earlier. My quota has reached its max."

"So you're just going to watch me eat then?"

"You watched me eat pizza."

"Touché," he said as he took a monster bite, and it was like tasting a bit of heaven. This woman sure knew her sweets. "Dang that is good. Just what I needed to end my day."

"I'm glad. I know you had a full weekend."

"I did, but a lot of issues are behind me now, so I can finally take a deep breath. Now tell me about this Valentine's Day themed FHE."

"A few of the wards got together for a singles mingle. I wasn't going to go, but I was kind of obligated to since I signed up to help weeks ago."

"Really, any prospects?"

"None so far. But I was busy making sure everything went smoothly behind the scenes anyway."

He raised an eyebrow at her, wondering if she had wanted to see him all along and was just using the leftovers as an excuse. After all, she didn't live in the city and getting there involved a long bus ride no one would randomly take unless it was their original intent.

"And visiting me was just a last minute thought?" he boldly asked.

"Of course," she said, but her blush gave her away.

"Huh, and here I was hoping you got all dressed up just for me."

Addie playfully rolled her eyes. "Has that ever happened with past girls?"

"Happens about bout nine times out of ten. But that's just here at work," he said, and her eyes widened a little.

"I'm kidding," he laughed. "You're the only one. But your face was priceless."

"Oh you think you're so funny," she drawled.

"I do, actually."

"And how funny is this?" she said as her finger swiped along the side of his face, leaving a streak of chocolate frosting on his chin.

"Oh you did not just do that."

Logan took immediate action by scooping up a blob of frosting of his own. Addie squealed as she leapt from her chair to escape, but she could only go so fast in her heels, which gave him the upper hand.

She barely made it past the desk when he cut her off and pinned her against it. He held the frosting over her face while she attempted to push his arm away, both cringing and laughing at the same time. She could have wriggled herself free, but obviously she was the type to enjoy getting a frosting facial instead of worrying about it ruining her makeup, which is why he resisted just enough to see her squirm before going in and smearing it down her nose.

As he did it, her laughter only got louder and Logan had to shush her so his other co-workers working late wouldn't come in to investigate.

It was true, he hadn't brought any women into his office, so he wasn't quite sure what the rules were about that. He knew some of the worker's spouses visited on occasion, but their interactions weren't as playful as theirs.

"As much as I love messing around at work, I think we should get out of here," he said, but he made no move to leave, and neither did she.

She reached up to wipe the chocolate off his chin with her thumb. Her touch was slow and deliberate, and he didn't miss the way she glanced at his mouth as she whispered, "Yeah, we probably should."

Instinct was carrying him now. Not that he completely lost his wits about him, but he'd been looking for the perfect moment. And seeing her the way she was right now, looking amazing as always, a smile on her face, frosting on her nose . . . he decided to act on what he couldn't stop thinking about since—if he had to be honest with himself—the moment he first saw her on stage.

Logan slowly tucked a stray hair behind her ear, keeping his palm on her cheek. The way she closed her eyes and sighed from his touch was definitely motivating.

"I'd really like to kiss you right now," he said in a low voice, as if it were a special secret between them. "But I only will if you want me to."

The corners of her lips turned up. "I wouldn't still be here if I didn't."

Logan paused a moment to smile and take a deep breath as his hand circled around her back, pulling her close. He made sure to keep his hands where they should be, making it clear that his intentions were honorable.

She was only a breath away now and all this build up had raised the anticipation enough to not waste another second.

He leaned in just as her eyes fluttered closed and he tenderly touched his lips to hers. The kiss started out soft and searching, until it deepened into something more natural and passionate, and Logan could feel a familiarity that he hadn't felt with anyone else before.

Lingering alongside it, he felt the same desire that came with being affectionate with women he had chemistry with. Only now it was mixed with emotion and real respect for all that she was, which made it so much more powerful.

Holding her closer and tighter, Logan realized where his feelings were headed and as hard as it was to do so, he figured now was the best time to stop.

As he pulled away to gauge her expression, her eyes slowly opened, and she had that look that told him they were on the exact same page.

"Wow," she breathed, and he chuckled in agreement. "Is there anything you're not good at?"

"I try a lot harder when it's with someone I really like," he said, lacing his fingers with hers. "Come on, I'll drive you home."

Chapter Eighteen

❧

Addie hung up the phone after a short conversation with her mom. She'd managed to find a payphone and called to tell her she made it to Texas safely. Addie was glad for it, but she still worried about her critical circumstance and if her surroundings would only bring her down after the hard work she'd spent getting back on her feet.

Although Addie could see some of the changes her mom had made these last few months, she had a long way to go and Addie wasn't going to get her hopes up just yet. Instead she kept her in her prayers and trusted the Lord to take care of her in the right way she needed.

Addie put away her phone, packing up the stuff she brought for her lunch, and headed back to the classroom. The kids were at recess, so she had some time to clear her desk and send a quick text to Logan, who'd asked how her day was going. She told him about the projects they'd been working on, specifically their Valentine's Day boxes for the party tomorrow.

She sent him a picture of the tissue paper, tin foil, and glitter messes over all their desks, which got the response,

> Looks fun. I'll have all the execs do
> that for our next meeting.

Imagining a group of grown businessmen cutting up paper hearts in a boardroom made her giggle out loud.

Addie texted back with,

> Hey, whatever spreads the love in spirit of the holiday ;)

> And everybody could use more of that. Question: what school do you work at again?

> Lincoln Elementary. Why?

> I have a co-worker who lives in your area and he has a daughter who goes there.

She was about to text a response, but the bell rang for the kids to come inside.

She dreaded having to jump into math, but they were behind on their lesson, and testing for midterm report cards was coming up soon. It was crunch time, so she quickly told him she'd call later and shoved her phone into her desk before the kids came in.

She had a strict rule of no cell phones out during class, which she always found ridiculous considering they were ten-year-olds. But in this day and age, teachers were taking away smart phones from the kindergarteners. So to be the example, she never took out her phone in front of them.

As the kids trickled in, hanging up their coats and still enthralled in their recess chatter, Addie gave them a few extra minutes to finish up their projects until they dove into fractions. But if she had to be honest, she just wanted a few extra minutes to daydream. Logan's kiss had kept her giddy until two in the morning, and she still hadn't hopped off cloud nine yet.

It was usually this point when doubt started creeping in, but she wasn't going to have any of it. At least not today. If there were a small chance that things were going to work out with him, she'd have faith and focus on that part only.

The next day when she pulled into work, the first thing she noticed was the sea of red and pink attire the kids had all donned for the occasion. Many were carrying boxes and bags of treats with cards for their classroom parties. Addie had a few ideas to make her mandatory lessons more festive, but she was more excited for their cookie decorating party and not having to do any work.

When the bell rang, Addie went about her routine as usual until after lunch when it was time to share Valentines. She gave the whole half hour to her students, who moved about the room as they stuffed each other's boxes with candy and mostly Disney and superhero themed cards that were evidently popular this year.

While they were preoccupied, Addie started to get the cookies ready when a knock came at the door. She didn't really know what to expect, but it most certainly wasn't a flower delivery man holding a bouquet of white roses.

"Miss Garrison?"

"That's me."

"Happy Valentine's Day," was all he said as he handed over the flowers and left before she could say a word.

Addie immediately snatched the card from the top that read, *To Miss Garrison, may today be as sweet as it will be tomorrow. Happy Valentine's Day. ~L*

So that's why he asked which school she worked at yesterday. Suddenly Addie felt like a seventeen-year-old girl who had just been asked to the prom. It was after hearing the giggles coming from her students when she remembered where she was and soon the questions were pouring out.

"Who's it from, Miss G?"

"It is from your boyfriend?"

"Does he love you?"

"How much did he spend on the flowers?"

Finally, Addie raised up her hands and said, "Tell you what, you guys won't know anything unless all of you get an eighty percent or higher on Monday's test."

The majority of them groaned in response, but dishing out details was somehow on the list of incentives that got them to study more. It was a silly one at that, but Addie was willing to use any academic artillery she could think of.

While leaning back in her chair, she secretly pulled out her phone and wrote Logan a message.

> You are the sweetest person in the whole world. Thank you for the flowers. Roses are my favorite.

"Yep, still on cloud nine," she said to herself, pressing *send*.

❧

Logan was heading out for a late lunch when Addie sent him an unusual text. She had thanked him for sending her flowers, even though he hadn't personally done so. He went straight to Laura's desk to ask if she had done so on his behalf, but her answer was, "I wouldn't do such a thing without running it by you first. Are you sure you didn't do it, and just . . . don't remember?"

"I think that's a pretty hard thing to forget considering I've never sent a girl flowers in my life. That only means one thing . . ."

"That she's crazy?"

"What? No. That another guy sent her flowers and she thinks it's from me."

"Oh yeah, that makes more sense."

"What do you think I should do?"

Laura took a minute to think while Logan contemplated how Addie thought he was the sweetest guy in the world for something someone else did, and now there was another person in her life that he was now competing against.

"Well it's obvious you should tell her they weren't from you and see how she reacts. If it was from another guy and she looks guilty about it, then she's seeing someone on the side. If she's genuinely confused, then there's another guy interested, but this is the first she's hearing about it. Either way, I think this is just another step toward defining the relationship."

Logan sighed. "I haven't had one of those in a long time."

"Do you like this girl?"

"Of course I do, and I would love to keep dating her and possibly get more serious with her. I just haven't done that in a while and I'm afraid of screwing it up somehow."

"Heartbreak is inevitable for everyone, but the last risk you take will be the one that's worth it in the end. She seems great, so give her the benefit of the doubt and try not to make it a big deal. Odds are she'll be the one that's more embarrassed and it'll work out just fine."

"This is why I made sure the company hired you. I had a feeling you had all the answers," he said, and she gave him a gracious smile before diving back into her work.

Logan dialed Addie's number that night, but it went straight to voicemail. About fifteen minutes later, she texted him saying she was at Broncos. Apparently the friend she had been practicing songs with was performing and he had asked her to help out last minute.

He wondered if it was the same guy who sent her the flowers and that knowledge irked him. He'd never been overly jealous before, and he didn't exactly have a legitimate reason to be. It wasn't like he had asked her to stop seeing other guys, nor were they an official couple. But now it was hard not to be a little possessive as he thought about the two of them on stage. They sang well together and they had something powerful in common that he didn't exactly share with Addie.

He thought over his options and decided on the one that was probably the worst idea he ever had. But maybe if he played his cards right, it wouldn't end up being a disaster.

After eating a light dinner and changing out of his work clothes, he put on his jacket and headed out into the cold Chicago night and hoped for the best possible outcome.

Addie was fixing the mic stand when Leo walked over to plug in his guitar for his preshow warm up.

After their final sound check, people began trickling in and the DJ put on background music until the show finally started.

Addie was only helping out with two of the songs. One was a song that Leo wrote himself, and Addie had tweaked it here and there. The other was one she had originally suggested. It was a duet between the two of them, and it was one of her favorites.

When it was time for Addie to go on stage to do the background vocals, Leo introduced her as the lovely Miss Addie G. and she walked out under the warm lights to do the set.

It was always a rush to appear in front of an audience and hear the crowd cheering. In a weird way, Addie loved the nervous tension that came with it. It always made her feel more alive than anything else.

The song went off without a hitch and Addie was pleased it worked out so well. Most of it rested on Leo's shoulders anyway.

But she was happy to help him succeed with it, and she was flattered that he respected her opinion.

When her contribution was over, she went backstage to hang out until the show ended. She thought about joining the crowd, but wanted to call Logan back and have the chance to talk to him. Unfortunately it went to his voicemail and she sighed, feeling a little disappointed, but not discouraged. She'd see him after the show anyway.

Trying to lift her own spirits, she headed outside to the van where Leo was loading some of his equipment.

"Hey, rock star. Need some help?"

"Me and my boys got it," he said, taking a long swig of whatever liquid he downed in one gulp. "But there is something you can do for me."

He stepped closer into her space, and she didn't appreciate the heavy scent of alcohol on his breath.

"I doubt that," she said. "Sleep it off, Leo."

"Wait a minute," he spat, grabbing her wrist. "You've been flirting with me ever since we started working together. When are you going to give it up?"

"Stop," she ordered, rotating her arm to forcibly loosen his grip.

She managed to break herself free, but before Leo could take another step, someone came from behind her and shoved Leo away from her vicinity.

Addie finally had a chance to get a good look at the guy's face, and was shocked to see it was Logan. There was an intensity she hadn't thought possible for him to have, one that almost scared her, and that's when she tried to intervene. But before she could step between them, Leo threw a punch to his ribs, which sent Logan straight to the ground.

Addie never witnessed anything like this before, so she didn't know what to feel or how to handle the situation exactly. But seeing Logan on the ground and holding his side like that, something was definitely more wrong than what it appeared to be. And if being a teacher taught her anything, it was to exercise control in any way no matter what the circumstances were.

Thankfully one of the guys he rode with rounded the corner just in time to grab Leo from behind and drag him away from the scene. Once he was gone, Addie dropped to his side.

"For the love of . . . What the heck was that, Logan? Are you okay?"

"No," he grunted, gasping in a harsh breath. "This is where I . . . punctured my . . . side . . . a few months ago."

"Oh no," Addie breathed. "That's it, I'm taking you to the hospital myself. Where are your keys?"

"Right here," he said, pulling them out of his pocket. At least complying with her demands.

She tenderly helped him to his feet and carefully walked outside to the parking lot where his car was parked. He got into the passenger seat and she hurried to start the car while Logan grunted in pain.

"Do you know how to drive a stick?" he said in a strained rush.

"You're lucky I do," she said as she shifted gears and pulled out onto the main road.

Once he was admitted into the E.R., she sat in the waiting area, finding herself alone with nothing but time to think. Logic told her he'd be okay. However, feelings of doubt were now creeping into her thoughts and she hoped this wasn't a sign. That getting hurt wouldn't somehow affect their budding relationship. But for now, she had to get through tonight and she knew they were in for a long one.

Happy Valentine's Day . . .

Chapter Nineteen

After X-rays, painkillers, and some poking and prodding, Logan finally relaxed as he waited to be discharged.

Thankfully nothing had been severely damaged. The blow only bruised his currently healing side. But not much could be done besides rest and not overdoing it.

Logan opened his eyes when he heard someone pull the screen open. He expected it to be the doctor, but instead it was Addie, looking temperate and exhausted at the same time.

"You're still here," he whispered.

"I drove you, remember?" she said, but the humor didn't reach her eyes.

"I feel terrible that you're spending the night here. You must be tired."

She just shrugged. "Don't have to be at work tomorrow, so it's fine. Are you in any pain?"

"Aches a bit, but I'll live. Still feeling pretty stupid."

"Don't be. You were only trying to help and I'm so sorry you ended up like this. It's my fault—"

"No it wasn't. I probably could've handled that better, but all I could see was him grabbing you, you telling him to stop and instinct took over. I had it coming, but I don't regret it at all."

"I'm still sorry it happened. If there's anything I can do . . ."

"I'm sure I'll think of something," he teased, trying to lighten the mood.

"Were you there to see the show?"

"I'm afraid I missed it, but I already know you sound like an angel."

She laughed. "What painkillers do they have you on?"

"No, really," he chuckled. "I'm more coherent than I sound. To prove it, I can tell exactly what you're thinking right now and . . . you're worth it, Addie. A trip to the hospital will only make for a funny story one day. I'm not going to run away."

She didn't mean to, but she let out a heavy sigh of relief. "That means more than you know, Logan."

Right then he extended his arm and beckoned for her to stand up. When she did, he scooted over as far as he could and patted on the empty spot next to him.

"Lay down next to me." She raised an eyebrow questioningly, but he could tell she wasn't opposed to the idea. "It's okay, we're not going to get in any trouble here. Trust me. I just hate you being so far away."

"I don't want to hurt you in any way . . ."

"The pain is on my other side. I'll be fine."

She still looked hesitant, but eventually she sat on the hospital bed and carefully turned so she could lie beside him. He took her hand while she nuzzled a little closer and suddenly all felt right again with the world.

"What time is it?" he asked.

"Almost two in the morning. Happy Valentine's Day."

Logan laughed as best as he could with a bruised rib. "Oh man. Not exactly what we planned for, was it?"

"What are you talking about? Anybody can give hearts and flowers. You were my knight in shining armor."

At the mention of flowers, Logan's stomach dropped a little knowing there was still an issue he needed to address. "Speaking of flowers . . ."

"Oh yeah, thank you for those by the way. I loved them."

"That's just it . . . I didn't send you any flowers."

Addie turned herself so they could talk face to face, likely wondering whether or not he was joking. But he kept his expression calm as he watched her put the pieces together.

"Oh no," she groaned. "The initial on the card said 'L' and I assumed it stood for Logan."

"I had a feeling it was that Leo guy who sent them to you."

She paused for a long moment until she said, "Maybe, but it doesn't change anything. I won't be working with Leo anymore. There are other ways I can be creative with music."

"I believe it," he said as they fell into a comfortable silence while he brushed her hand with his fingertips. Eventually the doctor came in to discharge him, and it began to downpour while Addie drove him home.

Although he insisted that she go home once they reached the parking garage, the pain medication was making him drowsy and she stayed to at least help him into the elevator and make sure he got inside safely.

"This is starting to become a habit," he said as he unlocked his door.

She gave him a weak chuckle. "I don't think we've ever done this before."

"No, I mean people having to drive me home from the hospital."

"Well let's not make it a habit between us, okay?" she said as they carefully made their way into the living room. "You have a nice place."

"Thank you, though it's not exactly suited for more than a single guy living on his own."

"Not like you need anything more than that."

"Still . . . it feels more like a place to crash than a home." He lowered himself on the cushion and kicked his shoes off. Addie watched him hold his breath while she helped him into a horizontal position. But once he was settled, he was finally able to relax.

"Home is where your heart is. My guess is your home is where your family's at. Where's a blanket?"

"In the corner." She moved to grab the folded up quilt next to the TV. Draping it over him, she knelt beside his head and ran her fingers through his hair. Once or twice, she leaned in to give him soft, brief kisses for no other reason than enjoying being close to him.

"I really hope I remember this tomorrow," he said. "I don't want you to fade away again."

"Again? What are you talking about?"

Logan knew he was spouting nonsense, but he didn't really have much control over it. He was tired and fighting to stay awake. But he wasn't going to fall asleep without reassurance that she'd be there the next day. He didn't want to wake up in another hospital and have it all go away.

"In my dreams . . . I see what my life could have been if I had made a different choice. If I had chosen to stay, I would have married you in a heartbeat."

"Oh yeah?" She sounded more entertained than intrigued.

"If I had stayed to buy you that doughnut . . . I would have married you."

She let out a soft laugh. "That would have to be some doughnut."

"I know you love doughnuts. You tell me its cupcakes, but I know it's really doughnuts."

Logan had the feeling Addie was scowling at him, but his eyes were closed as he started to drift.

"Yeah . . . but I never told you that."

He could only shrug as reality started to mix with his subconscious. He thought he felt her kiss him on the forehead before whispering a good-bye, but it could have been wishful thinking. The deeper he fell into sleep, the more the whole night felt like a dream, and soon it started to blend with the night of the crash.

Headlights shining through the falling snow, the sound of screeching tires and crushing metal infiltrated his mind as he felt his body being strapped down in a vice.

He tried to call out, but his voice didn't work. All he could do was wait out the chaos until the relief of Christmas lights and the singing angel arrived to sooth away his troubles. Only this time, he didn't see her as the woman he ran into twice, or even the woman he watched on stage. Painted in a different light, he could only see her as one thing: his wife.

Chapter Twenty

Now that spring was here, Addie could finally begin the weeklong break she'd been looking forward to since Christmas. For her first day off work, Logan insisted they celebrate by staying up extra late the night before to go to a concert together. Every minute had been a blast, and it definitely made up for the last several weeks.

Since Valentine's Day, Logan had been holed up at work or in his condo trying to take it easy. Addie visited on a few occasions, but mostly just to watch a movie and order in. Not that it wasn't wonderful being with him, but the commutes had worn her down to the point where she had to ask herself why she was doing this.

She cared about him a lot and always enjoyed being with him. There were times where his sporadic schedule irritated her, especially when he had to cancel certain plans last minute. But mostly she wondered where they were as far as relationships go.

He hadn't officially asked her to be his girlfriend, which left the unanswered question of whether or not it was a good idea to address it. With the guys in her past, bringing up the "define the relationship" talk had always ended bitterly. For one reason or another the atmosphere always changed when the word *commitment* was brought into the picture. So for now she figuring playing it cool was her best option.

One morning she had poured herself a bowl of cereal while she checked her phone for updates to see all the commotion happening with her friends and family.

She continued to scroll as scenes from last night played through her mind. It was a country music tour where Addie got to wear her cowboy boots and band shirt. She also got to see Logan wear flannel for the first time, which was when she concluded that he could wear a burlap sack and still look dreamy.

She giggled from the tickling sensation in her ear as she heard his deep voice sing along to the music. The notorious butterflies took flight when a slow song came on and he wrapped his strong arms around her from behind and swayed to the rhythm.

Hearing him sing, she remembered he still hadn't played her that song on the piano like he once promised. For a minute she felt kind of gipped, but of course she hadn't made the request since then and it really wasn't that important compared to the other things he did for her. But even during the loud performance, she could tell he had a musical ear and wondered if she would ever get to hear more.

After she got ready for the day, she walked downstairs to her apartment's community laundry room to do a load and read a book while she waited. The last time she left her laundry alone while her machine was in use, she noticed a few unmentionables were missing and she wasn't going to let some creep rifle through her clothes again.

Settling down in one of the chairs, she opened her book and tuned out the rest of the world while she dove into the story. She was about halfway through the chapter when she heard the door open.

Because it was a common area, she didn't bother to look up and see who it was. She expected them to go about their business.

But when she felt a strange presence approach her, Addie peeked at the stalking figure and then instantly snapped her book shut.

In a defensive act, she stood and stared with a straight face at the man she hoped to never see again.

"Addison. You are looking so grown up since I've last seen you."

"Lars," she choked, trying to keep her voice light. "What are doing here?"

He just chuckled. "I was in the neighborhood and came to see how you were doing."

Fat chance.

How in the world did he find her? More importantly, what did he plan to do next? Addie didn't want to find out, but going on with this nonchalance was killing her and he knew it. She wasn't going to give him the satisfaction. As shocked and afraid as she was, she had to think quickly.

"Let's sit down and catch up," he said, taking the seat next to hers as she slowly sat down with his arm on the back of her chair.

He looked fairly put together for a man who was in jail four months ago. Then again, any man who was practically a member of the mob always looked more put together than the average criminal.

Addie folded her arms, but tried not to look defensive. The more she challenged him, the greater the chance was of him trying to disarm her. "What brings you to the neighborhood?"

"Business," was all he had to answer with, and his looming stare that followed made her stomach churn.

"Oh. Any friends or family in the area?"

"I'd like to consider you family. Don't you feel the same?"

"Yeah," she said, but she had a good feeling this man knew she was lying.

"How's your mom?"

"I don't know. I haven't heard from her in a long time."

"That's too bad. I was hoping to reconnect with her."

"Why not go home to California and see her for yourself?"

"Because she doesn't live in California anymore."

Addie squinted to look confused by that. "What? Where did she go?"

"I was hoping you'd tell me."

"How would I know if I'm just now hearing about it?"

"You're a smart girl," Lars said, readjusting himself to face her directly. "And you have a soft heart. It doesn't surprise me that you would end up being a teacher. Let alone fourth graders in a forgotten community."

Oh no.

"We could play this game all day. But I know your mom was here, Addie. I know she's running from me and you know exactly why."

"You could have just called," she said, trying to be brave in the face of danger, but really she was scared senseless.

"If I did, I wouldn't have gotten to see the life you've built here. It's quite impressive. Lovely roommate with a successful medical career, talented friends with promising futures, and a handsome man with the money to wait on you, hand and foot."

She had a heart-wrenching feeling on where this was headed. He'd been watching her. For how long, she didn't know, but long enough to learn details that he could easily turn to threats.

He leaned forward to whisper in her ear, "Did you like the flowers I sent?"

It was all Addie could do to keep herself from getting sick right there. It was all becoming painfully clear now.

"What do you want from me?" she whimpered.

"I just want to know where she is."

"You'll hurt her if I do."

"I'll hurt you if you don't."

Addie prayed with all her might that the Lord would intervene somehow. If he walked away now, the threat would linger over her and everyone else she loved. She couldn't let that happen.

She needed guidance in every way and only one thought came to her.

"Come. Let's go for a walk," he said.

As much as she wanted to run, the small voice in the back of her mind was telling her to comply. Just for now to get them both out of the secluded room.

She nodded and stood to walk in front of him while his tight grip held onto her elbow. From the corner of her eye, she saw two men disappear behind a corner, and instinctively she screamed, "Help me!"

Lars reacted by covering her mouth with his hand, but a newfound strength pushed her to thrust her elbow into his gut, which barely loosened his grip until she stomped hard on his foot.

This maneuver pushed him to the ground and Addie made a break for it. She ran down the hall and around the corner until she nearly collided with the two men she saw earlier. Both appeared to be in their twenties and carried Latino accents, but she had the strong feeling to trust them.

"What happened?" one asked.

"There's a man back there who's threatening me."

"Where is he?"

"By the laundromat."

She didn't have to say more for them to push past her and investigate. Without thinking she followed them, not taking any time to worry about what kind of confrontation would be going down once she got there.

She arrived to see both chasing Lars down, which didn't take long due to the discomfort she inflicted. Both caught him by the wrists and kept him stationary until he quit struggling. He then began accusing Addie of attacking him for no reason, but that was likely due to the fact that being on parole and seeking out the daughter of an ex-girlfriend wouldn't look good in court. Thankfully the two men weren't easily swayed enough to believe him, and one pulled out his phone to dial the police while the other kept a watchful eye.

Assured the authorities were on their way, he guided Addie into the adjacent hallway where he asked her simple questions that kept her calm and collected until they arrived.

After she told the police their backstory of his connection to her mother and why he was after her, Ernesto and Diego, the two men who had helped her, chimed in to explain how they heard her scream for help. She was amazed at how sincere they were as they defended her like their own sister. It gave her a sense of peace knowing the Lord had orchestrated it perfectly so she wouldn't be alone.

Along with their testimonies, the police located a recording from a hidden security camera and there was enough evidence for Lars to be handcuffed and taken into custody. It was Officer Jensen who offered to escort her back to her apartment, and Ernesto and Diego were kind enough to follow suit, insisting they even carry up her laundry for her.

"Thank you for all your help," she said.

"Yeah, you are one tough chica," Ernesto said. "We're proud of you."

Now that the shock was wearing off, the overwhelming feelings of the day's events and what could have happened began to rush in all at once. Diego noticed and he offered her an arm, which once again, Addie accepted as he pulled her into a hug.

"Thank you," she blubbered.

"De nada, mija. We live in the building, so you let us know if you need anything, okay?"

Addie nodded while the men left with encouraging looks on their faces. Officer Jensen made sure she got in safely and promised to update her on what legal actions would take place and how she'd need to be involved. She knew it was far from over, but at least Lars was locked up for now on assault charges and would likely go back to jail for violating his probation.

The officer stayed until Savannah got home, and was nice enough to fill her in on the story before he left. Addie was tired of explaining and quite frankly, she just wanted to curl up under a blanket and escape into another world.

Although Savannah kept herself together for Addie's sake, she could tell she was beside herself with worry. But she didn't ask any more questions or beg for further details. Instead she brought out the frozen cookie dough and put some in the oven, then laid her big, red fuzzy blanket over Addie as she lay there curled up on the couch.

"Can I just say one thing?" Savannah asked. "Remember how you once said that you went from one guy to another because you lacked security in your life?" Addie nodded. "And you did it because you felt like you needed a man to help protect you from the world. But instead they only brought you down with it."

Addie knew exactly what she was talking about. She just wanted to know where she was going with this.

"I don't know if this will make you feel better or worse. But if this hadn't happened to you . . . you would have never known that you were strong enough to fight back. And you fought back hard and won. You won for yourself, your mom, and for anyone else who's been bullied by someone."

When Savannah put it that way, she could hear the truth in it, and it brought her more comfort than she expected.

"You're a good friend," Addie told her.

Savannah smiled and squeezed her hand. "What are sisters for?"

❧

Logan had just finished eating dinner when he got a call from Addie's number, but it wasn't Addie on the phone.

"Hey, Logan. It's Savannah."

Surprised, Logan responded, "Hey, what's going on?"

"Addie's not feeling very well. Emotionally, I mean, and I think you should come over."

"What do you mean?"

In a quiet voice, Savannah began to explain how Addie went to the laundromat where a man associated with her mom had cornered her, demanding to know her whereabouts. Logan remembered Addie mentioning her mother moving out of state for that reason.

At that point Logan was already getting his stuff together to head to her place, knowing how shaken she must be about now. But he froze as he heard her mention how physical it got and Addie's brave execution in defending herself.

Although he was glad to hear the story ending with the guy in handcuffs, Logan's heart thudded in his chest and anger welled up inside him. It was the same anger he had felt when he watched that Leo guy corner her behind the venue.

Although there was nothing he could do about Lars, he still had a mind to do anything he could to make sure Addie was safe and taken care of. During the drive, he came up with a plan that he hoped Addie would appreciate and accept. He made the necessary phone calls and had mostly everything worked out. He hoped he wasn't overstepping his bounds, but inspiration told him it was what she needed.

When he reached her apartment, Savannah let him inside to where Addie lay asleep on the couch.

"It's okay to wake her up. She'll be happy to see you."

Logan was glad to know she had good friends in her life to be there for her, and he quietly thanked Savannah before kneeling at her side to nudge her awake.

Her eyes fluttered open. "Hey."

"Hey, yourself."

"The tables sure have turned, haven't they?" she joked and Logan tried his best to smile.

"Come on, we're getting out of here," he whispered.

"Really? Are we going to Disneyland?"

"Something like that," he chuckled.

Without asking, he wrapped Addie with the blanket she had on like a cocoon and cradled her in his arms. He then stood to carry her to the door, and he thought she'd object, but instead she nuzzled herself against him as he told Savannah they wouldn't be gone long.

It was when they reached the stairs that Addie insisted on getting down on her own. But as soon as they reached the outside, Logan picked her up again and put her in the passenger seat of his car.

"So if not Disneyland, where are you taking me?"

"It's a surprise," he said.

❦

Addie felt a wave of nostalgia driving into the city where all the bright lights illuminated the streets. Wrapping her in a blanket and taking her on a late-night cruise was something her mother used to do and the gesture was comforting in many ways. Regardless of where Logan was taking her, she was happy to bask in the moment.

Once they reached a residential area where the slender houses were tall and pushed against each other, Logan found a parking meter and cut the engine. He opened her door and she stepped out to see a building that read in gold letters "The Church of Jesus Christ of Latter-day Saints."

"What are we doing here?" she asked. Logan only smiled, pulling out a set of keys to unlock the front door. "Do I want to know how you got ahold of those?"

"I stopped by the bishop's house and he agreed to loan them to me."

"Wow, that's very trusting."

He opened the door and gestured her inside. "We've gotten a lot closer these days."

Addie felt strange to be in a church building wrapped in a blanket and slippers. But she had little time to dwell on it when they walked into the Relief Society room and Logan sat down on the piano bench.

He beckoned her to sit down next to him and understanding dawned on her.

Without saying a word, she sat down beside him while he warmed up his hands, and when his fingers touched the keys, her heart melted as the beginning chords of her favorite song wafted throughout the room. She remembered telling him what it was like living with her grandparents and how sometimes they would take her to "Music and the Spoken Word" at the tabernacle in Salt Lake City.

She was very young the first time she'd gone, but she would never forget how much she loved hearing the choir sing "Consider the Lilies" and the spirit that emanated from them as they sang. It was the first time she truly felt it and it was the beginning of her testimony, which had only grown from there.

Watching him play it for her now, she could only look at him and see the real side of a man who cared about her heart more than anything else she could give him. They hadn't known each other very long, but somehow she was emotionally connected with him in a way she hadn't experienced before. She had opened her heart to others in the past, but she was truly recognizing what it felt like to have someone open his heart to her. Combining it with everything that made him so wonderful in her eyes, she couldn't deny that she cared about him. And maybe even loved him.

The song was nearing the final notes. Now that she made her internal declaration, she could feel the spirit enter the room and the tears began to pour.

When it ended, Addie was still taking it all in, hardly believing a day that had started off so horrible could end so amazing.

"I know I owed you that a long time ago," he said, keeping his eyes on the keys until he looked at her in a way he hadn't before. "But it was after that night in the emergency room that I wanted to do something a little more meaningful."

"It was perfect," she said, resting her head on his shoulder. He put his arm around her so he could hold her closer, and she felt more complete. "I know I should have said this sooner. But you are the most wonderful man I've ever met. I received many gifts over the years, but this is the best one yet. Did you really practice that in just a few weeks?"

"I practiced the best I could on the Sundays I've been here. It became one of the motivations to bring me to church. Free piano."

"Wow," she whispered. "It certainly paid off. This has honestly been quite the day."

"I hoped I could make it a little better."

"You went above and beyond. Thank you."

"And that's not all. I hate to bring it up now, but I heard about what's going to happen next with Lars and all the legal action taking place. I want you to know that you're not alone in this. I know a great lawyer who will help you and your mom. He's a very good friend of mine; he's reliable and trustworthy, and he will make sure everything works out fairly and in your favor."

"You're going to make me cry again," she said, the second set of tears already forming. He pulled her in once more, leaning down to kiss the top of her head. "Sometimes it's hard to understand why you go so above and beyond for me," she murmured.

"You're my girlfriend. I'd fly to the moon for you if I could."

She looked into his eyes and could only see sincerity, which put the goofiest smile on her face.

"Oh, is that what I am?" she teased.

"It is if you want to be."

"Then I say you take me home and we eat some more of Savvy's cookies and watch a movie. That way when I'm asked what I did tonight, I can say I spent the evening with my boyfriend."

"Sounds perfect to me."

Chapter Twenty-One

❧

Four months had gone by since Mark opened his call, and Logan still felt unprepared to face his siblings. But he was confident that their conflicts wouldn't resurface given the reason for the gathering.

Having never been on a plane before, Addie insisted Logan go to Mark's farewell without her, but he wasn't having any of it. He literally had to throw her over his shoulder to get her to the gate, which provoked her into giving him the silent treatment while she pouted in her seat.

But as the plane moved down the runway, she gripped his hand like a vice and finally accepted Logan's comfort and reassurance that she was perfectly safe. And once she believed it, he was comforted knowing she'd be there to support him through his own fears.

Besides his family, Logan's next greatest trepidation was knowing James was going to be there per his mother's invitation. He found out when he casually mentioned to her his frustrations in his failed attempts in contacting him. Apparently James had kept in touch with Logan's other family members over the years, which nobody had bothered to say anything about.

At this point all bets were off. He hoped James would be forgiving enough to hear him out; that his grudge would have relented enough to forgive him. If James hadn't reached out even after hearing he was in a coma, then Logan doubted he'd get through to him now. He just couldn't ignore the prompting that they needed to talk. Whether it was personal closure or restarting a good friendship, he had to be there.

When they landed in Salt Lake, Addie's grip on Logan's hand wasn't as tight as before, nor was she as pale. But the first thing she did after exiting the plan was order a chocolate milkshake. She slowly sipped it down until her attitude perked back up to the normal scale.

"Feel better?" he asked.

She nodded without taking her lips off the straw while Logan did his best to keep his laughter down. "I'm still mad at you. But you're really cute, so . . . " She took another long sip.

"Are you mad about the trip?"

"Oh no, this trip is going to be great for both of us. I'm mad that dozens of people had to see my backside in the air with me over your shoulder."

"Desperate times call for desperate measures. And admit it . . . you kinda liked it."

She gave him the stink eye in response, but eventually it melted into a smile. "Only because you're cute."

He only laughed and put his arm around her in response.

"Is your mom here yet?" she asked.

"I just got off the phone with her and she's on her way. She told us to be waiting by the baggage claim, so I say we head down there."

"All right, let's go."

They made their way through the terminal while Logan concentrated on his eagerness for the reunion. Had it been under better circumstances, Addie was right: it would be a great trip for both of them.

After retrieving their bags, they sat in the waiting area until Logan saw his nephew, Josh, bounding toward him with Evelyn in tow.

"Hey!" he yelled, jumping up to greet their tight hugs and simultaneous chatter. "You guys have gotten so tall. It's not okay that you're both are growing up to fast. But do you know what that means?"

"That you're an old man?" said Josh.

Logan rolled his eyes. "All right, that's it. Just because you're getting older doesn't mean I can't still tickle you."

Both the kids squealed as they fled from his grasp.

"You're quite the fun uncle, aren't you, old man?" said Addie.

"Oh, you're just asking for it now." He reached for her sides, which made her shriek and jerk from his grasp.

"Don't you dare, Logan!"

"What? Are you ticklish?"

"You know very well I'm ticklish, and we're in a public place." He could tell her feathers were ruffled, but he couldn't help but be thoroughly entertained by it.

"That didn't stop me earlier. Take it back." He reached out to grab her. She tried to dodge, but he was too quick for her to escape. His fingers pressed just under her ribs and she burst into laughter. "All right, you're very young and the handsomest man alive!"

Logan ceased to torture her, pulling her close to his chest. "Thank you," he said, giving her a quick kiss.

"Ewww, Mom. They're kissing," said Josh.

When they both turned around, Logan at last saw his sister standing with them with a wide smile on her face.

"Hey, little brother," she said.

Addie seemed to understand his thought process, because she stepped out of his hold so he could move into Brin's embrace.

Although Brin got the red hair gene from their mom, everyone always said how alike they were in looks; as if they could be twins. Quite often they pretended that were true in their youth. But they had two very different personalities in which their traits made up for each other growing up.

But after so much time growing apart, Logan was surprised at how easily they could let bygones be bygones and live right now for what it was. He hoped that would be the same with Taylor.

"I've missed you, Brin."

"I've missed you, Logan. We've all missed you."

"It's good to be home."

"You said home," she crooned, using the same dramatics Mark was known for, but Logan was too eager to make introductions.

"Where's Mom?"

"Manning the fort. I volunteered to come instead."

"Well in that case, there's someone I'd like you to meet," he said, gesturing toward Addie, who continued to stare dreamily at the scene.

"Hi, I'm Addie," she said, as both hugged each other like they'd been friends for years.

Brin quickly changed from emotional to ecstatic. "It's so good to finally meet you! Again, I think. Who knows how many times we've run into each other before now. But either way we've heard so many great things and we're happy you could come."

"Me too. You can thank Logan for making sure of that." He didn't miss the sarcasm, but at least it was in good humor.

"Where's Sarah?" Logan asked, seeing she was one short of having all her kids with her.

"She's with John at Mom and Dad's house, hopefully taking a nap. She's teething and the ride would have been a nightmare for all of us."

"What about Taylor?"

"He's there too, but he and Annie are staying at a hotel while their kids are bunking in the basement with Evie and Josh." Brin could obviously see the reason behind his curiosity and she was quick to reassure him. "They're not at the hotel because of you, Logan. Expanding families come with tight quarters."

"Understandable," said Logan and he left it at that.

When they got to the SUV, they all piled in with Addie in the front and Logan in back with the kids. She and Brin immediately dove into conversation, leaving Logan to chat with his niece and nephew about everything going on in their lives.

Evelyn was about to graduate from primary and start young women's soon. And Josh was excited for soccer season, telling him everything he knew about the World Cup and the teams he followed.

For Logan, the drive was long and loud, but it was the kind of noise he missed. He had a feeling Addie was enjoying it just as much as he was. But once they reached the Highland neighborhoods, there was a hint of longing in her eyes that Logan could empathize with. The wave of nostalgia likely hit him just as hard.

At the house, they brought their stuff in to find everyone scattered around the backyard eating burgers and playing in the sprinklers. Logan got the same ecstatic greeting from Taylor's kids before they ran back to their fun.

He stayed to chat with his dad, who was busy at the grill, and then later found Addie being gushed over by his mother in the kitchen. Quickly, her attention was diverted to him in the same way.

"Good heavens, it's so good to see you walking around," said Peggy, hugging him fragilely at first until Logan picked her up off her feet just to prove he was fully recovered.

"Well we all know Logan," came a voice coming up the steps. "Nothing could ever bring that kid down."

Logan turned to see Taylor, looking almost exactly as he remembered him. He still had the beard he'd started growing last year, but it was obvious he'd been attending the gym regularly. The small gut he had was all but gone and his build was more toned. He wondered what motivated him to get in shape, but he didn't care as much as he was happy to see him taking care of himself.

"Taylor," Logan said, putting on his best smile and moving in for a handshake.

Taylor reached out to return the gesture, which lasted only a second before he pulled Logan into a desperate hug that Logan returned equally. His mom, sister, and girlfriend attempted to inconspicuously leave the room but likely moved to a place still within earshot.

"When I heard about the accident . . . there was a minute where I thought you were going to die," said Taylor.

Apparently Taylor wasn't going to waste any time with small talk, and he preferred it that way. He had obviously prepared a speech like Logan had, and Logan figured it was best to let him say what he needed to say.

"And everything I said to you . . . out of anger and stubbornness, came back at me like a bolt of lightning. I'm sorry, Logan."

"I was the one who walked out on you guys, Taylor. I gave you a lot of reasons to hate me."

"I never hated you," he said, pulling back to look him in the eyes. "I was mad, yes. But I let that anger get the best of me. Annie suggested I see a counselor, which I've been doing these last few months. I got over a lot of things and discovered a lot of truth. But the most important was that you're still my brother, and I still love you. If I had expressed that over the years . . ."

"I still knew it. But you were right on many accounts. I was a big idiot who walked away from the happy life I could've had this whole time. I won't take that for granted anymore."

"Well then I look forward to getting to know you again."

"Same here, bro."

Nothing more needed to be said between the two of them once the family gathered on the porch. They all exchanged stories and his parents brought out every single baby picture they could find, but it was fun to reminisce and see Addie light up when hearing about his childhood.

The sun was beginning to set when his mom held out a picture of all four of her children covered in mud and Mark said, "That one's my favorite."

Everyone turned their heads to see him leaning against the doorway with his arms folded, looking amused.

"How long have you been standing there?" Brin asked.

"Long enough to enjoy the scenery. Been a while since I've seen this."

"Creeper," she teased. But everyone understood Mark's meaning.

He only shrugged and moved to Addie's side. "You must be the famous Addie G."

"The one and only," she said, shaking his outstretched hand. "It's nice to finally meet the famous spiritual trainer."

"Yeah," Mark laughed. "But I can't say I'll be the only one when I get to the MTC."

Addie shrugged. "The more, the merrier."

"I knew I had a good feeling about you."

"So where have you been?" Logan asked.

"Just officially saying good-bye to some friends who won't be at my farewell. Tonight was the only time I could that."

"Did one of these friends happen to be a girl?"

"No," he drawled, but the shift in his eyes read otherwise.

"Ooh, that's a big fat yes," Addie chuckled. "Your face is as red as a cherry on an ice cream sundae."

"I take it back. You all stink," Mark said, which provoked another round of teasing and laughter.

When the sky grew dark, everyone eventually said their goodnights and went their separate ways to get the kids to bed.

Addie and Logan stayed in the family room and ended up watching *Star Wars: A New Hope* at her insistence once she saw the first editions Henry had on videocassette.

When the movie ended, they both stayed cuddling on the sofa while they stared at the twinkly lights on the fireplace mantle in comfortable silence.

"Something about this is so familiar," Logan whispered.

"Did you spend a lot of time with girls on this couch when you were younger?"

"No," he laughed. "I don't know exactly how, but I did spend some time on this couch before, contemplating my life and deciding what I wanted for my future."

She'd been leaning on his chest while he unconsciously toyed with her hair. But now she sat up and turned to face him. "What do you want for your future?"

"A lot more than before."

"Care to elaborate?"

"It doesn't matter right now. What does matter is that I have a beautiful woman with me and I should be putting all my focus on her."

"You know how to say all the right things," she said, as he sat up to pull her close to him. "But don't think I won't ask about it later."

"I know. I just want to enjoy this moment exactly the way it is right now." He leaned in to softly kiss her lips, and meant to only leave it at that. But before he could stop himself, the kiss deepened and sparked into something more meaningful.

He could feel a warmth spread from his heart throughout his entire body and he broke away just enough to rest his head against hers. "I love you," he said, hoping it wasn't too soon for him to say.

There was a long pause and Logan opened his eyes, hoping he wouldn't see her panicking from his declaration. But within a few seconds, her face broke into a soft smile. "I love you too."

Hearing her say it brought back that euphoria in an instant, and this time she leaned in to kiss him with more fervor. But what came with tenderness and longing, was a desire that Logan could feel pushing him toward dangerous territory, and he had to do the right thing by holding himself back.

Addie seemed to read his mind. "It's hard for me too, Logan." He gave her an incredulous look, still feeling like the recovering scoundrel. "Hey, I'm serious. I know what it's like to get carried away. It's enjoyable for a reason. But in all my past situations where I felt pressured, or wasn't in the right mind to stop, I've never had love provoke me to want to . . . share that bond with someone, until now. And maybe someday, under the right circumstances, we'll get to."

"You think so?"

"I hope so," she said, but both of them finished her sentence, "under the right circumstances."

"I guess that gives us something to think about," he said.

"I guess it does. But we can talk about it another time. It's getting late and your family has nine o'clock church."

With a final kiss goodnight, Logan drove her to her grandparents who lived close by, and returned home to sit back on that couch and think. It was the kind of déjà vu that hit him harder than ever. But he could feel a difference in which he was far happier on the path he was on now.

He knew exactly what he wanted for his future, and it served as his motivation, especially since all of his decisions included a certain someone who had just told him she loved him back.

The thought made his spirits soar and there was no doubt he had the answer to the biggest decision he would ever make. He just hoped when the time came to make it, she'd say yes.

Chapter Twenty-Two

❦

Getting everyone to the church building on time was a task Logan didn't think would be possible with all the chaos that ensued that morning.

Brin and Annie were frantic getting all the kids ready while Taylor and John put breakfast together. They eventually took over so their wives could do their own hair, but Brooklyn ended up spilling juice on her dress, so Taylor offered to watch Sarah while Annie fell behind schedule to clean her up.

Logan's job was to keep the boys looking nice in their suits, which was easier said than done, when they wanted to go outside and play with their nerf guns in the dirt. He wondered how kids could have so much energy at eight-thirty in the morning, but at least he accomplished the task by redirecting them to play a game of Mario Kart.

Henry had already taken Mark to the church building so he could be sitting on the stand before sacrament meeting started, but it was two minutes to nine when everyone finally walked inside the cultural hall to the saved seats in the front pews. Addie was already there waiting for them.

"Early morning?" she asked.

Logan let out a heavy breath in response. "So much crazier than I expected."

"Just wait until you meet my family. So. Many. Babies . . ."

"Can't wait," he chuckled, lacing his fingers with hers.

When the prelude music ended and the bishop got up to speak, the room quieted down as much as it could in a family ward.

At this point in time, Logan accepted having to pass the sacrament along without partaking, but it was always a letdown for him, especially in the presence of his family. Nobody gave him any looks and Addie was fully aware of his situation, but each time he was reminded of the meeting he'd had with the bishop and the stake president a few months prior. It had been a humbling and painful experience reliving his past mistakes; one that he knew was necessary. It just opened his eyes wider to the reality of what he had given up. And to get it back, he had to put a lot more time and dedication into understanding the process of repentance.

Although it hadn't been an easy course, he had a lot more respect for the things that once blessed his life with true happiness. Like going to the temple, for example. He looked forward to going there again, and hopefully bringing Addie with him.

To start the meeting, a couple youth speakers each did a five-minute talk on enduring to the end. The first was a Mia Maid whose eyes were glued to her notes the whole time. The second was a teacher who said "um" and "like" in every sentence, to the point where he saw Addie keeping a long tally sheet in her notebook.

As Mark got up to speak, Logan noticed his hand shake a little. He had never been one for crowds, but they briefly locked eyes for a moment and Logan gave him a nod of encouragement.

As Logan contemplated Mark's words, his first thought was how impressed he was at Mark's eloquence and understanding of what he knew to be true. When Mark paused briefly, Logan could see the confirmation in his eyes as he bore witness of Jesus Christ and the Atonement. He went on to talk about the Savior's life and what He had endured until the very end.

Although Logan knew he was blessed to have good and caring people in his life, Mark's words were an added reminder since the crash that he wasn't alone in his pain—that Christ had a true understanding of his suffering. That knowledge encouraged him to pray for peace, which had come about in so many ways since then.

After sacrament meeting was over, Mark stayed after to talk and shake hands with everyone in the ward. Most of his family had already gone home to prepare for the luncheon. Addie and her grandparents left with Brin to give them some extra hands, but Logan stayed a bit longer to see if he could find a familiar face in the crowd.

According to his mother, James had said he would be here, but it was more than likely he would make his appearance, congratulate Mark, and leave before Logan had the chance to see him.

Heading toward the south entrance, he was surprised to pass Mark in the hallway, who stopped him long enough to shake his hand and pull him into a brief hug.

"Excellent talk, little brother."

"I'm glad you could be here for it. Where did everybody go?"

"They're back at the house, but Dad's still here and said he'll give you a ride back."

"Cool, are you coming back with us?"

"No, I'm actually looking for someone," Logan said, wondering if his search was useless. "You didn't happen to see James, did you?"

"James . . . McCovey?"

"Yeah, was he here?"

"I talked to him for a few seconds, but he left right after."

"Dang," Logan sighed, feeling the disappointment crush his spirit a little. I guess I'll see you at home then."

"Sorry, man. See you later."

Logan walked the grounds to think for a bit, and went back inside to sit in the foyer. Deep in thought, he almost didn't notice anyone walk in through the doors. But when the person sat down in the armchair in front of him, Logan's focus snapped to attention.

"Hey, Logan," said James, looking both serene and serious at the same time.

Logan opened his mouth to speak, but no words came out. After a solid minute, he somehow managed to say, "I thought you left."

He shook his head. "I talked to your mom this morning. She said you were looking for me."

"I had this whole speech prepared . . ."

"So did I . . ."

Logan had encountered awkward silences before, but this one really took the cake. Someone had to say something, so it might as well be him. "I know saying I'm sorry isn't going to make up for how I screwed up."

"You're right," he said. "But these last five years have been good to me, Logan."

"Have they?"

"I was angry with you for a long time. When I got kicked out of school, I thought it was the end of my career, the end of my reputation, and I thought I was going to have to start over from scratch. But with the help of many different outlets, I've managed to get my degree and I'm working at a decent job in the field I want to be in."

"Are you working for your uncle?"

"I am. It pays well and I like the environment."

"That's good," he said, taking a deep breath before he asked the question that had been nagging him for months. "Where have you been, James? Why did you ignore all my attempts to reach out to you?"

James sighed, looking both sad and conflicted. "Like I said, I was . . . angry. My brother tried talking some sense into me, and eventually I decided to call Peggy and see where you were at in life. I swear I didn't even know about the accident until recently and I'm really sorry I wasn't there for you, Logan. I just didn't know how much of a friend I could be to you, jumping back in so suddenly with an old grudge hanging between us."

"I understand. I could have contacted you years ago, but it took a coma to motivate me. Disasters shouldn't have to be the thing that brings people together."

"Funny how they do though. It's like God wants us all to get along, or something," he chuckled. "I hear you're doing well."

"I am. Again, it took a coma to do it, but I give a lot of credit to the woman in my life."

"Addie?"

"Beyonce."

James snorted and Logan broke into laughter with him. There had been an inside joke in their apartment at Dixie where one of the girls had put up a life-size cardboard Beyonce in their kitchen, but no one bothered to get rid of it. It became the subject of talk for the rest of the year.

"Addie is pretty much the best thing that ever happened to me," said Logan.

"Are you going to marry her?"

"Yes, but she doesn't know it yet."

"I was engaged once."

Logan raised his eyebrows in surprise, but he wasn't exactly shocked. "What happened, if you don't mind me asking?"

James shrugged. "She wasn't ready for marriage. She wanted to finish school and try being independent for a while. We took a break, but eventually we became too distant to reconnect. I wish all the best for her, but it just didn't work out."

He was trying to pass it off with nonchalance, but Logan could tell he was still heartbroken by it. "I'm sorry to hear that."

"Me too. I don't say it to discourage you. I just know what it's like to love someone and it's a great feeling, especially when it does work out in the end. And I certainly hope it works out for you."

"The same to you." When James said no more on the subject, Logan moved on to say, "Would you like to come to the lunch we're having later?"

"I wish I could, but I'm actually headed to a homecoming at my cousin's ward, ironically. But it was good seeing you. One of these days we'll really catch up."

"Definitely," he said, giving him a friendly handshake before he walked out the door.

Logan returned home feeling much lighter than before. He approached Addie standing on the grass and pulled her into a tight hug for no other reason than to just give her attention. Of course being outside, surrounded by everyone he knew, a few people witnessed their tender moment and Mark started chanting, "Kiss, kiss, kiss, kiss!" and soon everyone else joined in.

Addie's embarrassment was clearly written all over her face, but without hesitating, Logan dipped her over his knee and kissed her hard on the lips, which led to a loud round of applause.

Pulling her back up, she giggled and said, "Wow, I don't think I'll ever get used to that."

"Why not?"

"Because kissing you always feels like the first time."

"Smooth," he laughed.

"I learned from the best."

Chapter Twenty-Three

❧

Meeting Addie's family was just as crazy, if not crazier, than being with his own. She had a lot of cousins who each had their own list of questions that really put him in the hot seat.

The atmosphere itself was also chaotic, but still warm and loving, with someone always laughing in the background or children playing a game.

He'd seen the way Addie interacted with her friends, but she was lot more vibrant with her family. She seemed more in her element and Logan enjoyed every minute of it.

When they returned to Chicago, life went on as it usually did. Addie got a summer job working as a part-time nanny for a few kids in her building, which kept her busy. Logan was also busy at work, attending multiple conventions in different states, giving dozens of pitches to different companies.

On one particular July afternoon, Logan went in for a meeting with his boss and received news that left him both flattered and deflated by what was coming up in the future. He didn't exactly have a choice in the matter if he wanted to keep his job, but it was something that neither he, nor Addie, would like.

What was worse was that her birthday was coming up. He had a thought-out plan to surprise her for it, but with this new project, he doubted he could get away long enough to pull it off.

That night, Logan invited her over and made a nice pasta dinner. He was glad the food turned out well and that she seemed to enjoy it, but he was taken off guard when she opened her mouth and said, "So what's the bad news?"

He nearly dropped the dirty dishes in the sink. "Bad news? Why would you think there was any?"

"I've noticed whether it's cancelling plans, going out of town, or having to dive into a project for a week . . . you've always cooked for me. Don't get me wrong, you're a good cook, but I think we should cut to the chase. That way the dessert will soften the blow."

Her tone was almost teasing and her face was amused, but she did have a point and he felt bad for having a job that would put her out frequently. At least she was understanding of his job's importance and didn't give him a hard time about it . . . often.

Logan sighed and sat down at the table, taking her hand in his. "My job is sending me to New York. There are lot of companies who need improving of their financial departments, and they want me to help start a new branch and get it going."

"I see. How long is it going to take?"

"A few months; three at the most."

Addie closed her eyes and let out a shaky breath. She was quiet for a long minute and Logan gave her time to process. Without saying a word, she calmly stood up and walked to the sink, turned on the water, and began to scrub the dishes.

"Addie, I can get those."

"No, I'll do it."

"Addie, please sit down."

"No, Logan," she said firmly. She was upset and he knew better than to tell her what to do when she needed her space, but he couldn't stand to distance himself when he knew how deeply this was affecting her.

Without a plan in mind, he stood up and slowly came up to her from behind, wrapping his arms around her torso. She didn't stop her scrubbing, but eventually he heard her sniff and could feel her body shake in quiet sobs.

He pulled her tighter and finally she stopped scrubbing to lean her head back against his chest. "It's not fair," she said in a small voice. "I know it's how you make your living and they're only utilizing your talents, but . . ."

"You want me here," he finished. "I know. I want to be here too."

"Do you really?"

Logan stiffened and stood back to turn her around so he could look into her eyes. "You don't think I do?"

"I know you want to be with me. It's just . . . old childhood feelings resurfacing. My dad left for long stretches of time and he never came back. You're leaving for long stretches of time, and I can't help but wonder if something will keep you away for good. I know it's an irrational fear—"

"It's not irrational," he interrupted. "You have every right to be upset, and I can honestly tell you that I don't like it either. I'm doing it because it's a heavy requirement, but once it's all said and done, I'm not going anywhere."

"You can't make promises like that."

"Of course I can."

"No you can't!"

Logan almost took a step back at her outburst, but all he could do was watch her as she buried her face into her hands and slumped against the counter. Finally she looked at him with watery eyes and his stomach twisted in anticipation of what she was going to say.

"You're ambitious, Logan. You're a hard worker. But sometimes I wonder if you and I want the same things."

"Where is this coming from? Not too long ago we started saying that we love each other, and now you're pushing me away."

"You're right, because that's what I do, Logan. Every time I open up to someone I fall for, they leave. And when they leave, I automatically close myself off because it hurts so much less. I don't want to do that with you, but I am really struggling here."

He partially grasped what she was trying to tell him, but he was having a hard time truly empathizing. He had failed relationships in the past, but never had anyone left him in the dust the way Addie described.

Logan decided to take a risk and approach her. She held up her hands as a warning to back off, but he knew what was wrong and he wasn't going to let her do this. "Addie, if we're going to talk about this, we need to be touching."

She furrowed her eyebrows. "I don't see why that's necessary."

"Your mind and your heart may be closed off, but not your spirit. In order for you to really hear what I'm saying, I need you to at least hold my hand."

Reluctantly, she extended her palm and Logan decided this was the best he could do for now. He laced his fingers with hers and took a step forward. "I know you've lived a life where you weren't allowed to get your hopes up. You expected everything good in your life wouldn't last forever. And you were falsely led to believe that you're not worth sticking around for. But for me . . . I hope that when I get back, you'll be here waiting for me . . . and the good things that come after will last forever. Because you're worth it, Addie."

He used his free hand to touch the side of her face, and he was relieved to feel her lean into him, relishing his touch. "I love you, and I believe we can make this work. All couples face hard things and if we can get through this, we can get through anything else that comes our way."

"I love you too."

"Do you have faith like I do?"

She thought deeply about it for a minute, but eventually she said, "I do. And you're worth it to me too."

"That's all I need to hear."

❦

Two weeks later, Logan was on a plane to New York. The new school year was going to start soon and Addie was working as hard as she could to learn the new curriculum and redo her lesson plans. As annoying as it was, it kept her mind off of him leaving and that was all she needed.

Later that night, Logan called to tell her he landed safely and that he was headed to the condo he'd be staying in until the company was satisfied.

Pressing *end*, she picked up a rag and wrung the cloth in her hands. "Stupid job, in stupid New York, for a stupid three months."

Savannah put down her cereal spoon and eyed her with a worried look. "You're going to kill the poor dish rag."

She chucked it in the sink and then dramatically put her head down on the kitchen table. "This stiiiiiiiinks," she groaned.

"So if Logan is in New York, who's taking his place here in Chicago?"

"Do you remember when I told you about the falling out he had with his friend back in the day?"

"Yeah."

"Well they're on really good terms now and Logan suggested his company hire on James temporarily until he gets back, but if he ends up liking the job, he'll stay on permanently. He's even staying in Logan's condo while he's gone."

"Wow, that's quite the turn of events for them."

"Totally. I kind of want to meet him. I was thinking of taking some cookies over so he feels more welcome in the city. Want to come with me?"

Savannah moved to put her bowl in the sink. "Why would I do that?"

"Moral support." She pushed out her lip. "And I'm super lonely."

"I also make better cookies than you."

"Well that too, but I seriously don't want to go by myself."

She exaggerated a heavy sigh. "If I must."

"Perfect! He gets here on Wednesday, so we should go during the weekend."

"The things I do for you."

❧

"Hang on, doesn't that one crazy chick live down this hallway?" Savannah whispered as they walked the hallways of Logan's apartment building.

"Sheila? Oh no, not anymore. She up and left a few months ago. Moved back to Aspen, I think. Logan wouldn't have suggested James live here if that weren't the case."

"Good thinking. He would have sent him straight to the lion's den."

"No kidding. Anyway, this is it," Addie said, stopping at the door. She knocked while Savannah held the plate of cookies.

When the door opened, Addie put on her brightest smile, but was welcomed by a man staring at her roommate like he'd been clubbed over the head.

"Savvy?" he breathed.

"Jimmy," she responded, wearing almost the same expression.

Addie squinted in confusion, remembering Savannah talk about the man she dated seriously back in California. The man who had proposed to her before she turned him down and moved across the states. "Jimmy? As in . . ."

Neither of them acknowledged her. In fact, neither knew what to say at all. One minute she was bringing a plate of cookies to a total stranger, and the next minute, said stranger seemed to be Savannah's sort of ex-fiancé!

Addie stared at the two of them, wondering what she should do next. Thankfully James looked her way and finally acknowledged her presence. "Hi . . . um, I'm James. You must be Addie," he said, shaking her hand. "Logan's told me so much about you."

"Same here. It's nice to meet you. Um . . . we thought it would be nice to officially welcome you to the neighborhood, so these are for you," she said, nearly shoving the plate into his hands.

He stared down at the plate for a second and then smiled, but it looked very forced. "Thank you, that's very kind of you." He looked back at Savannah. "I assume you made these cookies." All she did was nod. This was the first time Addie had ever seen her speechless. "Then I know I'll definitely enjoy them."

She just nodded again, which made it very clear her senses were broken and it was time to get out of there.

"Well we won't keep you," Addie said. "Have a great day."

"I will. Thanks again."

The ride home was brutally quiet. Addie rarely ever saw her best friend in a negative mood, but after they got home she disappeared into her room and didn't come out for hours.

She didn't know if it was best to give her space, or if she could use a friend to talk to. But right now she figured the best idea was to call Logan and tell him what happened. Being involved with James, or rather Jimmy's life, he'd be interested to know about this freaky coincidence.

"Hey, pop tart," Logan answered, finally picking up the phone after the third try. "Are you okay?"

"I'm fine, but Savvy sure isn't. And since when did you start calling me pop tart?" she asked, getting sidetracked by a nickname he never used before.

"Since now. Wait, why? What's going on?"

She decided to ignore his first comment and talk about the important matter at hand. "Did you know that Savvy got her BSN in nursing at a university in California?"

"Yeah, I remember her saying that . . ."

"And you know how James finished his degree from a university in California as well?"

"Where are you going with this? Are you thinking about setting them up?"

Addie almost laughed. "It's too late for that, because they're already acquainted."

"How so?"

"Keep thinking about it. It'll come to you."

There was a ten-second pause until Logan exclaimed, "No way! Savannah is his ex-girlfriend?"

"Bingo."

"Oh, what are the odds?"

"Right?" Addie exclaimed.

"So what happened when they saw each other?"

"Oh my heck, it was the most awkward moment of my life. I felt like the biggest third wheel. They just stared at each other in silence. Thankfully he was polite, but I believe it was for my sake. I got her out of there as fast as I could."

"Did James look upset at all?"

"No. Thankfully, just stunned. I think you should call him."

"I don't think that's the best idea. If a man's in shock, he usually wants time alone to process it."

"Baloney. In times like these, friends need emotional support."

"You just want me to get more details and tell you about it afterward," he corrected.

"Well, yes, but—"

"And you're going to Parent Trap them back together."

Sometimes Addie resented how well he knew her. "You weren't there, Logan! Behind those expressions were bleeding hearts still longing for each other. And what are the odds of them getting together in California and meeting again in Chicago? I'm serious. Look at us, for example. Fate intervened, so what if fate is making a double-whammy?"

"No wonder you and Mark get along so well," Logan chuckled. "All right, fine. I'll call James and see how he's doing. But if he refuses to talk about it, there's not much I can do."

"I'm only asking you to try."

"Fair enough. How was the rest of your day?"

"It was good. Now call him."

"Tomorrow. I meant what I said about processing, and I have a better way of going about it." She was impatient, but Logan likely knew better in this situation. "Right now I'm more interested in talking to you."

"Fair enough," she sighed. "How's life in New York City?"

"It's . . . okay, so far. I'm mostly just working, so there isn't much time to do anything in the big city. Not that I really want to."

"You don't want to see any Broadway shows or go to the Empire State Building?"

"Not without you."

Addie blew a raspberry into the receiver. "I love you, Logan, but just because you have a girlfriend doesn't mean you can't have some fun without me. You'll go crazy if all you do is work. Plus if you don't bring me back a snow globe of the Statue of Liberty, you might as well not come home," she teased.

"I guess I have no choice then," he chuckled, but then his voice quickly sobered. "I love you too, by the way."

"Can we video chat tomorrow?"

"Why not right now?"

"I gotta see if Savvy's okay. Guys may need their solitude, but Savvy and I work a bit differently."

"True that," he laughed. "At least I'll have something to look forward to tomorrow. 'Night, babe."

"Now about the pop tart thing."

He laughed. "Cheesy, right? I heard a coworker use it over the phone to his wife and nearly choked on my lunch. I'm not going to make that a thing."

"You sure? Because I'd be more than happy to call you up on speaker phone at work—"

"Please no, I was just teasing you. Don't call me pop tart."

"Darn, and it was just starting to grow on me."

"Goodnight, Addie." She could hear the smile in his voice.

"Goodnight, honeybun," she cooed.

Addie could picture him shaking his head but smiling when she hung up the phone. She held it to her heart like it was some kind of lifeline. Whoever said distance makes the heart grow fonder might have been onto something.

With a deep breath, she approached Savannah's door and quietly knocked before cracking it open. She found her sitting on her bed, crocheting the blanket she had kept unfinished in her closet since they moved in.

"Needed a distraction?"

Savannah didn't even look up. All she did was mutter, "Needed to keep myself busy."

"Isn't that the same thing?"

"A distraction would have kept me from thinking about Jimmy. But since that's proven to be impossible, this just keeps my stress level down . . . while I think about Jimmy."

Addie sat on the edge of her bed and picked up a ball of yarn. She had never seen her best friend so distressed since they met. "I know you probably don't want to talk about it, but it might make you feel a little better."

Savannah's hands froze and she shoved her project to the side. "How in the world did this happen?" she exploded. "How could Jimmy, of all people, end up here? It's karma, I tell you. I left him standing in the rain, breaking his heart, believing there were things I needed to do before I got married, and now fate has brought him here to show me what I gave up."

"I don't think that's how fate works."

"Yeah, well it's certainly not bringing us back together. He was not happy when I left and there is no way he would take me back now."

"Do you want him to take you back?"

"No. Yes? Maybe. I don't know," she groaned, grabbing the nearest pillow and buried her face in it.

"Well let's work this out for a minute. Did he write you off after you left? Block your number? Send all your stuff back?"

She lifted her head. "No. He hated the fact that I left, but he wasn't cruel. In fact he sent me a two-page letter of how he'll always care about me and hoped I'd find what I'm looking for."

Addie exhaled. "Wow."

"I know. I'm the villain in this story! I broke the man's heart and he was nothing but sensitive."

Addie took a moment to think about her situation and only one thought came to her. "You know what you need to do," she said calmly, gently resting her hands on her shoulders. She had her attention, but now it was time to show her some sense. To do that, she squeezed harder and shook her with all the strength she had. "You need to get a grip!" Savannah's eyes widened. Usually she was the one to express the dramatics, but now the tables were turned. "You of all people know when life gets weird, you get weird with it!"

It wasn't the most profound thing Addie could say right now, but at least it got a smile out of her. "Look, you've given me enough pep talks to know what's happening here. It's like bungee jumping. You know what you're getting yourself into, yet you jump anyway because there's a possibility it's going to be the biggest thrill of a lifetime, and if you don't do it, you'll regret it for the rest of your life.

"You have one day to freak out. I mean it's Jimmy for crying out loud. But if there's a slight chance that if you talk to him, and it leads you to something great, or closure maybe . . . you can at least move forward. And my guess is you've already thought about everything I just said, so do I have to be the friend that pushes you off the bridge?"

That won her another smile, which gave Addie more hope.

Savannah groaned. "How do I even approach this? Do I call him? Knock on his door again?"

"That . . . is a very good question," she said, having no real plan in mind. "But I have an idea in the meantime. Instead of getting ice cream like we usually do, let's use our money on something lasting and go shopping. We haven't done that in forever."

"You hate shopping."

"Not at the bargain shops. We always find cool, vintage stuff there. Come on, please?" she begged.

"Fine, but if I pick something out for you, you're getting it without any argument."

"Deal," she said, hoping this would start off her plan in bringing the two together. She knew there was a chance it wouldn't work out, but Savannah had been the one to bring her to Chicago and she ended up finding the love of her life. If there were any possibility she could return the favor and see this mess turn into something much better, she would do everything in her power to see it done, even if she had to try on a hundred frilly hats to do it.

Chapter Twenty-Four

❧

On Sunday afternoon, Logan called James like he promised Addie and he answered right away with a, "Hey, what's up?"

"Just wanted to see how you're holding up back home."

"I'm holding up just fine. Laura's been a big help and I'm really liking the view from your window."

"I'm glad you're settling in, though I'm looking forward to getting back to my comfort zone."

"New York not as cool as they say it is?"

"No, it's awesome, but it's like when you're a kid and you move to a different school. The new kid on the block is usually left eating alone in the lunch room."

"I hear ya on that."

"So anything else exciting going on besides work?"

"You mean when your girlfriend and my ex-girlfriend showed up on the doorstep?" James answered bluntly.

Logan had a feeling this wasn't going to be an easy conversation to have. ". . . Yeah, I heard about that."

"It's not something I want to get into right now."

"I figured, but I think you should know that right now, it's crunch time."

"What does that mean?"

"I'm just saying you might want to be prepared before she knocks on your door and you stare at her like an idiot again."

"Wow, you really know how to make a friend feel better."

Logan ignored him and continued. "I don't know much about your situation, but you can't tell me that on your way to Chicago, you didn't think about Savannah at least once."

"Well . . . yeah. I mean I still think about her every now and then."

"Do you still like her?"

"I . . . maybe. But she did leave me high and dry and I doubt she'll ever come near me again."

"If I learned anything about women from my mom and sister, it's to always expect the unexpected. From what I hear, she's still single and . . ." Logan wasn't sure if he should say this. He didn't want to put things out of context, but decided to take a risk. "She's still into you, bro."

"Your source?"

"Her best friend, which happens to be my girlfriend."

"You sure she's not trying to pull a Parent Trap?"

"Addie's not the type to create drama, but in my opinion, there's one way to find out. You could talk to her."

He was silent for a moment until he asked, "How would I go about that?"

"That's the best I got for now. But if something comes to mind, I'll let you know."

"Thanks . . . I guess."

"Anytime."

Logan hoped he didn't just open a can of worms, but James had a good head on his shoulders. Whatever came next, he was confident that things would turn out all right. If he and Addie could make it through, so could they.

❧

Addie had all her school binders sprawled out on the floor as she tried to organize them before the academic year started. But she had them organized weeks ago and was looking for an excuse to keep busy while she waited for Savannah to return from her "date."

A week after her interlude with James, Savannah found the nerve to call and invite him to lunch. To both of their surprise, he accepted, but Savannah was beside herself taking a full hour to decide on what to wear, and two more to style her hair.

Neither of them really knew what to expect from this, but Addie secretly hoped the two of them could forget about the past and start over. It was wishful thinking and probably something that could only exist in a fantasy, but so was two people winding up in the same city with feelings that obviously still lingered. Something good had to come from this.

After two hours of waiting around the apartment, Addie went for a run, stopping at the grocery store for a few things, and came home to find Savannah on the couch looking solemn and ready to vent to her how badly it went.

"Oh no," Addie said, moving to hold her like her mom could if she were there.

"When I decided to move to back to Illinois . . . I really thought it was what I was supposed to do," Savannah said. "I felt like I needed to find some independence and really be on my own. And I've matured. I've solidified personal beliefs that were still a bit iffy before. But I felt like the Lord needed you here too. I don't regret it, which is exactly what I told him. And of course I apologized for hurting him. He said he already forgave me. And then . . . I said it. I said I was still in love with him."

Addie winced, knowing this probably wasn't going in a good direction. "What did he say?"

"Nothing. He seemed so shaken up and flustered by it all, I thanked him for lunch and hightailed it out of there like an idiot. I really think I blew it, Addie. Seeing him was a big mistake."

Addie wished she had a comforting response, but at this point there wasn't much she could do to intervene. And inspiring Savannah to go for it in the first place had likely made it worse.

"Is there anything I can do?" Addie asked, feeling a bit help-less on her friend's behalf.

"No," she said. "But thanks for trying."

❦

Logan had just walked out of the gym when his phone went off.

"Hello?"

"What's Savannah's address?" asked James, not bothering with pleasantries.

"Why? Is something wrong?"

"Nothing's wrong, but time is really important right now, so I'll explain later. I just need to know where I'm going."

"Yeah, sure, give me a second and I'll text it to you."

"Thanks, I owe you," he said before ending the call.

"No problem," he said to himself before typing out the direc-tions. Right away, he sent a text message to Addie,

> Incoming. James just asked for
> your address and sounded pretty
> urgent.

❦

Addie tried to stifle a gasp when she saw Logan's message. She glanced over at Savvy who moved to a laying position, holding a pillow to her chest. She didn't know if telling her James was likely on his way to the apartment was a good idea or not, but concluded it would stress her out for something that was inevitably going to happen.

The next twenty minutes were intense. Savannah started a movie and Addie had to force herself not to glance out the window for incoming taxis. But just as she expected, a knock came at the door and she answered to see James standing in the doorway, dressed nicely, but out of breath from the five-floor sprint.

"Is Savannah here?" he asked, getting straight to the point.

She only had time to point at the couch where Savannah was at full alert, staring into his eyes while he silently stared back.

"I'm just gonna . . . yeah," said Addie, backing away into her room.

She didn't want to eavesdrop, but even when she tried to listen in, their conversation was too quiet.

About an hour later, she finally heard the front door open and close, giving Addie reason to come out of her room to investigate.

She didn't have to ask to know how it went when she found Savannah standing up against the door, gazing dreamily into space.

"He kissed you, didn't he," Addie said.

All Savannah had to do was giggle before the two of them started their happy dance.

"We have a lot to talk about still. But in a nutshell . . . he's willing to see where it goes if there's still something between us. His first idea was to test the spark, and . . . let's just say the spark was definitely there."

"Can I just say," Addie started, flopping on the couch where Savannah joined her, "life is great."

"Cheers to that."

Chapter Twenty-Five

❧

*H*alloween was right around the corner and Addie had just about had it trying to teach the new curriculum. This year had turned out to be more challenging, but it wasn't her student's overall attitude that got to her as much as their scores and comprehension. As a Title I school, most of the children struggled more academically when their parents were always working to put food on the table.

She'd been staying extra hours after school to get planning done and help her students with their homework. On this particular day, it took Layla an hour just to understand one math concept, which made Addie miss the train. And to add to her grumpiness, she got a text from Logan saying he had an unexpected problem to take care of so he wouldn't be able to talk to her until tomorrow. What was worse—and yes, it got worse—his trip had been extended into December, so a few more weeks of separation now turned into a month and a half.

Her discouragement level was on the rise and it was during moments like these when she started having doubts about the future. She loved Logan with all her heart, but occasionally a nagging thought would gnaw at her brain, causing her to wonder if their relationship would be the same after he came home. At this point she continued to pray and read her scriptures, hoping encouragement would follow, but the comfort always seemed to fall short.

At home she did a quick workout and ate a protein salad for dinner. She refused to wallow and eat ice cream in Logan's absence, only indulging when it was absolutely necessary. That usually fell on nights when Savannah wallowed, but lately there hadn't been any reason for it. Since she and Jimmy had been spending most of their time together, Savannah was either with him or floating on cloud nine at the apartment.

Not that Addie was complaining. She was truly pleased to see her friend blissfully happy and hoped everything would work out for her. She just hated coming home to an empty place most nights with no one to talk to.

After cleaning up the kitchen, she slumped on the couch to read a book. But when she turned on her iPad to open her kindle, there was a notification saying she had a video message.

Seeing Logan's username, she eagerly opened it up and pressed play.

The video started with him propping up his phone while he moved to sit on the bench that was in front of the most beautiful black grand piano she had ever seen. It looked like he was in the lobby of a hotel, but her focus was less on the décor and more on the beard that had started to grow since she had last seen him.

His hair was also a bit longer and it was the first time she had ever seen him appear so rugged. To Addie it made him look roguishly handsome, and she couldn't help but giggle like a teenager with a hardcore crush.

"Hey, Addie. I know it's been a while since we've had the chance to talk, but to make up for it, I wanted to play a song that I wrote for you," he said, and proceeded to lift the cover off the keys.

When she started playing, she noticed it was a melody she had never heard before. It was intricate and beautifully composed. It reminded her of something John Schmidt would play, and it surprised her how much he had improved in his skill this past year. It was the most wonderful thing she had ever heard.

"I know it doesn't make up for a whole lot," he said. "But it's definitely a promise that I'll do everything I can to make it up to you when I get back. I love you, Addie. Sweet dreams."

Addie replayed the song two more times before she closed her iPad, thanking her Heavenly Father for, once again, giving her the reassurance she needed.

She knew the time zones put them one hour apart, which made it one o'clock in the morning in New York, and he was likely sound asleep. She thought about leaving a message, telling him how amazing he was and that the video he made meant the world to her. But the gears of her creativity began turning and she suddenly had a better idea.

Pulling out her pen and notebook, she began scribbling down words she pulled out from the more poetic part of her heart. She hadn't written down her own lyrics in years, but right now she felt the need to get it copied from her mind before she forgot it the next morning. She could already hear a tune flitting through her consciousness, showing her the exact chords she'd use for each line.

After work the next day, she pulled out the box that kept the old ukulele she bought when she started college. The chords were iffy at first. Some of the notes didn't sound as well as she thought they should, and there was a lot of rearranging she had to do, but eventually she was able to get it all organized to the point where it sounded pretty good for the project she was about to complete.

She remembered telling Logan that she knew how to play the ukulele, but never got around to actually showing him her skill. This would be a first, and she hoped he'd like it.

She set up her iPad on the desk and pressed *record* before she sat cross-legged on her bed and took a deep breath . . .

❧

When Logan finished work for the day, all he wanted to do was go back to the condo and relax. He had just closed his briefcase when Rob, another member on the team, came in and knocked on the conference room door. "Logan. A few of us are going out for steak. Want to join us?"

Logan hesitated, reluctant to say yes after spending a long day fixing their rookie mistakes. But if there was the possibility of getting on their good side, they just might start taking his advice the first time before acting on arrogance like they had done today.

"Steak sounds really good. When are you guys leaving?"

"We're meeting in the lobby in ten minutes. I'll let them know you're coming."

"Cool," he said, hoping he wouldn't regret this.

At the restaurant, Logan looked at the menu and was impressed with their selection. Although it was a bar and grill, and the ambiance wasn't exactly family friendly, the food looked delicious and his mouth watered at the idea of a good steak.

While he selected his entrée, the three guys (Rob, Danny, and Stephen) chatted about sports-related topics that didn't center toward his interests. He was more of a hockey fan anyway, and he doubted any of them would share his opinions on the Chicago team this season.

When the waitress came to take their order, they all took turns requesting their drinks until Danny added, "And four beers, please. On me. You're welcome, guys."

"Actually, three beers," Logan corrected. "I'm good."

The waitress nodded and headed back toward the kitchen while Logan looked back at three sets of eyes staring at him; as if denying a free beer was a sin against masculine nature.

Suddenly uncomfortable, Logan shrugged. "I don't drink."

"Really?" Rob said. "That's not what we heard."

Logan scowled. "What have you heard?"

"You used to seal deals over a drink all the time back in the day."

"Yeah, well . . . that's not my style anymore. After my car accident, I turned over a new leaf, you could say."

"It's just a beer, though." This came Stephen, who had been the least talkative next to Logan until now. "It's not like we're planning on getting wasted, and none of us are even driving."

"I get your guys' logic, but I'm fine. Let's just enjoy our meal."

The finality in his words seemed to drop the topic and the conversation thankfully moved on to something else. When their drinks came, Logan sipped his diet coke while they gulped down their beers and bragged about past girlfriends.

Although their words were crude and somewhat insulting, Logan remembered the days where he'd been just like them, boasting about his conquests and drinking the amber liquid that he suddenly found himself craving. But the more he looked at them, the clearer he could see the person that he used to be, and the scene made him sick to his stomach.

He imagined someone talking about Addie like that, and suddenly he wanted nothing more than to get out of there.

Excusing himself to the bathroom, Logan rushed to the nook that was hidden from anyone's view. He leaned against the wall and closed his eyes, breathing in deeply. As timing would have it, his phone vibrated in his pocket and he pulled it out to see he had a text. Attached was a video file and the text read,

> Watch this when you get home tonight. Love you!

Logan was tempted to open it now, but whatever she wanted him to see, he didn't want his current company to taint it. So with newfound courage, Logan walked up to the waitress and asked for a to-go box before heading back to the table.

"Sorry guys, but I can't stay. Something important just came up."

"Like what? You got a phone date with your girl tonight?" said Rob, which sounded more like jab at his ego than a general question. Rob didn't know how that information got passed around, but he didn't appreciate the mockery in his voice.

"As a matter of fact I do."

"Oh come on, when was the last time you had a guy's night? Don't you ever get tired of spending every free minute with her?"

Logan winced. "No, actually. I don't."

"Whipped," Stephen coughed before gulping down the rest of his drink.

This was followed by Danny making the sound of a whip cracking, which sent everyone into a fit of laughter.

"It's just the honeymoon phase," said Rob. "He's young and in love, but give it time and he'll come around."

"No, I think it's more than that," Stephen added. Logan was surprised that he would come to his defense. Unfortunately that wasn't the case when he added, "Have you seen the pictures of her he has in his office? That phone call might be more explicit than he's admitting. In this case I think we should be high-fiving him."

Logan's knuckles turned white from squeezing his fingers into tight fists as they continued to speak about her in the crude way they had before. His anger rose by the second and it took everything he had not to start a verbal fight. When their food finally arrived, Logan stood to put on his coat, making it very clear he wasn't staying to hear more.

"Wait, are you really leaving?"

"I said I had things to do, and I'm not going sit here and take this," he said honestly, feeling like he had to make a point instead of just being polite.

"Aww, come on, man. We were just messing around."

"I can take a joke when you're only making jabs at me. But the second you talk about my girlfriend that way, I won't tolerate it. You are representatives of a major company and what you do on your own time is your business, but you should always treat your coworkers with respect. You never know who's going to report your behavior to the one who decides whether or not you have a job."

Logan didn't stay to hear their response. He took his food box and headed to the front counter to pay his cut of the bill, leaving a generous tip.

When he got back to the condo, he changed out of his work clothes and threw his food in the microwave. He flipped through the channels and found a rerun of *Duck Dynasty* to watch while he ate. The steak turned out to be just as delicious as he expected, even though it was reheated, and finally he was able to relax for the first time all day.

It was after he finished eating that Logan remembered Addie's message, and he shut the TV off and pulled out his phone.

As we pressed play on the video she sent, her face suddenly showed up on the screen, dressed in the band T-shirt she got from the concert they went to.

"Hey, Logan. I know I could've called to tell you how wonderful you are for sending me best song in the world. But I thought this would be better. I wrote this just for you."

He watched her pull out a ukulele that he didn't know she had and situate her fingers. She took a deep breath and began strumming a tune that was mellow and slow, but still carried an upbeat rhythm that matched her personality somehow.

After playing a few chords for the intro, she sang,

Oh darlin, what can I say? The way you got me on the first day
I'm not the type who usually calls dibs

I saw no point in waiting so long, to end up like this cheesy love song
And looking back I'm so glad that I did

Cause you're my knight in shining armor, strong and riding free
To rid the world from evil, along the way to rescue me
Baby, I'm one stressed out damsel, and I know the future's hazy
But you know it's true, and happy too, in a world that's built on
crazy

No one's perfect. That much I know, but your good looks are not
just for show
I wouldn't change a single hair on your head
Everyone says it's stuck in the clouds, but they are only just jealous
right now
So how about you listen to me instead?

Cause you're my knight in shining armor, strong and riding free
To rid the world from evil, along the way to rescue me
Baby, I'm one stressed out damsel, and I know the future's hazy
But you know it's true, and happy too, in a world that's built on
crazy

With a final strum, she smiled and blushed bright red. "I know, it's super corny, and there's a reason why I'm not famous, but hopefully it made you smile. I love you, and I can't wait until come you home."

Logan was disappointed to see the video end, but after such a conflicting night, he felt rejuvenated and lighthearted. It was one thing to hear her sing covers for a crowd, but another when she used her own imagination. But even though his spirits were lifted, his heart ached with a sense of longing that put him back in a depressing mood. It was enough to tempt him to go to his boss and say he couldn't do it anymore. But he wasn't a quitter and Addie would never encourage him to be.

He dialed her number to prove it, and once again it went straight to voicemail. He thought about leaving a message, but he was done playing phone tag and decided to wait until tomorrow morning to call. He wondered what she could possibly be doing right now since she didn't mention having anything planned on a Thursday night, but whatever it was, he hoped she'd call back soon.

❦

When Addie came home from grocery shopping, she was surprised to see a gaggle of people in her apartment all sitting in a circle with playing cards. Apparently Savannah and James had invited a bunch of people from the ward over for a game of Scum.

Although she wasn't much of a card player, when it came to Scum, her strategic and competitive side came out and she always managed to stay in the highest ranks. Many had said it was a good thing no one gambled because they would all lose their money betting against her.

After putting her groceries away, she joined their game and was happy to have a nice distraction. She hadn't heard from Logan yet and she wondered if he had a chance to see her video message. She was getting so tired of missing each other due to their busy schedules and the time difference, but since there wasn't much she could do about it, she focused on the game, which led her to one more victory to put on her belt.

"I feel hustled," said Bryan, who was apparently brand new to the ward.

"It's only hustling if you're playing for money," Addie declared.

"True. My pride is hurt, but well done."

When a few people announced they had to leave, the game paused so people could chat and say their good-byes, which drew

Savannah's attention away for James to conspicuously lean over and whisper, "We don't have much time, but I need your help."

"With what, exactly?"

"I want to propose to Savannah this weekend."

"Are you serious?" Addie exclaimed, trying hard to keep it in a whisper. When he nodded, she clapped her hands in excited approval.

"Listen," he said with a hint of urgency in his voice. "Can you bring her to the park this Saturday at twelve o'clock?"

"I'm sure I could. Neither of us work that day."

"Exactly. It doesn't matter how, just make sure you're both there and then make up some excuse to leave for a minute. That's when I'll come in."

"You got it."

"Perfect."

As timing would have it, Savannah's guests had all left and her attention was brought to them. They made sure to appear as if neither of them were planning something totally sneaky, but Addie didn't wipe the silly grin off her face in time.

"What are you smiling about?" Savannah asked.

"Oh, um . . . Logan just sent me a cute text."

"You guys are just as gross as we are," she said, leaning over to kiss James on the nose.

Addie forced a chuckle to acknowledge the exaggerated cheesiness, but in reality, it was like a dagger to the chest—a painful reminder that no matter how many times they serenaded each other, they were still hundreds of miles apart.

Once the majority of the group left, a few had stuck around to talk, which left Addie in the corner with Bryan who kept her engrossed in conversation. She had no problem answering questions about her life. In fact, it was nice talking with someone who was interested in getting to know her.

But halfway through, Addie realized what was happening and suddenly she began to panic. During her inactive days, she couldn't remember a moment where there wasn't a guy around to give her attention. She had thrived off it, mostly to temporarily fill a void brought on by loneliness and the need for validation.

Obviously that wasn't the case anymore. But right now Logan's absence had left a small void in her heart, and suddenly she found herself enjoying Bryan's company a little too much.

She let Bryan finish his thought, but once the topic reached a good stopping point, Addie said, "I hate to do this, but I have to get up early tomorrow."

"Oh, no worries. I have to get going anyway, but I really enjoyed talking to you."

"Me too," she said, not bothering with a . . . "we should do this again," or "let's talk more."

"And I've definitely learned a thing or two about Scum."

"I bet you did."

"How exactly did you do it?"

"Sorry. I'm taking the secret to the grave." *Oh my heck. Seriously, take a freaking hint.*

"Oh, come on. You're not going to help a guy out?"

"Nope."

"How about if I buy you dinner? Are you free this weekend?"

Yes, she thought before mentally kicking herself in the shin. *No you're not, Addie! Logan's the love of your life and you'd never do anything to sabotage your relationship. You've overcome this once, which means you know you're strong enough to avoid it.*

"Actually, no," she answered.

"How about next week?" *My, he's persistent.*

"Bryan . . . I think you're great, but . . . I'm just going to be blunt and say I have a boyfriend."

"Oh," he said, the confidence in his eyes considerably dimming. "That's probably something I should've asked before."

"Or something I could have brought up earlier. I'm sorry."

He shrugged as if it were nothing, but she still felt bad. "Don't worry about it." He said. "Not the first time it's happened, but it was still nice getting to know you."

She nodded. "Same here."

Once everyone was gone, Addie went to her room and didn't hesitate to call Logan after she missed him during the party. But when he answered with a groggy, "Hello?" she looked at the clock and realized in was almost midnight in New York.

"I woke you up. Dang, I'm sorry, we'll talk tomorrow."

"No, I'm awake," he said, which followed with an audible yawn.

"It's fine, Logan. Go back to sleep."

"Not until you sing to me."

"Seriously?"

"Seriously," he said with a sleepy laugh. "You woke me up, so I think it's fair that I get a live performance of that amazing song you wrote for me."

"Oh my heck," she chuckled, delighted that he liked it. Or at least he said he did, but it lifted her spirits either way. "Do I really have to?"

"It's my song, and I want to hear it."

Addie sighed and began her second performance. In her opinion, it didn't sound as great without the ukulele, and half-way through when he tried to sing along she couldn't contain her laughter. But the whole time she was reminded that goofing off with Logan felt better than any interaction she possibly had that day.

They stayed on the line for another twenty minutes catching up on their day, which eventually turned into whispering sweet nothings until they said their final goodnights.

Though she still didn't care for the separation, she managed to go to bed with a smile on her face, reassured that just a bit more patience would make it worth it.

Chapter Twenty-Six

$\mathcal{T}$ime didn't exactly fly by, but there was a lot going on to make the month of November bearable.

Just as James had planned, Addie feigned the need for some fresh air despite the chilly weather and convinced Savannah to go on a walk with her. They sat on the bench in the park and talked about trivial things for a few minutes until she got up to throw a piece of trash away. Right then she and James made the switch and Addie pulled out her camera as promised.

She didn't exactly hear what was being said, but was able to capture the rapidly changing expressions on Savannah's face as he appeared and got down on one knee.

It went from surprised to anticipation, to emotional, to giddy, and then full on thrilled when she let out an enthusiastic, "Yes!"

It was only a day later when plans started being made, and there was a lot to be done considering they wanted a Christmas wedding.

Everybody questioned if it was possible to put one together so soon. But if it weren't for all their friends and family wanting to be a part of it, they would have likely ran off and eloped.

Thankfully Savannah's parents lived in Illinois, and they helped with most of the major decisions. Even though it wasn't quite Thanksgiving yet, somehow everything seemed to fall into place when her mom managed to book a hall already decorated for the Christmas holiday.

On top of planning, Addie kept herself busy working on projects. One of which was directing the Thanksgiving pageant this year at her school.

She only had two weeks to teach the kindergarteners a few songs that would be performed for the school and their families the day before they went on break. While her own students were at lunch, she visited their classrooms to guide the music until their own teachers knew it well enough to take over.

When they had their first dress rehearsal, everything was as she expected it to be . . . a mess. Though the kids had the music down, they were all over the stage without a clue how to stand still. Several fights broke out over who got to be the turkey while the rest of them decided to play a game of tag.

She somehow managed a compromise and she had a few other teachers to back her up. But after an hour of shouting instructions over their giggling and chatter, she was close to losing her voice.

Eventually they managed to do a full run-through without any mishaps, which gave Addie hope that their performance would go just as smoothly. But she prayed Alex wouldn't feel the need to give Sarah a wet willy during the pumpkin number again.

When the day of the pageant arrived, the whole school gathered in the gym, which also served as their auditorium. The families sat in the overflow in the back with their phones and video cameras ready.

Addie stayed in the wings, keeping the kids settled until she heard the principal say in the microphone, "On behalf of the school, we'd like to welcome you all to our annual Thanksgiving pageant. All the classes and teachers have worked very hard putting this together, and we look forward to their performance.

We just ask that you put your phones on silent, and students, we expect you to be on your best behavior."

When he walked off the stage, the audience applauded and Addie made her way to the front row below the stage.

The curtain opened up and all the kids were ready for their opening number. Leading the music for a bunch of five-year-olds was nothing like leading the choir at church. Waving her arm didn't do much, but reminding them to smile, mouthing the words, and giving them a thumbs up made a big difference.

When it was time for the kids to change into their costumes and act out the first Thanksgiving, Addie sat back and watched with her fingers crossed. A few of the girls were noticeably nervous, and one of the boys tripped on the stage, but he happily jumped back up with a smile on his face, and the cheering that came after motivated him to finish the scene.

It was a bit of a task to get all the kids seated on the floor, but once everyone settled down, the rest of the grades each took a turn doing their own performances. Some were musical numbers and others were skits. But overall, it was wonderful to see the whole school participate and to see her own class display their talents.

When it ended, the principal took the stage for the closing remarks. "I think I'm speaking on behalf of everyone when I say what a real treat that was. Let's give another big hand for our talented performers." Once again, the parents and students clapped while most of the younger kids giggled and blushed after a job well done. "I'd also like to acknowledge our teachers, especially Miss Garrison, for helping with the kindergarten classes. In fact, could you join us here on the stage?"

Addie blushed when everyone cheered on her behalf, and moved to stand in front of the audience. She didn't think she deserved that much recognition was but was grateful to be acknowledged.

"First of all," he started, "Not only did Miss Garrison work very hard to put together this production, but after only having been with us for a year and a half, she has already made a huge impact on our school. The students and staff love her. She always aims for the highest goals and never falls short."

There was a brief pause, which gave everyone the cue to clap and cheer again. Once more, she gave them all a bright smile, happy to be appreciated, but hoping her praise was nearly over.

But when she was about to retreat back to her seat, a voice behind her said, "Can I add to that?" And her heart nearly skipped a beat.

She turned around and slapped her hand over mouth in a useless attempt to hold down her surprise and emotion. Because casually walking toward her with a microphone in his hand was Logan, looking more pleased and amused than ever.

Apparently everyone was in on it, because amongst all the cheering and giggling, every teacher sitting by their classes had the "we knew the whole time" look on their faces.

"Oh my heck," she said over and over again, both laughing and crying at the same time as he pulled her into tight a hug.

Immediately her senses were filled with his familiar feel and aroma. She pulled back to notice he was clean shaven and his hair was newly cut. She had almost forgotten how handsome he was in person, and here he was!

Logan's eyes sparkled when he took her hand and raised the mic to his lips. "Well for starters, Miss Garrison really is an amazing teacher. But personally she is the smartest, kindest, funniest, most beautiful, talented, and loving person I know. I'm so blessed to have her in my life, and . . ."

And then it happened. Just when she thought she had the biggest surprise of a lifetime, Logan lowered himself onto one knee. At this point it was all she could do to keep herself from breaking down completely.

"Addie, I love you so much. And I want to be with you forever," he said tenderly, and suddenly it was just the two of them alone in their own bubble. "If you say yes, I promise I will spend the rest of eternity doing everything in my power to make you happy. Will you marry me?"

Heart beating, hands tingling, and tears streaming, Addie struggled to get a word out. But from all the pent up euphoria, she let out a joyful laugh, and it wasn't long before a few kids started chanting, "Say, yes! Say, yes! Say, yes!" which had spread throughout the entire student body.

"No pressure," Logan chuckled, but she could see the sweat beading on his forehead from her lack of response.

Not making him wait any longer, Addie nodded her head and said, "Yes" before he stood to hold her close as if his life depended on it.

"I love you," she said in his ear, and just like he had done at Mark's farewell, he threw her into a dip, giving her a long overdue kiss that made the audience go wild with catcalls and groans.

Given their time apart, she wished the kiss could've lasted longer. But with the hundred or so pairs of eyes on them, Logan handed off the microphone and took her off the stage into the wings where a door led to a quiet empty hallway.

"I can't believe this is happening. How long have you been planning this?" she asked him.

"About a month now. I hated lying to you, but I wanted you to be extra surprised, so I said my trip had been extended. I didn't know how I was going to do it at first, but as soon as you told me about the play, I made a few phone calls."

"You little sneak," she said, giving him a playful punch to his side, but she quickly sobered. "I couldn't have asked for a better moment."

He took both her hands in his, resting his forehead on hers. "If I ever have to leave again, I'm taking you with me. Because guess what? You're going to be my wife."

"You're going to be my husband!" she giggled.

Right then she hoped for another kiss, but a squeal suddenly sounded from down the hallway as Savannah scurried toward them to give her a bone-crushing hug.

"You're here too?" Addie chuckled.

"Of course. You filmed my proposal. Someone had to film yours," she said, waving her camera. "Can't wait to put this in your wedding video."

"I'm so stinking happy right now, I can't even stand it. I wish I didn't have to go back in there."

"Psh, you don't," Savannah said. In her giant tote was Addie's purse and coat, which she thrust into her arms. "You two lovebirds are free to skedaddle out of here."

"But my class—"

"Is being taken care of. The whole school was in on it, Addie. Like they're gonna make you stay after a big thing like that. Now jump in that getaway car and go celebrate before I make a scene."

Logan raised his eyebrows and held out his hand. With another wave of giddiness, she took it and they both ran down the hall.

"You're the best!" she called out to her.

"You know it!"

Once they exited the front doors, they made their way through the brisk November weather to the parking lot where his car was waiting in the back.

"We have to hurry," he said as he moved to open the passenger side door. However, he didn't open it right away. Instead, he took her face in his hands and gave her a searing kiss that made her forget about the chilly weather, and everything else altogether. "I've missed you," he breathed. "But really, we have to hurry."

He wrenched the door open and Addie laughed as she got in. "I missed you more."

"That's arguable."

Once they were out of the parking lot and headed down the main road toward the city, Addie finally said, "Well, fiancé, what exactly are we in such a hurry for?

"I don't want us to miss our flight."

Addie's eyes widened. "Our flight?"

"Of course. It's Thanksgiving and everybody is gathering at my parents' this year. It's kind of a big deal and they want their future daughter-in-law to be there."

"But I don't have anything packed!"

"Savannah took care of that," he said, pointing to the back where her two suitcases lay on the backseat.

"Of course she did," she chuckled.

"I hope this isn't too much for one day."

She shook her head in amusement, lacing her fingers with his. "I couldn't have asked for better."

◈

Their flight got in late, but Logan's family was awake and excited to see them now that she was about to become a part of it. As soon as they walked in the door, all the adults crowded into the front room to give hugs and congratulations.

But just when things began to settle down, she heard a quiet voice behind her say, "Hi, Dumpling."

Addie turned around to see Linda standing at the end of the hallway, looking more healthy and radiant than the last time she saw her.

"I know you don't like it when I surprise you like this, but they called—"

"Mom!" Addie squealed as she rushed into her mother's arms.

She obviously wasn't expecting such a greeting. Since she left California, their connection had been severed so badly, she hardly felt any longing over the distance between them. But after all the recent changes, she truly missed her. They had grown closer through emails and phone calls, but right now she didn't see the hollow shell of a brokenhearted woman. She saw her mom.

"I'm so glad you're here," Addie said. "I take it Logan pulled a few strings."

"He's really special, Addie. I know I raised you to believe that all men have an agenda, but he's all good from the inside out."

"I know."

"And you're getting married!" she screamed, waving her arms like the eccentric woman she still knew and loved.

After some small talk and getting the next day's schedule figured out, Addie settled in the guestroom at her grandparents' and checked her bag to make sure Savannah had packed all the essentials. Thankfully she knew her well enough to pack everything she needed and then some. But when she dug deeper, she noticed in the side pocket was an envelope with a sticky note that said, *It's up to you, but something told me it was time for you to read this. Have a lovely trip! ~Savvy*

Peeling the note off, she saw that it was the letter from her father.

Addie stared at it as she slowly lowered herself onto the edge of the bed. It had been sitting in her desk drawer, meaning to be opened at the right time, and Addie had never felt sure of when that might be. She was a little shaken that Savannah would feel the need to make sure she read it. But whatever inspired her, she had to agree that now felt like the best time to see what her father had to say.

With steady hands and an anxious heart, she carefully tore the seal and pulled out the two pages of lined paper that had his handwriting on it. Inside was a picture of him holding her as a baby.

She stared at the photo, taking in his smiling face and all at once, her childhood came rushing back at her.

Going back to the letter, she began reading,

My little Addie,

By now you're probably not so little anymore. You're a grown woman taking on the world each day as they come. But as I write this, you're still my little girl who likes to play with Barbies and dress up as a princess for tea parties. I write this because in my line of work, there may come a time when something will happen to me and I won't come home. I may not get the chance to tell you face-to-face what every young woman needs to hear from her father before she makes big decisions in life. It makes me sad to think that would ever happen, but in case it does, I want you to know this.

You are a beautiful daughter of God. I love you just as He loves you. And as you grow and progress, there will be moments where darkness will do everything to make you believe otherwise. But if you work hard to make good choices, you will always find peace and happiness.

As a grown woman, you will be making decisions like attending college, choosing a career, finding a husband, and starting a family. Because I know you're smart and determined, I'm not concerned about where you'll end up when it comes to school or finding a job. But I want you to find somebody who makes you laugh and listens to your problems without trying to fix them. Who talks softly to you and never raises his hand when he's angry. Who takes over the dishes even though it's your turn and reads the kids a bedtime story even though he's had a long day at work. Who holds your hand in public and never stops telling you you're beautiful.

It's always the little things that make the biggest difference. There was a lot I had to learn when I first married your mother. I was very young and I thought I had it all worked out. But as I adjusted, and you came into our lives, I realized that we never stop learning. So always have that mindset, and make sure he does too so you both can grow together.

I am so proud of you. No matter where you are in life, I will always be proud of you. Even though my life on earth may be over, I'm always by your side watching over you. I know it didn't work out

the way we wanted it. But God knows what's best, and everything
works out the way it's supposed to. Sometimes we don't ever find out
why, but if we have faith, we'll see how it ultimately blesses our lives.
Whether it's in this life or the next.

I love you, princess.

~Daddy

Addie sniffed as tears flowed down her cheeks. She pressed
the letter to her heart and whispered out loud, "I love you too,
Daddy."

Right then she couldn't help but cry mournful tears at the
loss of her father; wishing he could be here during happy occasions like these. But almost immediately the thought came to
her that he was. He had been with her every step of the way, and
she had always felt his presence whenever she had faced a critical
choice in her life.

And feeling that same warmth now, her tears turned into a
celebration of eternal life and the miracle that he could be there
for her in spirit and they would be reunited in heaven.

ॐ

The next morning, Peggy, Brin, and Annie were getting a head
start on dinner while everyone enjoyed a light breakfast, watching the Macey's Thanksgiving Day parade.

Linda was peeling potatoes, telling the other women about
her life in Texas, which Addie briefly overheard as she came up
the stairs.

"Why didn't anybody wake me?" she said groggily after a
ten-minute planned nap turned into an hour.

"A smart person never pokes the sleeping bear when she's jet
lagged," said Linda, which earned a few laughs.

Addie just smiled and shrugged as she sat on the barstool.

Just by the sound of his steps, she knew Logan was approaching her from behind, and as she predicted, he wrapped his arms around her torso and nuzzled her neck.

"Good morning," he hummed, and she giggled from the tickle of his morning scruff.

"Good morning, and happy Thanksgiving."

"Happy Thanksgiving. I certainly know what I'm grateful for today."

"Me too," she sighed.

"Gross," Brin groaned.

"I'm going to take a shower," Logan said. "But before I forget, after dinner, there's a place I want to take you. Are you free tonight?"

"I may have to move things around, but I think I might be able to fit you into my schedule."

"Always so accommodating," he said before giving her a quick kiss and heading back up the stairs.

Addie sighed in satisfaction and blushed when all the women smiled as if they had just witnessed a scene from a Nicholas Sparks book.

As the day progressed and everyone gathered together to enjoy a wonderful meal and share what they were thankful for, Addie basked in the idea that this is how it would be from now on—being a part of a big family and eventually adding to it with their own children in the future.

Just after the sun set, Logan reminded her of the place he wanted to take her to and they discreetly left the house to sneak off to the unknown.

"Should I even ask where we're going?" she said.

The look he gave her clearly meant he was keeping his lips sealed, and she figured she was just going to have to get used to his surprises. But since his surprises never disappointed her. She didn't complain.

When they ended up in a neighborhood in Draper, Addie was a little confused as to who they were visiting since he never mentioned having friends or family in this area.

He parked in someone's driveway and took her hand as soon as they got out. She thought he was leading her to the backyard until she noticed behind the house was a forest of trees.

Because the weather had dropped that afternoon, a thin layer of snow covered the ground and flurries danced in the air, making the atmosphere look more mystical in nature.

"Where are we going?"

"You'll see," he said. "It's not much farther."

They stopped in a small clearing, and Logan looked around expectantly as if something were supposed to be happen.

"What are we waiting for?"

He looked at his watch. "Just a few more seconds. Okay, five . . . four . . . three . . . two . . ."

Right on cue as Logan reached the end of the countdown, every tree in sight simultaneously lit up, causing her to gasp as she watched her surroundings turn into something straight out of a fairytale.

"Oh my goodness," she breathed.

"What do you think?"

"This is amazing," she said, completely enchanted.

"Whenever you show up in the good dreams I have, for some reason I usually see you here. Ever since then I've had the strongest desire to share this with you."

"You have given me so much, Logan. Sometimes I feel like it's too much when I have so little to offer."

"You've already given me everything I ever wanted," he said, pulling her close to kiss her forehead. "Will you marry me?"

"I think we've already done this," she giggled.

He smiled, "It's not official until I put the ring on your finger," he said, pulling out a black velvet box.

He lifted the lid showing her the silver band with the solitaire cut diamond in the center. It was simple and elegant, which was just what she preferred.

"When you told me to bring you back a souvenir from New York, I went and got this for you the next day. I still got you a snow globe if you don't like it."

"I love it," she laughed. "It's beautiful."

The ring fit perfectly as he slipped it on her finger, making it official.

"And I know just where to take you on our honeymoon," he said, pulling her into his full embrace.

"After all the wonderful things this last weekend, let me guess . . . Atlantis?"

He leaned down to kiss the tip of her nose. "I was thinking . . . Disneyland."

Addie jumped up in the air with a loud, "Yes!" and Logan caught her, swinging her around in circle, making all the lights blend together in a sea of color.

Even though the future wasn't certain, Addie had complete faith that after all the hardships both she and Logan faced in their lives, everything had worked out according to plan. She couldn't wait to see what the rest of the plan entailed, but thankfully they had an eternity to find out.

Epilogue

*O*ne year and six months later . . .

Logan sat back in his chair and closed his eyes, remembering all that transpired from the moment Addie agreed to marry him to where he was now.

During the holidays after his proposal, he and Addie had attended James and Savannah's wedding. Although the happy couple stayed in Chicago for a while, they decided to relocate back to Utah where James kept his job with the company in a different branch. Savannah easily found a nursing position with better hours, and the last he heard, they were both settled into their new home in Holladay.

The June after Logan proposed to Addie, they were married and sealed in the Mt. Timpanogos Temple. He remembered how beautiful she looked that day, how happy she was on the dance floor with all the nieces and nephews, how hard she laughed when they shoved the cake in their faces, and the way she gazed at him as if he had just given her the world.

Now, one year later to the day, his gratitude toward his Heavenly Father, his family, and his friends for helping him get here had never stopped increasing.

He also had someone else to thank as well—someone he never had the opportunity to meet, but knew had a great deal of influence in his life.

When Addie showed him the letter from her father, he ached for her loss, but was touched that a father had his heart in the right place to do that for his daughter. However, when she showed him the picture, Logan recognized him immediately, and had said the name, "Tommy" before Addie had the chance to explain.

Although it wasn't much of a surprise, both equally agreed his near-death experience had been a miracle in more ways than one. And from that point forward, Logan's nightmares had all but stopped.

Logan walked through his parent's home where a large crowd had gathered to celebrate Mark's homecoming.

Throughout the two years he spent in Japan, he and Logan stayed in close touch, but Logan was pleased to see the positive changes his mission had made in him.

As he made his way to the backyard where most of everyone stood talking to one another, he leaned against the house as he observed Mark talking to a few of his friends from high school.

He wasn't quite out of the handshaking phase yet, and Logan chuckled to see him get caught off guard when a girl went in for a hug.

As she walked away, Logan stepped up behind him. "It's a good thing you've been released. How scandalous would that have been?"

"Shut up," Mark said, still looking a bit scandalized, but the humor was there. "Wow, I've missed everything. Everyone I know is off on their own missions, going to college, and even engaged already. And here I am without a clue of what I should do with myself."

"Well you should probably get working on that."

"What, no speech on how I'll have plenty of time to figure it all out?"

"I could," Logan shrugged. "But what kind of brother would I be if I told you everything will work out eventually? You've been released to the wolves, dude."

He huffed a laugh. "Fantastic."

"At least you have time, and take as much as you can. That's the first lesson when it comes to figuring it all out. Make decisions too quickly and you might end up in a place you think you can't turn back from."

Mark nodded in agreement and then his smile turned a bit more genuine. "I see the student has surpassed the teacher," he said, bowing his head out of cultural habit. He said something in Japanese, but then translated it to, "My work here is done."

"Always so dramatic."

"Hey, this is a big day for me. I'm not your spiritual trainer anymore. So I'll be as dramatic as I want to be."

"I thought that became official the day I got married?"

"But I wasn't there for that, so it doesn't count. And it's a crying shame too, because I had a really good speech prepared."

Logan raised an eyebrow at that, but a thought came to mind that made him see the situation from a different perspective.

When Logan woke up from his coma, Mark didn't hesitate in pushing him to make the changes he needed in his life. He was also the one who prompted him to seek out the woman he saw in his dreams. But above all that, Mark had become his closest friend and although James had made a good best man, he wished his brother could have been with him at the temple to see the real victory that he encouraged. And he sensed Mark had wished the same thing. Even though his mission was important, he could tell Mark felt a bit left out when it came to family events he couldn't be a part of. But whatever he had planned to say, Logan still wanted to hear it now.

"You know . . . today happens to be our anniversary."

"Is it?"

Logan nodded. "And if we had gotten married today, instead of a year ago, I would have asked you to be my best man."

"Your best man? Really?" he asked, as if it would have been a privilege to receive the title.

"You played a big part in our whole love story. Something tells me that speech would have been worthy of sharing."

Mark could have used the opportunity to make a comedic retort, but instead his face softened as he put his hand on his shoulder and said, "Thank you. It means a lot that you see me the same way I see you."

They both stood in meaningful silence until they started chuckling, which turned into a fit of laughter. Although they enjoyed their spiritual talks, as brothers, they couldn't stay serious for long.

"Hey, everybody!" Mark suddenly called. "Listen up. There are few things I'd like to say."

"Mark, what are you doing?"

"Better late than never, right? And since it's my party . . ." Mark turned his attention back to the crowd who had all quieted down to listen. "I know today is my homecoming, but it also happens to be the same day my brother married my sister-in-law a year ago. Although I couldn't be there for their wedding, I did get the opportunity to watch Logan fall in love with an incredible woman who has made a great addition to our family.

"Ever since I was little, I looked up to Logan as my hero and never stopped seeing him that way. My best memories are the times he came to visit and spent endless hours talking to me about life and hearing what I had to say. He helped me find my voice and the will to stand up for what I believe in. He's survived traumatic ordeals and has worked hard to overcome many trials, and if it weren't for him, I wouldn't have gained the testimony that I have now."

While friends and family clapped, Logan felt a tug at his heart, not knowing until now just how much Mark looked up to him.

He searched the crowd to see Addie standing by the refreshment table, beaming at the two of them.

It amazed him how marriage could bring two people so close as to teach them to communicate without words. He gave her a look that asked for her permission to use this opportunity to tell everyone the kind of influence Mark had on him, and she nodded with her approval.

When the clapping quieted down, Logan put his arm around Mark's shoulder and said loudly, "Mark has always been the one to put on a good show, but he never says anything that strays from the truth. I am blessed to have him as a brother and a friend.

"What a lot of you may not know is that I was in a bad car accident, which put me in the hospital for a while. But after I was released, Mark stayed by my side until I could recover on my own. And during that time, I heard about this beautiful and talented woman that I had recognized from my past, and he was the one who encouraged me to step out of my comfort zone and introduce myself to her. In fact, when I started to chicken out, he threatened me, 'You're going to see that girl again, Logan. Don't make me come back there.'"

Logan paused when everyone, including Mark, laughed in response, and then continued to say, "With his intuition and faith alone, he was able to foresee something that has truly blessed my life. At the time my testimony had significantly faded, but he made it his personal goal to break past my stubborn barrier and help me find the happiness I'd been missing out on.

"I now have an incredible wife who I love with all my heart." He looked back at Addie in admiration. "And I'm really excited to tell everyone that come next spring . . . she'll be bringing our first child into the world."

It took Mark a few seconds to register what he had just said, but when he did, he nearly jumped back in surprise. All the family and guests cheered, crowding around Logan and Addie to give their hugs and congratulations. His family was beside themselves, especially his mother, who had adopted some of Linda's enthusiastic tendencies.

"I'm going to be an uncle," said Mark.

"You're already an uncle."

"I know—I'm just extremely happy for you, brother. You're going to be a dad!"

"I'm going to be dad," Logan breathed, realizing how good it felt to say it out loud.

When Addie had told him the news, he thought he'd feel a rush of anxiety at the idea of becoming a father and raising something so pure and innocent. But instead he felt peace and a surprising wave of excitement that they were going to start their family.

Later that night, after everyone retired for the evening, Logan took Addie's hand and guided her into the sitting room where their family piano stood.

"Are you going to play me something?" she asked expectantly.

"Actually," he said, taking out his phone and hooking it up the speakers on the shelf. "I brought you in here for a different reason."

"Oh? And what might that be?"

"Will you dance with me?"

Dancing at random moments wasn't an uncommon thing for them, so Addie didn't hesitate to say, "Why, I'd love to."

He turned on a classical tune and pulled her into a waltz position, gently swaying along to the rhythm with ease after all the practice they had.

"How are you feeling?" he asked, knowing her morning sickness had been rough before they flew out here.

"Really good. I've had more energy today than in weeks, and I was able to keep Mom's potato salad down. The pickles in it were delicious."

"She didn't put pickles in it."

"I know, I did. I think those cravings are starting to kick in."

"Yes! I've been waiting for the day I'd get to do midnight craving runs for you."

Addie shook her head and laughed. "Who knew you knocking me over would lead me to blissful eternity with you?"

"Well I had to get you to fall for me somehow."

She chuckled before her face softened. "In that case, thank you. For not giving up on me."

"And thank you," he whispered, placing a kiss on her forehead. "For bringing me home."

He then leaned down and softly kissed her lips, feeling a greater love and passion for her since their first. He had meant what he said about living this moment before. It confirmed that he was exactly where he wanted to be. But better yet, it was never going to end.

Discussion Questions

1. What themes were largely highlighted in the story?

2. What were the lasting consequences of Logan's choices before the accident?

3. How did those consequences affect the people in his life?

4. What influences inspired Logan to change his lifestyle for the better?

5. How did Addie's relationship with her mother affect her throughout the story?

6. Would Logan and Addie's relationship have lasted without the time and experiences that occurred before they actually met?

7. What important roles did James and Savannah play in the story?

About the Author

Chelsea Curran lives in the desert valley of Arizona. Though secretly a romantic, she used to spend most of her time brooding over the idea of love until her college roommates (now best friends) introduced her to the exciting and fantastic world of romance novels. When she's not teaching, dancing, painting, laughing, or baking cookies, she's in her blanket fort giggling over the handsome hero capturing the fair lady's heart. And no matter how old she gets, that will never change. Countless authors have inspired her to write stories for those who seek the same ideas that brought her comfort, joy, and hope for the future. By experience, she believes one good book can change a person's life forever.

Scan to visit

www.chelseacurranauthor.com